Absolution

THE AWAKENING SERIES

Absolution

ASHLEY LUCERO

Book design by Maureen Cutajar
www.gopublished.com

ISBN: 978-0997201680

Acknowledgments

Thank you to my parents Michael Pearson & Wendy Pearson, thank you for your undying support through all of the ups and downs writing this book. I hope that one day I am able to repay the strength, faith, love and support you have always given me.

Thank you to my husband Steven Lucero, whom after countless numbers of sleepless nights pushed me to continue to pursue my passion in life. Thank you for not giving up on me and for the thousands of pep talks and kisses. I love you dearly!

A gigantic thank you to my editor E. Lee Caleca, whose invaluable writing notes and editing skills breathed life into this book and made it real. You are amazing!

Finally, to my brother, Brandon Pearson, you always watched over me and I know you still are. Your strength, encouragement and brotherly love will always be remembered and I will always hold our brother-sister talks, and memories together close to my heart. I hope that you've found the peace and happiness you truly deserve. Until I see you, have a cold one for me. This is for you. Semper Fi, we will never forget.

Without their support this book would not have been written.

 Prologue

Hastily, I gathered what little belongings I owned and shoved them into my bag. I snapped the gold pendant and chain from my neck and slid it into my pocket. They would be here any minute now...I had to hurry. Several bangs sounded on the door before it was abruptly kicked in and two men advanced into the room.

"This isn't something you can run from, Nathaniel, punishment must be given," one of the men stated as the other man, who I confirmed was Ezekiel, continued his approach.

"That order is wrong, you know it is! She isn't supposed to die," I exclaimed as my attention turned towards Ezekiel who paused at my comment.

"It's not your decision who lives and who dies, Nathaniel! You broke a direct order! You will be punished for it!"

I shook my head. *This wasn't right, this can't be happening.*

Ezekiel's eyes looked pained as the other man nodded for him to continue. His creamy plush wings extended on either side of him and I knew this was it.

"This won't be the last of me," I affirmed, looking at the men.

Ezekiel's hands raised and I was met with excruciating pain across my body followed by a flash of blinding light and the feeling of falling. Without warning, my body hit asphalt as the pain seared through me once more causing me to convulse and vomit. My wings splayed out behind me and I watched in horror and screamed aloud as they burned before my eyes until nothing was left.

I lay there; trying to process the permanent dark substance that now resided in my veins and the pile of ashes from my wings. I was a fallen one now. I would have to find her.

Chapter 1

It was the first day of junior year, and there was nothing I wanted more than to pull the covers over my head and sleep away the day. But the unrelenting 'beeping' of my alarm clock refused to be ignored and made me get up. Groaning, I barely managed to pull my exhausted body from my bed and start the shower so I could get ready. I stepped into the hot water and let it revive my senses. Then it was on to hair, some make-up, and an outfit; the usual routine every girl has.

As I swung my creaky closet doors open, an array of clothes came into view. I studied what consisted of my wardrobe for a while trying to decide what I was in the mood to wear today. The colors stared back at me – black, blue, red, green and a rainbow of others. After an eternity of trying on different shirts I finally decided on a pair of denim blue shorts, black flip flops, and a plain green off the shoulders shirt. As I stood in front of the mirror checking once more if this was really the outfit I wanted, I stared at the girl in the mirror.

She had a well-proportioned 5'6" frame and a slim body, with long straight blonde hair that framed large round eyes. Red and brown highlights had the effect of emphasizing the brilliant emerald color of those eyes, and played against her caramel skin as it cascaded around her shoulders and down her back.

My parents had always told me I was beautiful, or as my mom

would say, 'a beautiful green eyed vixen,' but I'd never thought that I was anything too special. I could name a hundred other girls who were drop dead gorgeous. I didn't think I was the best, but I didn't think of myself as ugly either. After all, what parent doesn't tell their child they are beautiful?

As I pondered thoughts of beauty, the clock flipped to 7:15 AM. Crap. I'm going to be late. And on the first day of school too. I quickly grabbed my binder and purse and dashed out to my car while yelling good-byes to my father and brother. If I didn't like the way I looked it was too bad, and besides, I didn't really care what other people thought about me anyway.

The sun shone brightly as I ran outside and a few puffy white clouds scattered the sky, reminding me that summer was over now, and it would be fall before I knew it.

As I drove to school obeying the speed limit of 45 MPH and being careful not to go over, I dialed my best friend Kate's number, noticing she had already called me once.

"Alex!" Kate's voice echoed through my ear as I cringed from the loudness and repeated the favor.

"Kate!" I screamed back.

Kate and I have been best friends ever since the seventh grade. She knows all about me and my family just as I know everything about her and hers. She is about an inch shorter than me, with long, dark brown, naturally wavy hair that comes to the middle of her back, and a curvy slim body that mirrored my own. After a couple of seconds of laughter, the questions came flying.

"Where are you? You're going to be late on the first day of school!" She shrilled on the other end of the line. "Listen lady, if you're not here in one minute I have to go. I can't be late, my parents will crucify me!"

Kate's parents, Mr. and Mrs. Jackson, had always been more along the lines of the strict type. Rules like 'don't be out past 12:30 PM curfew', or 'make sure you're home by 5:00 PM for dinner', were the typical forte at the Jacksons. Other than that though, her parents were pretty cool. Strict, yes, but I viewed them as my second family so they never really bothered me. Plus, they make the best dinners I've ever had, and seeing as my family doesn't cook except on holidays, I relished the dinners I had at their house.

Growing up our family dinners consisted of 'whatever you can find'; rules were in place, but were breakable and lax. As long as my parents know where I am, and when I'll be home, they don't have a problem. They expected what every other parent does, get good grades, be safe, etcetera. Etcetera. Basically though, as long as my brother and I are safe we can do as we please, within reason of course.

"I'll probably be late so you can head in without me if you want, but I'll see you in math class, k."

Even though walking by myself was not something I extremely enjoyed, it didn't bother me that much and I didn't want Kate to get in trouble and not be able to hang out later.

"Ok I'll see you then!" Kate cheered until all I heard was the sound of a dial tone.

Mostly I was good at being invisible to others, walking fast to class, and saying hi to the friends I recognized in the hallways. As I parked my boat of an SUV in parking spot number 151 that was assigned as mine for the year, I glanced around to see if anyone else I knew was making a mad dash for the school doors to avoid being late. As far as I could tell I was around the only one, except for the smokers who gathered by the far end of the parking lot and who needed a morning dose of Nicotine before class.

I gathered my things and began speed walking inside. I still had a few minutes left. At least I could make an attempt at not being late to my first class of the day, which happened to be English; one of my best subjects. I have always been good at English, History, and Science; however, math is another story. My dad, a software engineer for a major company in Colorado called Deftech, obviously failed to pass his genius mathematician skills onto me. So getting a 'C' in math is a miracle.

As I briskly walked down the blue carpeted hallway, avoiding bumping into other students who were desperately trying to locate their classrooms, a familiar voice boomed from behind me.

"Well, well, well, what do we have here?"

I knew that voice. The voice of someone who has been one of Kate's and my best guy friends since freshman year. He also happens to be one of my brother's friends even though he is my age, and therefore, two years younger than my brother. I slowly turned and put my hands on my hips as a smile formed on my face.

"Well, well, well, if it isn't Trey Banoff," I retorted.

A crooked grin was plastered on his face and before I knew it I was engulfed in a gigantic bear hug.

"Trey...can't...breath," I managed to squeak out. He just laughed and let me go.

Immediately I gasped and air reentered my lungs. Now I was able to get a closer look at him, and yep, he was the same Trey I knew from last year and the year before.

Trey was one of our school's hockey players and was naturally well-built with broad shoulders in a six foot frame. His shaggy dirty-blonde hair was gelled into a mini Mohawk, and with puppy dog brown eyes, and that lopsided grin of his, he was what other girls at school called 'eye-candy'. However, as impossible as it is not to notice how boyishly cute and handsome he was, he and I saw each other as friends only.

After walking and catching up with each other's summer events, I realized Trey had English with me, and to my relief, the bell rang just as we walked into class. Ms. Nethers, our English teacher, eyed us disapprovingly as we each took an empty seat near the back of the room by one another. Her short curly brown hair and her dress that resembled more of a quilt than a dress made her look more ancient then she was.

She tipped her glasses down from her eyes.

"As I was saying, tardys can be made up before or after school, and unexcused absences will not be tolerated."

I tuned out Ms. Nether's lecture and groaned inwardly. Great, I thought, only 230 more days to go. I cringed inwardly at the thought of being in Ms. Nether's class for 230 more days, but at least Trey had this class with me so I had someone to talk to.

English, Science, and Social Studies went by in a hazy blur, and after hearing the rules and expectations from every teacher I was ready to go home, but alas I had one class left. Math. At least Kate had that class with me so it wouldn't be extremely boring.

I walked in to Mr. Kritch's math class and found an empty seat on the left side of the room a couple rows from the back. Pictures of 'Math is fun', and 'Success is through math' hung all around the walls, and it made me wonder how anyone could think math is a fun and exciting thing to learn.

As I turned to look at the students now pouring into the classroom I noticed Kate and Jesse standing by the doorway talking and giggling. Jesse is Kate's boyfriend, it's been that way on and off since they met freshman year. Kate immediately had a crush on the 6' brown haired, green eyed, jock and before she knew it, they were dating.

I had to admit they were an adorable couple, Jesse walked her to almost every class, and they would laugh, flirt, and dote on each other. But, they were also quite dysfunctional. They were constantly breaking up and then making up, and they would argue and bicker one minute and the next be apologizing and kissing. As perplexing as their relationship was to me, Kate had explained that that is what 'young love' is, and as long as they were happy I went along with it. As Jesse kissed Kate's cheek and sauntered off down the hallway Kate walked to the open seat next to me and sat down.

"So have you met Mr. Kritch yet?" Kate implored as a distraught looking man entered the room carting a stack of papers.

"My name is Mr. Kritch I am your math teacher. I don't accept late work, and as you can see I am a new teacher at this school and I have my hands very full right now, so if it's not a life or death matter, don't ask."

The man looked like he could have a heart attack any second, and I tried to wrack my brain and remember CPR in case he did have one. As he took a couple of breaths to calm himself down the class just stared at the old man. Obviously they were in as much shock as I was.

Mr. Kritch brushed off the stares and began with a lecture.

As I looked over at Kate with a raised eyebrow, she chuckled at my expression and whispered, "Well at least math class won't be boring."

"I keep waiting for him to have an aneurism or a heart attack." I giggled back before we were silenced by the frustrated glare Mr. Kritch sent us.

The rest of math class flew by relatively quickly, and before I knew it Kate and I were walking out the school's double doors to our cars.

As we weaved our way through the parking lot a familiar crowd of girls came into view. Beth Ryder and her posse advanced affably towards Kate who smiled and gestured in return. Beth and the four girls that followed her were what consisted of the popular girls at school, Kate had managed to befriend them and said they weren't as bad as they seemed, while I begged to differ.

Ever since Trey had refused to go out with Beth, she blamed me. Somehow it never occurred to her that stalking someone is not attractive, and instead, thought I had somehow dissuaded Trey from letting them go out. Needless to say she harbored much resentment towards me, and whenever an opportunity presented itself, she sought to destroy my reputation.

As she sauntered towards Kate and gave me the stink eye, I had to be thankful for the fact that Beth was somewhat smart. She never badmouthed me to my face, but only glared. She knew that I was not someone who should be provoked, so I was relieved I would not have to endure her; I kept walking to my car and told Kate I would call her later.

I have never been the type of girl who has gone out looking for a fight, but if the chance ever came, I know I wouldn't be the one to back down. I considered myself more of a peacekeeper. My father always tells me I'm 'hard core' but then others tell me I'm quiet, and fun to be around. I'm guessing that means I'm somewhere in between.

My thoughts began to dissipate as I pulled in the driveway and gathered my belongings to go inside; noticing that Trey's rusty, old, faded blue Ford was halfway on the curb outside our house.

We had recently moved, due to the pending divorce, to a farm house on the outskirts of town. It resembled more of a two story Victorian era home I thought, with huge white pillars that surrounded the wraparound porch and a barn painted the same identical eggshell white as the house that sat farther back to the right, complete with four horse stalls and a tack room. Dad said it had 'real estate potential' when we bought it.

I walked up the white wooden steps and opened the door to reveal my brother Derek and Trey in the living room den shouting and cursing one another as they battled in the PS4 game, Call of Duty. I smiled at just how into the game they were before heading upstairs to get rid of my things.

Derek and I didn't look much alike at all; he took more after Mom with her dark brown hair while I took after Dad. Even with the stresses of the divorce, I had to admit I liked the new house. The stairs are in front of the doorway as you walk in, with the living room den to the right and a spacious wraparound kitchen with stainless steel appliances to the left. Dad's office is located behind the stairs with a mini library in it, while upstairs, there are three bedrooms; the master is the farthest to the left, then comes my brother's room, and farthest to the right is my room.

Mom decided to live in downtown Denver in a huge loft. Derek and I each had a room there too so we were free to stay there whenever we pleased. My parents wanted my brother and I to not be affected by their divorce, so they told each of us that we could stay with whomever, whenever we wanted. As comforting as that is, it still didn't fix the 'living' situation. So, I decided that I would keep my things half at my mom's and half at my dad's. This way for a week I could live somewhere and the next I could live somewhere else; it made it easier than choosing which parent to subsequently live with.

Derek on the other hand is leaving for the Marines in two months, on October 10th, so until that time he is trying to balance the amount of time he has left between my parents, his girlfriend, and his friends.

After dropping my stuff and bouncing back down the stairs into the kitchen, I grabbed a handful of Oreos and a glass of milk and joined the boys in the den. Just as I was sitting down on the chair, Derek immediately jumped up with his hands in the air and shouted.

"I won! I finally killed you!" I started laughing at just how seriously they took the game, while Trey just scowled at Derek and me.

Defeated Trey looked at Derek and promised his revenge.

"Alright so you won this round, but next time victory will be mine."

Derek just smiled as he sat down and I rolled my eyes as I dunked a cookie in the milk and ate it. Boys are so strange, I thought.

After a while of all of us just hanging out in the den watching T.V., Trey said he had to leave before his mom had a huge fit for him not being home, and Derek went out to dinner with his girlfriend Jessica, so I was left to my own devices on entertaining myself. I decided I would read more of my book, Breaking Dawn, by Stephanie Meyer. I had read the other three books by her, and I was finally on the last one with only a hundred or so pages left. I liked the idea that Bella and Edward could be together, even though they were vastly different. I laughed inwardly. Well of course they're different, he is a vampire and she is a human. Besides, I was already this far into reading it, I might as well finish the series. I smiled as I grabbed the thick hardcover book on my dresser, and walked to my window. I pushed back the curtains and pulled up on the old fashioned window with no lock, it slid up with one swift shove. I stepped out onto the flat stone colored roof, and laid down facing the sky and began reading.

One of the things that I loved about my dad's new house was the roof. It was flat enough that you could move around and walk on it, and not have to worry about falling off. The view is breathtaking as well. I can see the entire backside of the property. Our two horses in the back by the barn, romping through the tall green bladed grass, the purple mountains that belittle the land far in the distance behind our house, and the deep pines that stretch out before, and cover them. Off to the left you can even see the bustling city of downtown and its sky-scraping towers. Before I knew it, the golden light of the sun that splashed across the pages of my book faded, and eventually grew dark-er and darker.

I had just finished reading the last page when I looked around at the vast darkness that seemed to envelope me. Lights sparkled to my left in the city far off in the distance and I had just enough light to jump back inside through my window. The wind had picked up a slight chill without the warmth of the sun's rays, so I shut my window and pulled the curtains, and I fumbled my hand across my dresser in search of my lamp. As soon as my blind hands found the switch, a dim light enabled me to go to my closet and find my pajamas to change into. Plaid green and pink shorts and a black t-shirt seemed comfy enough so I quickly changed, and headed down stairs when I heard a car pull up outside the house.

Dad's home, I thought as I rounded the stairs and went to the kitchen to fix myself something to eat.

Sure enough, the familiar boisterous 'Hello!' of my father echoed throughout the house as soon as the front door swung open.

"Hey!" I yelled back, until my dad joined me in the kitchen, laptop case and work bag in hand.

"How was work?" I asked him as I began to boil water for Fettuccini Alfredo.

He smiled. "It was long, but I finally got the lab rats to do some work after a while."

I smiled back. My dad always joked calling his employees 'lab rats' ever since he had watched the movie, *A Good Year*, with me one night.

"Well that's good," I replied.

As he began unpacking his laptop from its case, he inquired as nonchalantly as possible about my first day at school.

"It was alright, I guess," I replied, remembering Beth and her posse and some of my teachers.

I must not have fooled him, because when I looked up from the boiling water on the stove, a frown was covering his face.

"School was school dad," I said as I smiled.

He seemed to take this as an ok answer from me, and afterwards we changed the subject and talked about other things. We continued talking over dinner, and then we went separate ways as I headed upstairs to get ready for bed and he headed to his office to finish up some work. After brushing my teeth and removing my make-up I climbed in bed with my cat, Duck, who was already curled up on a pillow asleep, with his puffy charcoal grey tail covering his matching face and his one blue eye and one gold eye.

As I stared up at my ceiling I couldn't help but wonder if things were ever going to really change for me for the better. As happy as my dad and mom tried to act around Derek and me, worry and sadness seemed to be etched in the wrinkles in their faces from the stress of the divorce. And soon, Derek would be whisked off to boot camp where communication would be at a minimum.

Derek and I had always been a close brother and sister. He helped me when I needed it and I returned the favor for him. We usually hung out with the same bunch of friends and it would be weird when he left; quiet.

I began to realize just how alone I was really going to be and a pang of sadness hit me. I quickly pushed the feeling away and forced my mind to think of only the positive. Before I could think of another optimistic thought, sleep overcame my body, and I began to dream.

Chapter 2

It's October 20th; Derek left ten days ago. The house feels empty beyond belief, and it's unbearably quiet. Since dad usually works until late, I've been trying to keep my mind occupied with things to do. Trey has been coming over to the house whenever he can, to just hang out; he knows how close my brother and I are and how much I miss him.

As I sat staring blankly at the T.V., not remotely interested in what I was watching, I felt my cell phone's familiar vibration in my pocket. I pulled it out and checked the caller ID. It read, 'Mom's Cell'. I answered.

"Hey Honey!" My mom said in her usual chipper voice. "I have a surprise for you, and you can't say no, because it's already paid for. I'm getting you out of that house for a little while; I've noticed you've been distant, so I set up a massage appointment for each of us today at 3:00. I'm on my way over to get you now, so get ready, k!"

As I heard the dial tone on the end of the line I couldn't help but smile. Mom always knew how to cheer me up, and since I couldn't stand being alone in the house anymore; I jumped up from the couch and bolted upstairs to change before she got here. As I finished brushing through my hair I heard a car pull into the drive. I raced down the stairs, out the door, and hopped in my mom's little white Mini

Cooper. We talked a little about how school was going, which truthfully, school had been a bit of a relief since Derek left. I was able to get out of the house for awhile, focus on my studies and nothing else, and see my friends. Mom talked about her new store.

Since my parents agreed to get a divorce, my mom had opened a bridal store. It started off slow at first; finding an empty and available building on 16th Street mall was a chore in itself; but after the last four months of fixing up the place and bringing dresses in, sales began to skyrocket, and more and more dresses were brought in and sold to love-stricken brides. Today, The White Dove is one of the most successful bridal stores in Denver.

We pulled into a parking space in front of Massage Envy, and walked through the double glass doors and up to the counter to check in. The lady behind the counter was a middle aged woman, with shoulder length straight black hair and glasses. She smiled brightly, showing tan-worn wrinkles on the sides of her eyes and mouth, as she confirmed our three o'clock appointment. Afterwards, she escorted us to the back room to wait to be called. I sat down in the taupe colored room in a chair farthest from the entrance where a rock waterfall hung on the wall. I relaxed a little as I listened to the calm trickle of the water behind me, but soon enough was snapped out of my thoughts when I heard my name.

"Alex, Alex Constance".

I looked toward the short red-headed woman who had just called my name before gathering my purse and following her left, down a narrow hallway to a massage room. As we entered the room she began to politely ask me questions, and introduce herself.

"My name is Bergitta. So, Ms. Constance what are the areas you want us to work on today? Do you have any problem areas we should know about before hand?" she inquired.

I wasn't quite sure what to say, seeing as mom had been the one to set up the appointment, and the fact that I had no 'problem areas' I was aware of.

"Umm, maybe my neck and back need it the most, they tend to get tight when I'm stressed. I don't really have any problem areas though."

"Perfect. Alright, well get undressed and we'll start with you face down on the bed", the woman ordered politely.

I simply nodded in recognition as she turned and left the room. I began to undress and slipped under the soft, warm, white, sheets before she entered the room again. As Bergitta began to massage my back and neck, I drifted off to sleep, and before I knew it, I began to dream.

As I dreamed, I heard a voice calling my name softly in the distance.

"Alex...Alex...Alex..."

I strained to hear the voice more clearly in the pitch black. I recognized that the voice was definitely male and I tried to follow where the sound was coming from in the distance. I began to feel around with my hands in the darkness, and then the sound stopped. Out of nowhere a cold breath blew on the back of my neck. I stopped dead in my tracks, the hairs on my neck where standing straight up and my breath caught in my throat. Someone was behind me.

Whoever was behind me whispered huskily, "Alex."

I finally mustered enough courage to turn around, but when I turned around I was met with nothing but blackness once more. I squinted in the dark; nothing.

All of the sudden my eyes were met with another pair of eyes. Brightly glowing in the dark in front of me were the most vivid eyes I had ever seen. Intense ice blue rings sparkled before me, and I soon realized I was staring up into them. I got the impression it was a male; he was tall; over six feet I gathered, give or take a few inches, but I could only see his eyes. And just like that, he was gone.

I woke up in a flash to someone lightly shaking my shoulders. I turned to find Bergitta staring at me with concern.

"Are you alright Ms. Constance, I think you fell asleep and were dreaming, but your whole body went ice cold and rigid."

I stared back at her, before managing to squeak out a reply and give a fake smile to let her know I was ok.

"I'm fine. I just...I was just dreaming, that's all."

"Alright, well we're all done, so I'll let you get dressed and you can meet your mother up front alright?" she replied warily.

"Alright, sounds good, thank you Bergitta," I replied.

Then she exited the room. As I was dressing, I couldn't shake the image of those eyes out of my head, or the guy's voice. I finally just decided to forget about it. After all it was only a dream; it wasn't real. I smiled at myself for being so childish, and walked out the door where my mom was standing talking to a woman, probably a prospective client who was soon to be married I gathered, judging by the humungous rock on her left hand's ring finger. I stood beside my mom as the two women talked about what dress would be perfect, when I felt a breath on the back of my neck again.

The same feeling that I had in the dream came back to me, and my eyes widened. I turned around blocking out the chatter and laughter of the women, and looked behind me, nothing. Alright, I thought, that was intensely creepy, but before I could return my attention to my mom and the woman, the icy goose-bumps crept up my neck again and I began to scan the end of the hallway.

My eyes stopped abruptly when they landed on a guy leaning against the exit doors. He was over six feet tall, with short, midnight-black, messy spiky hair. He was dressed in all black; black boots, a long sleeved black shirt that was rolled up on his forearms, and black pants. However, I could not make out his face; it was bent as though he was staring at the ground in front of him, with his hands loosely hanging in his pockets. I stared at him until eventually, he slowly lifted his head and stared straight back at me, with an expressionless face. His eyes however, were what caught my attention.

Bright blue icicles that glowed brought me back to my dream I had had minutes ago. It was him, the same man from my dream. My head began to swarm with thoughts, how could this be possible? Am I going insane? Am I still dreaming? This is not possible.

I stared back at the man; my thoughts scrambling, until I felt a light tap on my shoulder. My mom was trying to get my attention to introduce me to the soon to be client of hers. I shakily held out my hand and congratulated the woman on her engagement, completely ignoring what she was saying back to me.

It wasn't until the woman began to walk away that my mom turned to me, concern written on her face, and asked, "Alex, honey are you ok? You look like you've seen a ghost."

I blinked my eyes a few times, turned around and found the guy still leaning nonchalantly against the exit door staring at me. Only this time he seemed to be smirking at me. I scowled back, and then turned to my mom who was still waiting for an explanation of my weird behavior.

Then I asked her, "Do you see the guy at the end of the hallway, he's just been staring at me the whole time."

She seemed confused, looked down the hallway, then back at me and replied, "Alex, what guy at the end of the hallway? Nobody's there honey."

I swung back around to find the guy still standing there staring, he looked at me once more, smiled, then turned towards the exit sign and disappeared.

I was stunned, but before I could decide if I had just hallucinated or not I turned back to my mom and said, "Oh, never mind, I thought I saw someone, but I guess not, sorry."

She seemed to think for a moment, before blowing it off, smiling, and asking, "So, did you enjoy your first massage?"

Chapter 3

The ride home was hazy at best. I tried my hardest to focus on the things my mom was telling me about, but all of my undivided attention was focused on the intriguing yet frightening stranger who apparently I saw 'disappear'.

I must really be losing my mind, I thought as my mom pulled into the drive of my dad's house. As I began to shakily get out of the Mini Cooper my mom seemed to sense something was not right with me. Before I could shut the shiny white door she looked at me worriedly and spoke.

"Alex, honey do you feel alright? Ever since we left the massage place I feel like you've been zoning out. And now you look like you could be sick."

Before I had any chance to disagree with the charges she had confronted me with, she gave me a stern look and said, "Why don't you stay downtown with me tonight, your father probably won't be home for awhile, and I don't want you here by yourself in your condition."

I nodded my head in acknowledgment, too exhausted from the day's strange and creepy encounter to argue, and went inside and threw some clothes and toiletries in my money green duffle bag. To be honest I was thankful that my mom had asked me to stay at her place tonight. I definitely did not want to be alone and see that guy again, even if I was crazy.

18

The soft orange glow of downtown Denver's lights illuminated the cars parked on the streets, and the howls of laughter and of stilettos could be heard up and down the streets as people mingled and walked downtown.

I always thought downtown Denver was so deceiving. From Arvada and surrounding areas it looked small; sure it has towering skyscrapers, but it is nothing compared to a big city like New York. However, whenever I actually am in Denver, it feels huge to me. Shops, restaurants, and clubs line the walkways, and it feels like a different world from the suburban, prairie Arvada life.

My thoughts quickly ended as we pulled into The Palace Lofts' valet wraparound drive; a guy in his late twenties jogged over to us and opened our doors.

"Welcome back to the Palace Lofts ladies, I'll take it from here." He winked at my mom and me as he smiled and got in my mom's car.

I just raised one eyebrow at him and thought, oh great another charmer, as my mom smiled fondly and we walked through the clear revolving door.

Inside, spotless creamy white carpet covered the floors, a gigantic chandelier hung above us in the arched ceiling. Each crystal seemed to shimmer at the slightest movement. A youngish girl a little bit older than me smiled at us as we passed the front desk and headed for the elevators. I pushed the up button on the wall and watched it go from clear to orange.

When Derek and I were little, we would always race each other to the elevators at a hotel, trying to be the first to push the button. I smiled inwardly at how the little things in life are the ones you sometimes remember the most.

The ding of the elevator announced that our ride was here, and my mom and I stepped easily inside the roomy black tiled elevator. Our ride ended as the ding of the elevator sounded once again, this time announcing our arrival to floor #7. We walked out of the elevator and I followed my mom down the hallway while she dug through her purse to find her keys. We stopped at a door with a golden plate on it that read, #53. Once my mom found her keys we were able to finally go inside.

My mother's loft is amazing. Or at least to me it is. It was one she had always wanted too, and with her flourishing bridal business she was able to get it for a reasonable amount. With over 1,100 square feet, wood floors throughout, three bedrooms, two baths, and a balcony that over-looks the city, it is easy to see why she always dreamed of living here. The kitchen came complete with stainless steal appliances, and a dark cherry wood that matched the dark, golden, granite countertops.

I walked to the right, past the kitchen and Derek's room, to the room I used when I stayed at my mom's, while my mom walked in the opposite direction to her room. I flicked the light switch and it be-came illuminated in a bright yellow glow. Some of my clothes I had left were scattered on the floor by a desk in the far corner, as a plain blush colored bed lay in front of me. The room was a lot plainer than my room at my dad's house, but I didn't mind. One of the bonuses to this loft was that not only did the master bedroom have a private bal-cony, but my bedroom did as well.

I opened the double glass doors removing the cream drapes in the process. Instantly, the cool October air met my skin. I leaned against the balcony's fence and closed my eyes, just relaxing and listening to the sounds around me. I picked up many sounds, most of them were cars and people, but another sound caught my attention and I pricked my ears to listen more. It was faint at first, but then I soon realized the sound was heading towards me, and getting closer at that.

I opened my eyes and looked towards the sound to discover a crow, as black as night, flying straight towards my balcony. The sound that had started out faint was now a decipherable 'cawing'. As strange as this crow was acting, I couldn't help but be curious, so instead of run-ning inside and shutting the doors like any other person might have done, I just kept staring at the crow.

It flew over to the balcony and perched itself on the right corner of the iron railing. It hopped on its feet a little while before flapping its wings and cawing directly at me. As I examined the bird over with my eyes to check for injuries and such, a habit of mine since I wanted to become a Zoologist when I'm older, I noticed a white folded sliver of paper that was on the bird's foot. Cautiously, I reached out toward the bird, and seeing that the bird wasn't going to bite me, slid the paper off its foot with ease.

I unfolded the tiny sliver of paper that looked as though it had been ripped from a larger piece of paper. Only one word had been written, in fancy cursive writing. It read, 'Soon'. I was startled when the bird cawed one last time and took flight. It flew in between the buildings until it was no longer in my line of sight. I looked down at the sliver of paper I still held in my hand, my mouth agape. 'Soon'.

With the dream at the massage place and this cryptic message, I began to silently freak out. I went back inside and shut and locked my balcony and bedroom doors, while calling good night to my mom.

I began pacing back and forth still clutching the ripped note. Alright, I thought, there has to be a reasonable explanation for all of this. Things like this just don't happen, especially to someone like me. As I wracked my brain for nonexistent answers, I began to yawn. I stopped pacing and lay down on my bed placing the note on my nightstand in the process. As I began to drift off into unconsciousness, one final thought entered my mind before sleep overtook me; 'What is happening to me? And 'Soon' for that matter.

Chapter 4

The next morning I awoke to the smell of fresh coffee being brewed. I lazily opened one eye as I looked at the clock, and groaned when I found it read: Saturday October 21st, 8:00 AM. As annoyed as I was that it was a Saturday and I was up at 8:00 AM, my thoughts quickly flicked to a strange and somewhat frightful dream I had had during the night.

A black crow delivering me a message that read only, 'Soon', and a fairly handsome guy smirking at me and calling my name in the darkness.

At least it was just a dream I thought as I shrugged and began to make my bed. As I threw decorative pillows on the bed and arranged them one by one, a sliver of paper on my dresser caught my attention. I eyed it cautiously, as if it was a dangerous predator.

No. No, I thought. It can't be. Can it?

My trembling hand slowly reached for the crumpled note. I slowly began to unravel it, and to my horror it read the one word I was dreading, 'Soon'. I felt my stomach tighten and let the tiny piece of paper drop to the floor. For a minute I stood unmoving, shocked. "What in the world is going on?" seemed to be the only thought repeating in my mind. I was shaken from my thoughts, when I heard my mom call from the kitchen.

"Alex, honey, are you up?"

At first I couldn't decide if the right thing to do was approach my mother and tell her everything that had happened from yesterday to today, about seeing the guy, and the crow delivering the note; but I immediately thought against it. If I wasn't even sure what was going on and I didn't understand it, freaking out my mother wouldn't help me find the answers I needed to the questions I had. So, I decided I would play it cool. I'd pretend everything was perfectly normal on the outside, even though on the inside I was screaming at the top of my lungs.

"Yeah mom, hold on just a sec, I'll be right out, k?" I yelled back.

I didn't wait to hear a reply, I needed to get rid of the note, or at least hide it somewhere until I could think about what I was going to do with it. I searched for crevices and boxes where I could stash it, and decided upon a book. I put the note inside my Wuthering Heights English book and stuffed it into my purse for later. Taking a deep breath, I gathered my composure so my mom wouldn't suspect a thing, and walked out to the kitchen.

My mom was quietly reading one of the latest bridal magazines and scribbling tiny notes in a notebook spread out across the counter. I poured myself a cup of coffee, knowing perfectly well my hand was shaking the entire time, and filled the rest of the cup with coffee creamer; it might not help with my shakiness, but at least I'd have an excuse for shaking.

I have never been one of those people who could drink straight black coffee. The smell alone is way too intense for me; my coffee usually consisted of half coffee, half cream. I sat on a barstool across from my mom as she started asking about my plans for the day. Honestly, I hadn't really thought about it, I mean with last night's activities my mind had been pretty preoccupied. However, I was sure I had about 10 missed calls from Kate wondering why in the world we weren't hanging out.

"Um," I replied, "I'm not really sure. I need to call Kate. She's probably called a ton wondering what I'm doing".

I smiled at the end, and mom smiled with me.

"Don't bother. She already called me this morning when she couldn't get a hold of you." She laughed. "She's already on her way over here to pick you up."

I laughed, but before I could ask how long ago she called, there was a knock on the door.

"Speak of the devil." I said as I skidded across the hardwood floor.

"Good Morning!" I screamed and smiled as I opened the door.

Kate screamed a huge good morning in return as I motioned to where the coffee pot was. Almost instantly, Kate was telling stories left and right about last night and her and Jesse's anniversary date. My mom seemed to struggle to keep up with what Kate was saying; to her she probably felt like she was listening to a tea kettle blaring on the stove top announcing animatedly that is was boiling. I just smiled. It was usually easy for me to follow along, but that was just because Kate and I were more like sisters than friends. She'd start a conversation and I'd usually know how she was going to finish it; so most of the time we were usually on the same page with one another.

"And so then he got all mad and said we were just not going to bother with it at all; he takes me home and we had a huge fight and everything. He drives me crazy! And then this morning I get a surprise visit from him. He has a card and flowers and everything, and tomorrow night we're going out again to make it all up."

Kate took a sip of her coffee and let out a huge sigh as she waited for our reaction.

"Wow," I said as I smiled. "That's one for the books." We all laughed and Mom mumbled something about young love.

"Well get your stuff, we're going to the mall so you can help me find an outfit for tonight." Kate stated enthusiastically. It was more of an order than anything else.

I laughed. "Is this at all optional?"

"Nope," she replied matter of factly.

I nodded my head and went to my room to grab my stuff and quickly get ready. Maybe what I need is a girl's day out, I thought. It could help keep my mind off other things, which I am refusing to think of, because stuff like that doesn't exist. I tried to reason with myself, as I pulled on a pair of Miss Me's Buckle jeans and a white t-shirt that had large sparkly black wings down the back. I hurriedly grabbed all my things, hugged my mom good-bye, and ran out the door with Kate. We pulled into the parking lot of the Flatirons Mall, and headed inside. The shops were bustling with people as they were every Saturday.

Hours had passed, and eventually Kate and I were completely shopped out. I had managed to find several cute shirts on our shopping escapade though – a blue long sleeved shirt with white feather designs down the arms and back, and a dress shirt that was emerald green, V-cut in the front, and had an open back to it that would go perfect with a pair of leggings. Afterwards we decided to go to my dad's to grab a snack, and then Kate would have to leave to get ready for her and Jesse's makeup date.

The house stood empty as we pulled into the drive, and my thoughts went to wondering how my brother was doing. It had been three weeks so far, and we still hadn't heard anything from him with the exception of one letter when he first arrived at boot camp letting us know he had made it to the base. I sighed softly and grabbed my bags. We headed inside and struggled into the kitchen with our purchases while I wondered where my dad might be. I hadn't seen his car in the driveway, however my question was soon answered when I found a piece of paper on the counter; it read:

> Hi Alex! I heard you stayed at moms last night since you weren't feeling well, but I hope you feel better and had a great day. I had to go out of town on a last minute business trip, so I won't be back until Monday, but if you need anything, Renee's number is in my office, and you have mine as well. Love you!
> -Dad

Kate read the note after me as if she had the same question I did, then asked how that was going with Renee. As I poured each of us a glass of V8 Splash and handed her a bag of pretzels, I shrugged nonchalantly.

"I don't know. Good I guess."

Renee was sort of dating my dad now. I had met her a few times; I was always polite. After all, as long as he's happy that's all that matters, but Renee was just a lot for me to handle at the moment. It was hard for me to even think of my dad with another woman, and with Derek gone and the divorce still fresh, the last thing I wanted to deal with was my dad's new girlfriend. Kate seemed to understand and didn't push the subject any further. Instead, I changed the subject to her date with Jesse tonight, and for the rest of the time we talked about that.

It wasn't long before we said our good-byes and I told her to tell me all about how her makeup date went. As I closed the front door a pang of loneliness hit me. I never noticed how flamboyant our house had seemed prior to the divorce, or Derek leaving. It was always filled with people, my mom, dad, Derek and I accompanied by Kate and Trey and all of our friends. That's just how it was; that was our normal.

Somehow now, standing in the hallway alone it seemed deserted and as empty as ever. Not wanting to bear the silence anymore, I decided I would go upstairs and turn on some music in my room and busy myself. As I walked into my room I noticed immediately my alarm clock sitting in the middle of my bed. I cocked my head, and with a confused look on my face, went to it.

That's weird, I thought. I don't remember moving my clock.

I shrugged it off and picked up the alarm clock and placed it in its rightful place on my night stand, before turning on shuffle on Spotify and going to take a shower. After a steaming hot shower I went to my dresser and pulled out black sweats with a white T-shirt that said *I bite* in black letters. I smiled at the memory of my father buying me the shirt a while back, because he said it fit my personality to a T; at least in the mornings.

As I pulled the shirt on over my head I couldn't help but feel like something wasn't right, that awkward feeling people get when they know they're not alone.

Come on Alex. I thought. You're just being irrational. After all, you're seventeen years old, not five, you should be able to stay home alone and not be scared.

I turned around and started walking towards my dresser, feeling foolish that I had a feeling like that at all, when I froze dead in my tracks. My alarm clock was in the center of my bed facing me again. I stood stone still, my thoughts racing. The only way my clock could move from my nightstand to the center of my bed was if someone had moved it, and I, surely, did not move it.

Instantly every sensory organ in my body heightened; I couldn't even hear myself breathe. I stood statuesque, straining my ears to pick up any foreign sounds, my eyes to capture the slightest movement, or my nose to smell something out of the ordinary; nothing. Everything seemed to stand as still as I. My brain began racing through possible scenarios. Was someone in my house? Is someone, maybe Trey or Kate, just messing with me?

At that moment my fear turned to anger. I stormed outside the doorway to my room, then back in my room ready for a fight. I slammed open my window and stood back and yelled.

"Listen up! Whoever you are, and whatever you're doing, you better knock it off right now, because I don't play games pal!"

Fuming, I stood looking towards my window until I felt the familiar shudder I had hoped to never feel again. Before I had time to react to the shudder, I was jolted by a voice, one that was becoming all too familiar by now, sounding behind me.

"What if I like games, Alex?"

I didn't move. My ears had picked up that same soothing husky voice I had heard before; there was only one way to be certain if what I was hearing was real or not. I would have to turn around. I paused, then spun around and staggered, speechless, as I looked at the man from my dreams, my nightmares and from Massage Envy. He stood as real as ever leaning against my dresser with his arms crossed on his chest. He was wearing the same clothes as before and his face held the same smirk and chillingly icy blue eyes. Before everything turned black, only one thought crossed my mind. He is real.

Chapter 5

I awoke to the smell of mouth-watering bacon and eggs.

Dad's home early. And cooking? I thought, as I groggily opened and rubbed the sleep from my eyes.

There was only one problem, my dad should have still been on his business trip. I'm the only one home, and I'm not cooking. Adrenaline rushed through my body. As I was about to pounce from my bed and make my escape through the nearest exit, most likely my window; a voice stopped me in my tracks.

"Good Morning Alex, I'm glad you are awake."

My head instantly snapped towards the direction the voice came from, my doorway. The same guy from Massage Envy still dressed in his all black attire stood leaning against the door frame. The ashy and caramel lightness of his skin against the darkness of his clothes made him appear as if he came straight out of a black and white movie. Until I saw his eyes. In contrast to the rest of him, they were the only color, like some special effects technique. I would know those eyes anywhere – electric ice blue, with a ring of deep blue around them that pierced me where I sat in my bed, as if to keep me from even trying to move or escape. I had hardly noticed the huge tray he had been holding until he lifted it up and smirked at me; probably at my ridiculously freaked out expression.

He placed the tray on my night stand next to me, then dragged my desk chair to the side of the bed and straddled it. He crossed his arms over the back of the chair as he looked at me and smiled again, before breaking me out of my daze.

"I knew you were going to be surprised, even shocked, but I didn't know it was going to be this bad." He seemed amused.

I however, was not. His callousness and arrogance evoked my anger. My eyebrows furrowed and I rose from my bed and began shouting and yelling at him.

"Just who do you think you are?! Why are you in my house?! And cooking breakfast for that matter?! How dare you! Get out right now before I call the cops!" I fumed.

By the end of my rant I was in front of him, my arms folded across my chest and breathing heavily from the severe rush of adrenaline that had just flowed through my body. He seemed astounded that I had just yelled at him. His eyebrows were raised and a bewildered look had betaken his face. He quickly gathered his composure while getting up and shifting his weight from foot to foot, then stopped and looked me dead in my eyes. Intensity seeped from him and I was almost regretting what I had just done.

"My name is Nathaniel; I'm in your house for reasons which I can't explain to you at the moment. I made you breakfast as a nice gesture; which you're going to sit down and eat, and good luck calling the cops because no one will believe you, and when they haul you off to an insane asylum, guess what? You'll still have to put up with me. Now I'm tired, I'm going to go sleep on the couch, so don't get any cute ideas about trying to evade me or escape, mm, k sweetheart?"

With that, he turned and slammed the door on his way out. Now I was taken aback. No one has ever talked to me like that, especially some mentally unstable guy who thinks all of a sudden he can imprison me, cook, and sleep in my house.

I am so having a nightmare right now, I thought.

Stunned, I sat on the edge of my bed for about 30 seconds or so, replaying exactly what had happened from last night up to this morning, when my nose picked up the satisfying smell of bacon and eggs once more.

Hmmm, I thought. Even if Nathaniel is a jerk, who randomly imprisons people – if that's even his real name – I can still enjoy a freshly cooked breakfast in bed right? There's no harm in that.

As I sipped on some orange juice and bit into a piece of bacon, I pondered ways I was going to escape. I had to do something. There is no way some stranger is keeping me under house arrest. My parents can't even do that. I devoured my bacon, confused as to what Nathaniel meant by the cops not believing me.

I shuddered. Being stuck with Nathaniel sounded like a nightmare that didn't have an end. I pushed it to the back of my mind and began pacing. I had to try and call someone for help; I knew I could easily escape unscathed and unnoticed from my window, but it would be awhile before I could contact someone for help if I just ran, and who knew what this guy was capable of.

Silently, I placed my ear against my bedroom door and listened. It was quiet enough so I gathered my kidnapper had found the couch downstairs and already started snoozing. Ever so carefully I gripped the door knob and twisted it without a sound. Poking my head out to check if the coast was clear, I made a dash for my dad's room where the house phone sat on his nightstand.

My hands began to shake as I picked up the phone and dialed numbers rapidly. Nothing. Not even a dial tone. Still trembling, I traced the phone cord back to the wall. The line was dead. I wondered if he could have done this. My anxiety rose as I set the phone back down and rushed back into my bedroom shutting the door behind me quickly and quietly. I had naïvely left my cell phone downstairs. So much for calling 911 and having this nightmare end, I thought. I needed to get out of the house and away from my kidnapper fast.

I walked over to my window and looking out, saw the sturdy eggshell barn sitting several hundred feet from the house. If I could sneak out my window, scale the house without being seen and get my horse, I could ride to get help through the woods that backed the edge of our property. Town couldn't be more than five or so miles away, and Kate's house was just on the outskirts of it. I turned away from my window and sighed.

"Here goes nothing."

Chapter 6

I decided it might be good to bring my duffle bag, I could throw some useful things in there and when I make it to Kate's, I could bunk with her until my dad got home. I threw together random clothes along with a small amount of toiletries and other necessities. I was desperately searching for my purse when I realized I had left it downstairs along with my cell phone. Irritated that the one thing that could save me was inaccessible on the main level of my own house I zipped the duffle bag. There was no way I was going to ruin my escape by going downstairs to get my cell phone. I'd just have to wait till I got to the Jackson's. Lastly, I changed outfits. I ripped a pair of blue jeans off a hanger in my closet and pulled them on followed by a zip up hoodie and hiking boots.

Careful not to make a sound, I slowly slid my window open just enough to where I could get through, then shut it from the other side.

Now, scaling the side of a house sounds easy, even with a flat roof, but trust me when I say it isn't. Especially for someone who is afraid of heights. I was wondering if I had thought my plan through enough, but there was no turning back now.

I placed my duffle bag on my shoulder and gripped the cliché gutter rose vine trellis that my mom had bought for the side of the house back before they decided to get the divorce. When I was low enough I carefully dropped, making as little noise as possible. Once my feet hit the ground I was off. I cut through a portion of the fence and used the long grass as cover while I darted out to the barn. Inside, I heard the familiar whinny of my horse, Ajax, who must have noticed me come in. He is an all-black Frisian, with one of the longest curly manes and tail I've ever seen on a horse. My dad was fortunate to have had the opportunity to purchase him for half of what he was worth when a friend had downsized and sold his home, barn and land.

I smiled as I softly petted his black nose; the scent of old leather and hay filled my lungs. My dad and I each have our own horse. I started riding when I was 11 and ever since then, I've loved it, and Ajax and I have been inseparable. Quickly, I unlocked his stall door, grabbed a trusty Western saddle and bridle, and began to tack him up.

With six years of riding experience under my belt it took no time at all before I had Ajax all saddled and ready to go. I began leading him out to the back of the barn doors and that's when I heard it. My name being shouted angrily and what sounded like something breaking.

Oh my God, I thought. He knows.

I threw the doors open then, desperate to not get caught and fearing the consequences of getting caught; I jumped into the saddle. Ajax was high strung, feeling my nervousness and reared in the tall grass in the pasture just long enough for me to see Nathaniel; fury was etched in his every feature. He was glaring at me from the back of the house. I spun Ajax around and took off towards the woods. We crossed what was left of our property in a matter of seconds and before I knew it I was shaded in the thick cover of the woods. There was no way I was going to slow down though; I wasn't planning on stopping until I got to Kate's house or to a police station.

Ajax and I glided through the underbrush effortlessly, his long strides moving me away from Nathaniel, relieving some of my anxiety. That was until I had to slam Ajax to a halt. Two different paths leading in opposite directions lay before me. Since this was a national forest, hikers and trails enveloped this entire area, however I had heard my dad recently talking about new trails being made and to my dread, this junction was one of those.

It had not been here before and a helpless feeling sank in my stomach. If I took the wrong path it would lead me deeper into the forest and farther from help. The other path would lead me straight into town, which is what I wanted. The question was which path was the right one?

Ajax paced anxiously almost as if he could feel my tension. Normally, I knew which direction town was, the only problem was now that I was deep in a forest I had no idea which direction was which, especially with the twisting turns of the trails. I decided to rely on my instincts, which told me to go right. So once again I took off. I had slowed my pace a little to a casual canter after a while, and then slowed to a walk so Ajax could take a break. The last thing I wanted to do was to make him winded and tired.

It was silent in the woods except for the soft plodding of hooves on the trail, chirping birds, and the gentle wind that pushed the leaves of the trees making a rustling whooshing sound.

I loved the forest and how peaceful it was; you could get away and never know there was a bustling city just beyond it. I listened to the noises around me and after a while I picked up on the sound of rushing water. The Winding River; Derek and I had been fishing at the Winding Lake once when we were younger; the lake which the river flowed into, and then into town. I smiled and coaxed Ajax into a trot; if I could follow the river downstream it would lead me straight into town.

I ducked down closer to Ajax as he walked below trees and there it was. Ajax and I stood on the edge of a huge gaping meadow that was filled in the center with a lake and next to us was the Winding River flowing through it. I sat gazing for a moment, somewhat proud of my escape and how my plan was actually working.

So much for damsels in distress, I thought with a grin.

The last of the summer flowers sprung up everywhere throughout the meadow; visions of purples, blues, whites, and pinks were everywhere. And in the center, lay the pristine lake that seemed untouched. It was a beautiful sight, but crows cawing and flying out of a nesting tree nearby made me stop lollygagging and remember that Nathaniel was still out there looking for me.

I was anxious at first about exposing my position in the open meadow, but I had no other choice; besides, if Nathaniel was anywhere, he would be in town or on the outskirts of town waiting for me instead of deep in the woods, I thought. I glanced at the mountains and noticed the sun had already begun to set; I was losing light fast and if I wanted to stay on track and not get lost I needed to make it to town by sundown.

With that present threat, I trotted Ajax towards the lake and out of cover. The Crows were still making a ruckus and flying about overhead, but I wanted Ajax to get a drink of water before I pressed on. As Ajax half waded into the water and slurped and sipped, something familiar hit me.

A chillingly cold shudder made its way from my lower back to the top of my spine. It made all the hairs on the back of my neck stand on end, and in that moment, I knew I wasn't alone.

I frantically raised Ajax's attention and looked around for the intruder; for him. My eyes stopped to my left as I recognized the familiar outline of Nathaniel and my father's horse, Doc. Before I could react he was already galloping towards me, cutting the distance between me and him in half. Ajax seemed to understand what I wanted and raced away towards the direction of town. I was panicking; I had no idea what Nathaniel was capable of and after his little outburst this morning, I highly doubted I wanted to see anything more.

With the head start Nathaniel had had, I could feel him gaining on me; he was close now, way too close.

If I can just make it to the tree line maybe I can lose him, I thought.

My plan didn't even have a chance. I felt my body being thrown off my horse by an unrecognizable force. Cold water and darkness surrounded me; I swam towards the only source of light I could see.

I gasped for breathe once I hit the surface; realizing that Nathaniel had dove off his horse and tackled me into the lake. I didn't think, I just began frantically swimming to Ajax who was standing on the bank. I heard Nathaniel surface behind me and I pushed my body even harder praying I would make it to land. I stumbled on land and then went down roughly, only not by accident.

Nathaniel grunted as he flipped me over and pinned me to the ground as I struggled. He straddled my waist and held my wrists firmly on either side of my face.

"Get off me!" I yelled, furious he had caught me.

"No!" he yelled back, just as furious.

I struggled for a little longer till I realized I had already wasted a lot of my energy with no results, and I was exhausted. I stopped moving and lay there breathing heavily. He didn't relax his grip on my wrists when I stopped, but he seemed just as frazzled as I was.

There was a moment of silence before he stared me directly in the eyes and flatly said, "You're a slow learner. I told you already Alex, you can't get rid of me."

My eyes widened. I could feel my body start to go numb. Maybe it was my defiant nature or the fact that I have a problem with authority and being told what to do; either way, I couldn't just let myself be kidnapped. One thing was for certain, I was not going without a fight.

I kept still and didn't struggle. As he began to loosen his grip on my wrists I took a chance. I kicked him where it hurts and thrust my palm upwards on his nose before scrambling out from under him and jumping on Ajax. I heard Nathaniel gasp and groan in pain as I raced Ajax towards the woods. Silently I giggled.

I can't believe I just did that, I thought, giddy with exhaustion.

Ajax and I galloped away; I had no time to stop and find the trail to town, I just wanted to get away from Nathaniel as fast as possible; so Ajax and I took no path, instead, we rushed through the uncharted woods and were safe at last. Or so I thought.

Chapter seven

Darkness had fully enveloped everything and with it came an eerie silence. I was starting to regret not having taken a path when I escaped from Nathaniel at the lake. Flustered, hungry, annoyed, and tired, Ajax and I walked aimlessly onward.

"I know we're lost," I snapped at Ajax as he snorted and, annoyed, stomped his feet.

I could hardly see anything in front of us and toppled-over logs came as a surprise when Ajax climbed over them. We had meandered a little farther when, from what I could see, the scenery around us had changed drastically. Moss seemed to cover every surface and hung like thick spider webs from the trees, as decaying logs lay sprawled out everywhere on the forest floor.

Great, I thought sarcastically.

This was going to make moving through here an extremely tedious task. As I brushed a web-like piece of moss from my face, my senses spiked. I had that bad feeling again, the feeling that Ajax and I were no longer alone. I felt someone watching me and I strained my eyes to see farther ahead. There it was - the flicker of two round glowing lights; eyes. As fast as I had seen them, they were gone in a flash. That confirmed it.

I'm definitely not alone, I thought shakily, and tried to keep moving. A small opening forged and I had room to turn Ajax in a full 360 degrees to get a better look at my surroundings and my hunter. I stopped Ajax after a moment and listened. It was dead quiet. The only noises that were heard were the sound of my heartbeat pounding in my chest and Ajax's heavy breathing.

Suddenly Ajax whinnied loudly and began snorting and stomping his hooves. Obviously he was sensing something he didn't like at all; what scared me the most was I had no idea what it was. I tried to sooth and calm Ajax, but it was no use. I could see blue flashes of light wherever I looked around me. I tightly closed my eyes as I gripped the reins firmly between my fists and held my breath; I just wanted all of this to be over. I couldn't stand it any longer.

"Boo." Someone breathed huskily in my right ear.

I was startled so much I lost my balance and fell from Ajax who snorted and jumped away from me. I landed on my butt and frantically tried to scoot away from the ever advancing Nathaniel; panicking as my back hit a tree stopping my retreat. My stomach dropped and I felt sick with helplessness. I never took my eyes off Nathaniel's as he continued to move towards me. They were even more piercing in the dark and seemed to glow like bright blue fog lights on a car. But just as I thought those eyes were going to be the last things I was ever going to see, Nathaniel halted a foot in front of me, but the intensity from his face never ceased; I watched in a daze as he sniffed the air quickly and before I could register what was happening, a snarl ripped from the bushes to my left as a mountain lion headed straight in my direction.

Everything happened in a blur; one moment I'm a second away from death by a wild animal, and the next, a growl ripped from the throat of Nathaniel that seemed to match the big cat's. Dirt and debris flew and I watched in horror as Nathaniel got behind the cat on the ground and, wrapping his arms around the beast's throat, suffocated it. A moment later silence once again befell the forest and Nathaniel let the head of the mountain lion drop to the ground with a thud.

He hung his head so I couldn't read his expression and breathed heavily, while his body tensed and relaxed again and again. I sat motionless. I had no idea if what I just saw really happened or even what to think at the moment; I just gaped at Nathaniel with wide eyes.

After what felt like an eternity, Nathaniel finally looked up at me; he took a deep breath and began to take long strides towards me. From what I could see, his face had not softened an ounce since the fight with the cougar. I gulped. Nathaniel roughly grabbed my elbow and pulled me towards Ajax.

"Get on," he ordered, and firmly shoved me into the saddle, then jumped on behind me.

I was too shocked from what had just happened to even argue, not to mention the fact that I was petrified. Nathaniel just killed a mountain lion, I kept repeating in my head – with his bare hands.

He picked up Doc where he had left him tethered to a tree and began to lead us all home. We galloped silently, until the familiar glow of the barn and house came into view again. I had no idea how Nathaniel had managed to lead us safely back to the house so quickly when I could barely see where we were going, let alone navigate.

I was still hoping desperately that somehow all of this was a dream that I would soon wake up from and laugh about later. But I had a feeling this was not a dream and I was either being taken back home by a man with extraordinary capabilities, or by a psychotic killer/stalker. My eyes were fighting to stay open but I couldn't shake the possible scenarios of what might happen next. I had escaped, kicked and punched Nathaniel, watched him fight and kill a mountain lion, and was now caught and brought back to stay in an empty house with him.

Panic coursed through my veins and for the first time in my life, I was truly afraid.

Nathaniel dismounted and pulled me down after him. He untacked Ajax and Doc and put them in their stalls before he once again took hold of my elbow, practically dragging me through the pasture and back inside the house.

Once inside he pulled me up the stairs to my room and into my bathroom and began noisily banging and searching the cupboards. I flinched at the noise and stood back from him; noticing he had dropped his iron grip from my arm. He seemed to find what he was looking for and pulled out a first aid kit that I had always kept in case of emergencies. He threw the bag on the counter and turned towards me. I held my head high as he came forward, trying to let him see I wasn't afraid of him, however, I was so scared I thought I might faint.

He reached out towards my face and instinctively I flinched and retreated from him; backing away quickly. He stopped. It seemed to dawn on him that after what had happened earlier I was not comfortable near him. Nathaniel looked down at the bathroom tile for a moment taking in a deep breath before he looked back at me. He spoke evenly.

"Listen, I'm not going to hurt you Alex. I need to see if you're hurt. That's all. Please Alex."

His voice seemed almost desperate as he finished. I stood looking into his eyes for a moment; the florescent blue orbs that had moments ago been fires seemed a softer glow. They were not as intense as before and now resembled a cool water's blue.

"Ok." I managed to squeak out, and I hesitantly moved one step closer.

I still was ready to bolt at any given moment, but somehow I knew that what Nathaniel had said was truthful and I could trust it. Nathaniel slowly moved towards me and this time used both of his hands to check for injuries. He held up and checked both my arms before releasing them and using his hands examined my whole neck and face with extreme scrutiny.

My heart was pounding rapidly the whole time; he was so close I could breathe in his scent and feel his breathe on my neck and face. I felt a combination of dizziness and lightheadedness. He smelled of a strong mint and sweet aroma, mixed with a finer earthy smell, which balanced out how strong it was. I tried to preoccupy my mind as he once again cupped my chin and moved it up to expose my neck and throat, but nothing seemed to be working. It was like I couldn't smell, see, or hear anything else but him; he was everywhere; enveloping me like a drug or vaporous gas and keeping me firmly in his grasp.

"Good." He whispered.

Nathaniel's voice seemed to shake me from inside and snap me back to reality. He breathed a sigh of relief then released me from his grasp and motioned for me to follow him out into the bedroom. I stood dumbfounded for a minute regaining control of myself before I followed him out.

Pull yourself together Alex! I scolded myself internally. He kidnapped you, remember?

At the thought of that I put up my defenses again and prepared myself for the worst. He motioned for me to sit down on the edge of the bed as his face took on a contemplative emotion. He paced with long strides for several minutes in front of me, rubbing his chin as he walked. I raised my eyebrows, a little irritated at how he obviously wanted to tell me something but didn't.

"Take your time. I'm really quite comfortable." I said sarcastically.

This seemed to knock him out of his thoughts and he turned to give me an aggravated look.

"I'm glad." he retorted. "Because since I obviously can't trust that you won't try to escape again, you're going to be spending a lot of time in here."

My glare deepened and I rolled my eyes, waiting for him to continue.

"So, here is how this is going to go. I need your help and since you can't get rid of me you are going to help me. In return, I will answer any questions you may or may not have. I am going to accompany you anywhere you go until I no longer need your help and then you will never have to see me ever again. Deal?"

He stated more than questioned. Panic took over as I thought about Nathaniel escorting me everywhere I went, and with that thought, I hastily replied.

"No, that does not sound good Nathaniel! Are you crazy? I don't even know who you are! You can't follow me around twenty-four seven!" I yelled as my composure broke. "Besides," I said coolly, "my dad is going to be home tomorrow and he will certainly not approve of you being anywhere near me."

Nathaniel's face seemed unaffected by my comment and his small smile only proved to confuse me more.

"What?" I asked, truly curious as to what he seemed to find so funny.

"Alex, Alex, Alex." He breathed slowly. "There's a lot you don't know about me. I already thought of that; which is why you are going to introduce me to your father as well as everyone else, as your boyfriend. That way no one will get the wrong idea."

"You mean the idea of how you just appeared out of nowhere one day and decided to kidnap and use me against my will?" I interjected angrily.

Callously he replied, "Yep that would be the one."

Then a question popped into my head.

"Wait a minute," I said hastily, now truly confused. "At the massage place my mom couldn't see you at all. How could my dad and others see you then?"

He sighed a little.

"Yeah, unfortunately, we are only allowed one time where we can choose to be seen by only one person and no one else. I already used mine up that day at Massage Envy, so this is going to be our plan B."

"What do you mean, *our* plan?"

I spoke trying to get a hold on the downpour of information I was receiving. He shook his head quickly before replying,

"Nope, no more questions tonight, sorry Alex."

"But, wait," I pleaded wholeheartedly. "So if I help you you'll leave me alone right?" I questioned nervously.

"That's the deal." Nathaniel replied nonchalantly.

I thought about it for a minute. Whatever Nathaniel wanted my help with confused me, but the sooner I helped him get what he wanted the sooner he would be out of my life for good, and I could go on and pretend it never happened in the first place. Resolved, I replied.

"Ok, I'll do it, but I have one condition."

"Anything," Nathaniel replied, sounding somewhat curious and sincere.

"You have to promise me that this whole thing is just between you and me; you won't involve any of my family or friends."

Confirming he agreed, Nathaniel bowed his head a little and spoke.

"Agreed."

His confirmation eased my anxiety a little and I wondered what exactly I had just gotten myself into. Could I really trust that Nathaniel would keep his word? I could only wait and find out. Before I could think any more on the subject Nathaniel smiled and spoke exuberantly.

"Now for your punishment for the rest of tonight, until your father returns home..."

Oh great, I thought sarcastically.

My hopes of Nathaniel forgetting the day's earlier events shattered to a million pieces.

"I will be spending the night in here with you," he motioned around the room, "and I slept for a while earlier so I don't need to sleep tonight."

He smirked as he waited for my response. I almost gagged as he finished his speech.

The only response I could muster was "You've got to be joking."

His smirk deepened as he looked at my repulsed facial expression.

"Oh come on Alex. It won't be that bad. Besides if we're going to be dating by tomorrow, it'll be good for you."

Satisfied with himself, he smiled as he sat in my desk chair.

"I just threw up in my mouth. How do I know you're not some psychotic unstable killer who is going to murder me during the night?" I replied sardonically, hoping that if I was a brat to him he would prefer to sleep anywhere but in the same room with me.

He seemed irritated by my comment.

"Trust me," he said, mocking me, "I'm sure sleeping in a pile of needles would be more pleasant than sleeping in the same room with someone as feisty as you, but it looks like we're both stuck with each other, aren't we princess?"

With that he got up and finished his statement before he left the room.

"Oh, and by the way, if I was going to kill you, I would have done it in the woods where no one would find you and it wouldn't make a mess."

"Ugh." I huffed, appalled at his statement.

He is going to drive me crazy, I thought, but he did have a point about the murder thing. It makes sense that if that was what he was going to do, he would have done it already.

I stormed into the bathroom, did my usual routine of brushing my teeth and washing my face, and threw my hair into a messy pony before walking back into my room to change for bed.

Like he knows anything about me, I thought, feeling defensive. I can be quite sweet when someone doesn't kidnap me and force me to help them.

I threw on a plain purple t-shirt, double checking that Nathaniel was nowhere to be seen, and then pulled on my white Capri sweats. A knock sounded on the door as I went to my bed and began throwing all six decorative pillows off.

Nathaniel took my non-answer as a sign that it was ok to enter and shut the door behind him. I refused to look at him; my stomach was already in twists and knots thanks to the fact that I would have to be sharing a room with a male stranger tonight. When I noticed he was just standing there staring at me I quickened my pace and began throwing pillows to where he directly stood in my peripherals.

I heard him chuckle under his breath as he caught two and dodged the others that flew at his head.

"Nervous?" He arrogantly implied.

His comment made me want to throw something a lot heavier at him, but I resisted the urge and instead glared at him; refusing to add to his ego.

"Of what? You? I've seen better," I responded, unaffected.

He gave me a death glare back before beginning to remove his shirt.

"Um, what are you doing?" I asked him hastily.

"What does it look like?" He replied uninterested.

I shifted my feet uncomfortably.

"Well, don't you think you'll get cold? I mean the floor gets cold you know. You might want to keep your shirt on?"

The last part of my reply came out as more of a question than a statement, and Nathaniel seemed to smile and take enjoyment at how uncomfortable I was.

"Alex, Hun." He mockingly replied.

"Who said I was sleeping on the floor?"

He flashed me a grin as my knees almost gave out. Alarm flooded through my body as I tried not to freak out. I already knew that being close to Nathaniel made my mind dumb when it came to functioning properly, I couldn't imagine what it would do if I had to sleep in the same bed with him.

I made my voice as strong and defiant as I could muster and then replied.

"I did, and since you're such a gentleman, I'm sure you'll be glad to sleep on the floor. I'll even give you a pillow."

Confidently I smiled at him as he calmly walked towards the other side of the bed and got in.

"Whoever said I was a gentleman?"

My smile faded and was replaced with anger as a half-naked Nathaniel smiled. I grumbled about how much of a jerk Nathaniel was and reluctantly got into bed.

"Try and stay on your side of the bed tonight will you."

I retorted as I turned on my side with my back facing Nathaniel. He seemed unaffected by my comment, that or he just ignored it, as I heard him huff out a breath and say what I thought sounded like, "Sweet dreams Alex."

Soon, sleep overcame me and my eyes closed.

Chapter 8

I was walking through the woods. It was dark beneath the towering trees that blotted out the sun from above; holes in the leaves of trees and open gaps let in streams of golden rays that spilled onto the world below. I was lost. Just randomly walking and searching for a way out when a caw sounded from behind me. I turned around in time to see a black crow swoop below the tree line straight towards me. I stood frozen in place, and just as I thought the bird would ram straight into me, a flash of blinding white light flashed behind it as it cawed, making me crouch down and shield my eyes from the brightness.

When I stood up the crow was nowhere to be seen and the blinding white light had disappeared. I was still in the forest only now there were no golden rays of light; it was night. I looked up through a hole in the forest canopy, trying to locate the moon so I could have a little light and maybe have some way of getting out of this forest. When I finally found what I was looking for. I noticed that it was no regular moon. A blood moon eclipse had begun and before I knew it, the moon, once a bright gray and white, was replaced by a shining blood red and orange hole where white light shone all around it.

I was stunned by its dark beauty, until I was jolted from my thoughts when a black crow's screeching caw made me cover my ears. Everywhere I could hear voices saying 'Soon, soon, Alex, soon', and mixed with the crows cawing I couldn't take it anymore. I closed my eyes tightly and screamed.

I sat up in bed; a fresh coat of sweat covered my skin and I was breathing heavily. I jumped at the touch of Nathaniel's hand on my back; I had forgotten he was in the same room with me, let alone the same bed.

"Alex, what's wrong? Are you ok?" Nathaniel seemed genuinely concerned as he scanned the room with his eyes, and when they came up empty looked back at me.

"I'm, I'm fine." I shakily replied. "It was just a dream, that's all."

He didn't seem to believe me, but decided not to push the subject. I lay back down uncomfortably, and then turned to my side facing Nathaniel.

"I'll be awake for the rest of the night; sleep Alex."

I glanced at him once; almost giving him a silent thank you and feeling a strange pull towards him. A stranger was practically sleeping in my bed and yet for some reason, he felt trustworthy. I finished my thoughts and glanced at him once again before closing my eyes; his arms where folded behind his head as he stared at the ceiling. For a moment I wondered what he was thinking, until sleep took over once again and everything went black.

I was forcefully awakened; I groaned in dismay at the irritating jabs and shakes from Nathaniel.

"Ugh, go away," I protested. "You don't exist." Nathaniel laughed softly before returning to his previous task of poking and jabbing me.

"Wake up Alex." he crooned and warned, "Or I'll show you that I really do exist."

I mumbled something incoherent into my pillow as I tried to drift back to sleep once more.

"Ok, then," said Nathaniel as I felt the weight of the bed shift.

Finally, I thought, exasperated by his presence. Now I can get some sleep. Before I drifted off into the never-ending blackness again, I felt the covers being thrown off me and my body being lifted and thrown over a stone hard object.

"What the hell!" I screamed as I realized Nathaniel was carrying me fireman style. "Put me down! What is wrong with you?!"

Nathaniel laughed before arrogantly asking, "Do I exist now?"

"Ugh! I really wish you didn't!" I frantically replied as Nathaniel lowered me to the floor. I stepped back from him and tried pulling myself together. Nathaniel stood with his arms over his chest trying his hardest not to burst out laughing. Flustered, I stomped into the bathroom and closed the door so I could shower. Once I had finished with my normal routine, and successfully kicked Nathaniel out of my room so I could get dressed, I appraised myself in my bathroom mirror at the finished result.

Today, I decided to wear a white lace t-shirt top with a pair of holey, dark skinny jeans, and my buckle, knee-high black boots. I wondered how my dad would react when he got home and I had to tell him I was dating Nathaniel; or fake-dating him anyway.

I had a bit of a sick feeling in the pit of my stomach. I never lied to my parents; or anyone for that matter. It just didn't suit me. I shrugged it off. This should be interesting, I thought. Sometimes a girl's got to do what a girl's got to do, and I went downstairs to where Nathaniel was.

I found him in the kitchen, a full plate of freshly cooked eggs, bacon, and toast with strawberry jam had just been pushed to an empty barstool at the kitchen table. Nathaniel smiled as I walked towards the inviting smell with a curious look on my face, and sat down in the barstool. He then continued about his business; cleaning the pans and utensils he had used when cooking. He acted like this was a normal routine for him. As he finished cleaning, he grabbed another plate he had set aside for himself and began eating across from me.

"Thanks." I said softly as I took a bite of my strawberry jelly toast.

"No problem." he replied casually as he looked up at me before returning his focus back to his eggs. "I forgot how good this stuff tastes." He seemed to say more to himself as he scarfed down the rest of his food and closed his eyes to savor the taste.

I cocked my head a little at his statement. Nathaniel was more confusing to me than anyone else I had ever met. He was also probably the most interesting person I had ever met. But something kept telling me something wasn't quite right or normal about him. I couldn't put my finger on it.

"What do you mean?" I inquired. "Surely you've had to eat food every day, just like everyone else." Nathaniel looked up at me then, something in his eyes had changed; he looked like he was about to tell me something, but instead averted his eyes from my gaze and put his plate and mine in the dishwasher.

"Yeah, I guess so."

I was going to press the issue when the phone shook me from my thoughts. I reflexively jumped up and ran to the portable phone on the charger behind Nathaniel.

"Hello" I answered.

"Hey, Alex!" I immediately recognized my dad's voice on the other end of the line.

"Hey!" I replied a little nervous; I was hoping I would have a little more time to think of how exactly I was going to break the news to my dad that I have a fake boyfriend, who, up until today he had never heard of.

"I just wanted to let you know I'm going to be home within a few hours. Were you ok while I was gone?"

I thought about my answer for a moment and snuck a glance at Nathaniel who had his brows furrowed in a serious expression as he watched me talk on the phone.

"Yeah," I lied. "Everything was just fine, I'm fine; I just sort of hung out at the house and yesterday I took Ajax for a ride in the woods." Technically it wasn't a total lie, I thought. I did take Ajax for a ride, but that was only because I was trying to escape a guy who imprisoned me in our house.

I looked at Nathaniel again and this time his face had seemed to soften at what I had told my dad. He must have thought it somewhat funny, too.

"Good! Well I'll see you soon then, ok! And I have something to tell you when I get home, too."

"Ok, yeah, I have something to tell you, too. Well sounds good I'll see you when you get here," I replied. I hung up the phone after that and turned to meet the stare of Nathaniel. His eyes were an intense ice blue and they seemed to pierce right through me. I averted my gaze and looked at the ground and back up again. He was definitely making butterflies do twists and turns throughout my stomach by staring at me.

"So..." I said trying to break the awkward silence and forget about the fluttering butterflies.

"Two hours huh?" Nathaniel asked.

"Yeah," I replied a little shocked he had heard my dad say that on the other end of the phone.

"You're nervous about telling your dad aren't you?" Nathaniel spoke while appraising my reaction carefully.

"No," I hastily replied. He kept his gaze on me as I looked away and then back at him again. "Well, maybe a little I guess."

Believe it or not I haven't really had many boyfriends." Many was an exaggeration, I thought. I had only dated a hand-full of guys before, one of which was in junior high and it only lasted three days because we were too good of friends. I had avoided dating anyone at my high school due to the fact that I couldn't take anyone seriously enough. I am extremely picky, as Kate once confirmed.

Nathaniel nodded his head seeming to understand before he replied, "I know Alex. I know more than you think."

I glanced up at him again and was about to ask what he meant when I noticed he was wearing the same black attire as when I had first met him.

"Hmm..." I pondered.

"What?" Nathaniel uncomfortably tried to stand still as I walked around him appraising his outfit.

"First things first." I said. "We need to get you some new clothes." Nathaniel shyly looked down and back up at me.

"Yeah, I sort of left in a hurry," he muttered.

I thought he might be blushing, but before I could tell if he was or not he somewhat excitedly grabbed my purse from the barstool next to me and motioned me out the door. As I went to pull my keys to my Mitsubishi Endeavor out of my purse, Nathaniel opened the passenger side door to an all black 1967 Shelby Gt500 with a silver racing stripe down the center.

"There's no need," Nathaniel said with a cocky grin plastered on his face. My jaw dropped as I looked at the car; ironically enough, it was one of my favorite cars. I could not believe we were taking it.

"Is this your car?" I asked in awe as I walked around it admiring the beautiful sparkling black paint job.

"Mmm, technically it's on loan from a friend right now," he replied as he stood still holding the car door open for me.

"Nice friend; we're not going to get hauled off to jail when this friend finds out you 'borrowed' his car, are we?" I asked, raising an eyebrow.

"Trust me. He doesn't mind." Nathaniel replied coolly, watching me walk up and down the car. I smiled and happily got into the vehicle then. Nathaniel got in the other side and as soon as the engine roared to life we tore off towards the mall. He reached inside the glove compartment and searched for a paper bag, pulling out what looked to be like a black leather worn wallet.

Inside the mall, I waited patiently as he tried on another outfit I had thrown over the top of the dressing room door. Soon enough, he came out and I hardly recognized him. He looked different in the white long sleeve shirt with dark blue jeans. A grin was plastered on his face, and I knew he knew he looked good. I rolled my eyes not wanting to give him too much satisfaction.

"Looks good."

"Looks good?" he mocked, knowing all too well he looked like a stud. I refused to look at him knowing that if I did, he would see straight through my façade and know that I thought he looked damn good. He shook his head a little as he walked to the cash register and I followed.

The cashier, a bleached blond, practically threw herself at him the whole time as I stood watching with a disgusted look on my face.

"Gosh. It is sooo hard to find a remotely attractive guy here I was just saying to my friend back there until I saw you walk in." She purred as she purposefully dropped the leather jacket Nathaniel had placed on the counter and bent down to pick it up. I cringed.

Seriously? I thought sarcastically. Why doesn't she just invite him into the back for crying out loud?

I looked back at Nathaniel who seemed to smile but not say anything back. Annoyed, I looked away and tried to think of something else. As if that wasn't enough, the girl continued. "I get off at five, you should pick me up."

Ewe, I thought. Then before I could react to anything else the girl said, Nathaniel wrapped his arm around my waist and pulled me close to him before looking at the girl straight in the face and saying as frankly as possible, "This is my girlfriend, Alex. I'm sure you are a very nice girl, but I'll be honest with you, you're just not my type." And with that, he grabbed the bag of clothes still holding me under his arm and left the girl with her mouth hanging halfway open.

I didn't know what to say. I was a little shocked and didn't know what to think of the fact that Nathaniel had just introduced me as his girlfriend. My stomach was doing flip flops and I couldn't figure out if it was because I was nervous, excited, about it or sick, or petrified. Finally I mustered up enough courage to ask him as we got into the car.

"Why did you introduce me as your girlfriend back there?" I nervously inquired.

"Because," he said as he looked from me to the road and back at me again. "We're officially dating, remember?"

"Oh, right," I replied a little relieved, but uncomfortable with it still. I was going to have to get used to the whole fake-dating scenario if I wanted Nathaniel gone. I just wondered how much of a 'show' I would have to put on in order for people to believe it. And what would my best friend Kate think of all this? Surely she would be furious I had had a boyfriend and never mentioned him to her; we told each other everything after all. I would have to figure out a way to tell her.

I knew I could trust Kate, I just didn't know how I was going to tell her. And I'm sure Nathaniel would be none too happy when I did either. I decided I would find a way to make it happen; Kate knew me too well and would know something was up, so sooner or later I would have a chance to tell her the whole story; but first things first. I have to find out the whole story. Who really was Nathaniel? What did he need my help with that he couldn't possibly have gotten help with from anyone else? And what have I gotten myself into?

Chapter 9

We pulled into the drive and I could feel my heart start to beat faster as I realized my dad's car was already there. "Crap," I sighed.

Nathaniel seemed calm for the moment and turned off the ignition before walking around and opening my door for me.

"Ready?" He asked as he winked and gave me a small smile. I felt nauseous.

"No." I replied honestly, then added, "As ready as I'll ever be," before stepping out and walking with Nathaniel to the door. Here goes nothing, I thought as I turned the handle and we both stepped inside.

"Dad?" I called.

"Hey honey! I'll be right out. I'm just putting some paperwork away," I heard my dad call from inside his study. A second or two later he walked out and was talking before he stopped mid stride and stared at Nathaniel.

"Sorry I had to put some of my thin...Who is this?" His voice seemed to deepen as he scrutinized Nathaniel in the doorway. I walked a step forward and motioned towards Nathaniel.

"Dad this is Nathaniel, Nathaniel this is my dad." Nathaniel took a step forward as he smiled and extended his hand towards my father.

"Pleased to meet you, Mr. Constance, and I'm sorry for the intrusion." My dad eyed him one last time before he strode over and roughly shook Nathaniel's hand and grunted in reply, before turning to me and motioning me into the kitchen for a little 'chat'. I followed reluctantly behind my father as I turned around and gave Nathaniel a pleading look. He gave me a reassuring, 'you'll be fine,' look and watched me go.

Once in the kitchen, my dad turned and gave me a questioning look. "Who is Nathaniel?" he pried.

"Just a guy, dad," I unwillingly replied. I wasn't really sure what I should say to him about Nathaniel seeing as Nathaniel and I never discussed what was ok and not ok to say, so I followed my instinct.

"Are you dating him?" My dad questioned and his face scrunched in anxiety at my reply. Here's the big one I thought.

"Yes." I tried to be as casual as possible.

"Well, Alex, how come you've never mentioned it before? I come home and all of a sudden you're dating someone. I was only gone for a day you know."

"I know I'm sorry dad, it's just with the divorce and Derek being gone, I haven't really gotten a chance to speak with you about stuff like this. I'm sorry." I replied.

He seemed to take in the new information with thought before replying.

"I'm sorry, you're right. I guess I'm just not used to the idea of you dating. But he better treat you nice or so help me I'll..."

I put my hand up as I stopped him from finishing his sentence and smiled. "I can handle myself don't worry." I laughed. "And besides, he treats me like a princess." I lied. Yea right, I thought. He kidnaps you and now you're pretending to be his girlfriend so he will leave. I smiled a fake smile but my dad seemed to buy it.

"Well good," he huffed, "You're just lucky your brother wasn't here to meet him like this. I might have enjoyed watching that." He smiled at the end and dodged my reflexive slap on the wrist.

"Dad!" He laughed as he left the kitchen to go work in his study.

"I'll be in my office, you two, and I have the ears of a fox, the eyes of a hawk and a loaded 12 gauge." I rolled my eyes and I'm pretty sure I was blushing.

"Dad!" I yelled back embarrassed. There was no way he would have to worry about anything like that between Nathaniel and me. This was all strictly business. The sooner I played along and helped him with whatever he needed help with, the sooner he would leave; I reassured myself before walking out of the kitchen to find Nathaniel still standing where I had left him.

I motioned for him to follow me out the back door; he followed as I lead the way through the pasture and out to the barn. I pushed open the doors and he closed them shut behind me. I needed to talk to Nathaniel. To find out what he needed my help with. What did he want? And I needed to find out about his past, where he came from; basically the whole shebang. Not to mention there was still that other incident in the woods with the mountain lion that I needed clarification on. Like for example, how that was even possible.

I petted Ajax on the muzzle as I walked by and sat on a hay stack that lay against the wall. "Start talking." I ordered. Nathaniel hesitated and looked at me. "You promised," I stated, "and so far I've held up my end of the deal; I've lied to my father and told him we're dating and I'm helping you, so it's your turn to hold up your end."

Nathaniel finally nodded his head in agreement and walked over to Ajax who was shaking his head for attention. He softly petted his head as I began to question him.

"What's your real name?"

"Nathaniel Corvx Archais. But everyone knows me as Nathaniel Corvx." He stated without hesitation.

"What do you need my help with?" I inquired, happy with how he seemed to be complying so far.

"It's complicated," he said, as he turned to look at me. I frowned.

"It can't be that complicated," I urged. "After all, you basically hunted me down for my help, but I can't help you unless you tell me what it is I'm helping you with."

"It's not as easy as it sounds." Nathaniel huffed as he began to pace in front of Ajax and me. "You won't understand. It's something that happened a long time ago, before you were even born; something that I'm forced to try and fix now."

I scrunched my face; I hated the fact that Nathaniel kept telling me riddles instead of just spitting out what he needed my help with.

"Maybe I would be able to understand if you just told me, it's not a big deal you know. Everyone's been through their own hell," I interjected, a little frustrated.

Nathaniel seemed conflicted and aggravated as he eyed me while continuing to walk back and forth. He looked like a predator off of the Discovery Channel, selecting his prey and targeting it – or me in this case.

I shifted my weight uncomfortably when Nathaniel suddenly halted; he turned towards me with that same intensity I had seen in the woods and marched straight at me. My breathing escalated and came in rapid movements as he kept eye contact, cementing me where I stood. He stopped about a foot away, breathing heavily, and began to shout at me.

"Not a big deal? You have no idea what you're even talking about Alex," he accused. "You're the only person who can help me get back to the way I was, or at least get out of this hell hole I'm in." He spoke more quietly. "Trust me Alex; you don't know what hell is." He stormed out, leaving me shocked.

"That went well," I scolded myself. I eventually got my bearings again and left the barn. The sky had started to darken now and I didn't bother looking for Nathaniel as I hurriedly stalked back inside the house. At least I found out his whole name, I thought optimistically.

Nathaniel Corvx Archais. That's not a name you hear every day. I pondered over where Nathaniel could have grown up to have a name like that, and what could have changed him to who he is today. I wouldn't give up though, I had to know, and the more Nathaniel tried to hide his past from me the more it made me want to know everything. I would find out sooner or later, and till then, I would have to just play along, I decided.

It was quiet when I entered the house except for some music coming from my dad's study. The door was shut, but as I walked past it I smiled. I could faintly make out the artist, Meatloaf, and the song, Anything for Love.

My dad had always loved that song for as long as I could remember, and by hanging around my brother and my dad when I was little, I was basically raised on rock music.

My mother, on the other hand, had listened to and taught me all the best of country music, like Garth Brooks. I laughed at how I could remember her going all crazy whenever there was a live show with him; she use to tell me:

"There's nothing like a man who can wear wranglers."

I walked upstairs to my bedroom and flipped on my light while throwing off my shirt in the process, revealing a white tank top underneath. I jumped almost a foot when I realized Nathaniel was sitting on my bed; his face went red as he grunted and turned around.

"God! Nathaniel! You should warn me next time!"

"I'm sorry." He seemed to try not to laugh. "And I really didn't think you would just walk in and begin to strip," he stated, appearing amused and not at all sorry.

"I was not stripping!" I yelled enough to get my point across, but not enough to raise the attention of my dad downstairs. He laughed and went to turn his head around again when I caught him in the act and in a nervous appalled toned yelled, "Don't look!"

Nathaniel laughed a little.

"Ok," I said, finally satisfied that I had managed to throw on a red sweat shirt.

My face must have been a little flush, because as soon as Nathaniel turned around and looked at me he was grinning and saying, "You know Alex, I've seen it all before."

I wrapped the sweat shirt tighter around me before making an irritated sigh and stalked into the bathroom to get ready for bed. Nathaniel laughed as he followed me into the bathroom.

"What do you want, besides to try and annoy me?" I inquired. I was still upset with him for blowing up at me in the barn and for once again not telling me what I wanted to know.

He straightened towards me as he said, "I just wanted to say I'm sorry."

I put my toothbrush down on the counter and turned to face him. His eyes looked soft and sincere.

"It was not right for me to just explode like that, I just..." he seemed to struggle with his words, "you're my only hope. I'm sorry Alex."

I was a little surprised at his straight forward admonition, but satisfied. He stood uneasily waiting for a response from me.

"Ok, but if you and I are going to be putting on a show for everyone I need you to hold up your end of the deal; and soon." He shook his head in agreement; at least now I could know that he was surely going to tell me.

"A deal's a deal," he replied before walking back into my bedroom with me close behind.

"Now, as far as your sleeping arrangements go," I began. "Where are you sleeping, because I can definitely tell you if you're within ten feet of my room my father is not going to be pleased and may use that 12 gauge." I smiled, triumphant at the fact that I would finally be able to sleep in my own bed without a stranger.

"Well, your father already thinks I left for one; two, I told you you're kind of stuck with me, and three, it would take a lot more than a shotgun to get rid of me; besides I think it would be better if I stayed close, just in case."

"Just in case what?" I questioned, I didn't like the sound of that at all, and there was definitely something Nathaniel wasn't telling me.

"Oh, you know, my presence here has perhaps created a bit of a stir and I just think it would be better if I'm around twenty-four seven." He replied callously. "It's not optional Alex babe, sorry."

I groaned. Why did I have to be the only person who could help Nathaniel? This must be Karma, I thought, as I walked past Nathaniel and climbed into bed. Tomorrow would be interesting. I would have to introduce Kate to Nathaniel, as well as Trey, and I'm not too sure they're going to be too keen on the idea or very happy with me.

Nathaniel pulled off his shirt as I pushed all thoughts of tomorrow from my brain and snuck a quick glance. With perfectly toned abs that created a wave look across his stomach and well-built biceps, he looked as if going to the gym was his day job. I quickly averted my eyes before he noticed me peeking; God knows that would spike his ego another three bars and make him say some arrogant remark.

As much as I despised Nathaniel for pulling me into what I gathered was a huge mess, I couldn't bring myself to hate or loathe him. He seemed desperate for my help; what was I supposed to do? Turn away? I wanted to, something about Nathaniel told me that what I didn't know could hurt me, but something else told me that I had to help him no matter what. Whatever the correct decision was, it was too late to turn back now. I could feel I was already too deep in something I had no idea about.

Chapter 10

The beeping of my alarm clock began to shrill at the strike of 6:00 AM. "No," I groaned, "It can't be time to get up already." I had barely gotten any sleep last night thanks to my ever reoccurring nightmares. And Nathaniel was startled twice when I had woken covered in sweat and frantically flailing. However, the six AM wakeup call didn't seem to bother him an ounce; he was already up and out of bed.

"Alex." he warned, "Don't make me do what I had to do last time."

At the thought of Nathaniel picking me up like a ragdoll, I launched myself out of my bed and headed for the shower, mumbling "Alright, Alright," in an irritated tone as I passed him. I had finished with my morning routine, as Nathaniel double checked to be sure the coast was clear and my dad had left for work before we headed down the stairs. I was wearing my newly bought backless, V-front, emerald green dress shirt along with my black Meloni boots and leggings. My hair bounced as I bounded down the stairs and slid into the kitchen where I found Nathaniel. He was wearing an all red t-shirt he had bought when we went shopping, dark blue jeans, and a black leather jacket. I couldn't help but notice how the red t-shirt showed off his nicely defined arms, and how the leather jacket seemed to give him that bad boy look.

"You look nice," he said casually, as he poured me a cup of juice, and his eyes, I noticed, seemed to linger on my dress shirt and boots.

"Thank you," I replied. "So do you. I think we make an appropriate fake couple," I said as I smiled and I took a sip of juice. He grinned back at me, but we were startled as the doorbell rang and pounding sounded. With a confused look between Nathaniel and me, I told him I would go check who it was. I unlocked and opened the door to reveal an exasperated Kate, and a laughing Trey.

"Have you fallen off the face of the earth?!" Kate screamed at me as she pushed past me and headed in towards the kitchen, with Trey following close behind. Immediately I tried to block their way, knowing full well that Nathaniel was in the kitchen.

"Wait! Don't go in there!" I frantically exclaimed. Trey and Kate each exchanged a look, before Trey looked at me like I was crazy.

"Alex, this lunatic over here," Trey motioned towards Kate, "made me skip breakfast because she thought you had died because she hadn't talked to you in an hour, so I'm going."

He went to push past me, as Kate slapped him on the arm and said, "Well she could have been dead for all I knew, and besides I haven't talked to her in a day and a half, which for your information is about 2 years in girl time."

They both bickered and fought their way into the kitchen with me trailing behind still shouting at them not to go; we probably looked like a gigantic mob, ranting and bickering, and fighting. All of a sudden Trey stopped dead in his tracks and went silent and rigid, Kate started to question his rude behavior, until she looked at where his eyes seemed pinned and went quiet as well. I pushed my way through the both of them and found they were staring blankly at Nathaniel; or at least Kate was.

Trey looked like he was ready to engage in a fight at any second. And Nathaniel, who had started cooking another two plates for Trey and Kate I gathered, stopped and walked over to greet Kate and Trey. He wrapped his arm around my waist as he out held his hand to Kate.

"You must be Kate, Alex's best friend," he said before turning to Trey and repeating the same motion. "And you must be Trey. It's nice to finally meet the both of you."

Kate shook Nathaniel's hand with her mouth agape as Trey roughly shook Nathaniel's hand and questioned him in a deep voice.

"And you are?"

Nathaniel looked back at me as I stepped forward reluctantly and prepared to say it. I tried to put my best fake smile on and play it cool, because if I knew Kate – and I knew Kate – she would see straight through any façade of mine. I had to make sure my performance was flawless.

"Kate, Trey," I announced, "This is Nathaniel, my boyfriend." At the sound of that they both started talking at the same time, or more or less shouting.

"Your what?!" They yelled simultaneously. I flinched. I looked up at Nathaniel who seemed as composed as ever, however, his grip around me tightened a little as a sign not to panic. Too bad I was. I had to keep my cool though. Kate and Trey were still astounded at what I had just announced and were letting out questions everywhere.

"One at a time," I said smiling. Trey gestured for Kate to continue. I looked up at Nathaniel and asked him if he could give me a minute.

"Gladly," he smiled and returned to his task of making Trey and Kate breakfast.

Kate was shooting me death glares when I turned back around and Trey seemed none too happy either.

"What?" I asked as though nothing was wrong.

"What," Kate screeched, "is that?" As she pointed towards Nathaniel who was busy at work.

"I told you, that's Nathaniel; he's my boyfriend," I said trying to sound confident and not falter on the word boyfriend.

"Since when do you have a boyfriend and not tell us?" Trey accused. His big brown puppy dog eyes for a moment portrayed that he was hurt, but they went solid after an instant.

"No, since when don't you tell me?" Kate accused as Trey rolled his eyes at her.

"I'm sorry you guys." And I truly meant it. I hated the fact that I was lying straight to their faces because of something that I didn't even know about. "I just thought that with everything you both had going on I shouldn't bother you. Trey you've had hockey practice, Kate I know you and Jesse have been going at it recently, and honestly I don't want you guys to think that you have to babysit me since my brother left. That's why I didn't tell you."

They seemed to take in my speech for a moment as their expressions softened.

"Well you just freaked us out is all," Kate replied.

"Ugh, you think?" Trey remarked sarcastically as he scratched the back of his head and eyed Nathaniel behind me.

Then Kate being Kate piped up and asked, "Oh my God, dude, what did your dad do?" I laughed. I thought she would want to hear about that.

"He said as long as he treats me right he has no problem."

"And then?" She knew my dad too well obviously. I smiled.

"And I stopped him before he could finish telling me the *and if he doesn't part.*

Kate laughed as she nudged Trey who seemed to still be giving Nathaniel death glares.

"Does your brother know?" he asked.

I paused. Great, if he goes and tells my brother, Derek will be having Trey check in on me regularly, I thought. Not that I minded Trey, he and I are best friends, like me and Kate. However, I still had to deal with this whole Nathaniel thing and help him with whatever he needed so he would leave, and I wasn't sure pop-ins from Trey would be a good thing. But it was too late; Trey already knew the answer from my silence.

He laughed before shaking his head and saying, "Can I be there when you tell him?"

I glared at him. "Yes, because nothing is going to happen," I countered angrily. Trey just laughed some more before looking at his watch and cursing at the time.

"Shit, we're gonna be late guys. We better go." He grabbed some bacon from the plate Nathaniel had made before turning around with a confused look and asked, "So I guess we'll see you there?"

He eyed me carefully waiting for a sign that told him I didn't want to go with Nathaniel.

I replied, "Yep," in a casual tone. He hesitated again before grabbing Kate by the arm and directing her to the car as she busily texted someone, my guess was Jesse.

"See you at school!" she hollered from outside, adding, "And your new boy toy!"

I didn't know I had been holding my breath until I let out a huge gasp. I turned back at Nathaniel and looked up at him. I had never really gathered just how short I was compared to him until then. My height of 5'6' shrank dramatically standing next to his six feet plus frame. He was almost a whole head taller than I. I have to admit I was a little unsettled after that whole experience, but I was definitely glad it was over, and I think Trey and Kate had forgiven me. At least I hoped they had.

Nathaniel smiled as he clapped his hands and grabbed his keys. "Bravo." he said as he grinned and continued. "But I do think we could work on your acting skills a little better Alex; I thought you were going to lose it for a second," he teased as I got in the passenger side of the Gt.

"Just get in," I ordered as I half smiled, half glared at him. He laughed before running around to the other side and getting in.

We pulled into the school parking lot and immediately were stared at. Mostly, the car was the one getting all of the attention until I heard whispers from people as we walked through the school doors.

"They're staring," I said, embarrassed, as Nathaniel slipped his arm behind my back and led me through the hallway.

"They're just wondering who the new guy is," he stated as he looked down at me and winked.

"Well that makes two of us then," I declared as I raised my eyebrow and looked back up at him expectantly. He smiled before lowering his head to my ear and huskily whispering.

"Some surprises you have to be patient for; I'll be back to see you at lunch." Then he strode off.

"Wait!" I shouted after him. "Where are you going?" He looked back at me and smiled.

"To meet with some long lost acquaintances." He winked and then disappeared in the throng of students. I turned around and headed into my English class, wondering who on earth Nathaniel was going to meet and why he had chosen to go meet them alone. Then thoughts of what Nathaniel had said to me last night appeared in my head:

Oh, you know, my presence here has perhaps created a bit of a stir, and I just think it would be better if I'm around twenty-four seven.

I really hated the sound of that, and I wasn't too keen on the idea of Nathaniel going alone to meet them either. I knew full well that Nathaniel was able to take care of himself; I mean after all he did win a hand to hand fight against a mountain lion, but still. I was uneasy nonetheless.

I tried my best to forget about it as I sat down next to Trey who was shifting in his seat and glancing in my direction. I smiled a little. Kate and I could always tell when something was bugging Trey and he wanted to talk, because he had a tendency to shift uncontrollably and look heinously uncomfortable.

"What is it?" I asked as I continued to pretend to listen to Ms. Nethers ramble on about punctuation. I could see Trey looking at me then from the corner of my eye.

"I just, I'm just surprised is all." He said as casually as possible, but I sensed the disapproval in his voice.

"Surprised about Nathaniel?" I questioned. "Or about me having a boyfriend?" I definitely did not want to have this discussion with Trey at the moment. Besides, what did it matter to him who I date?

"I just think you should be careful. This Nathaniel guy seems like he's hiding something. I can feel it," he said as he furrowed his eyes in confusion.

You have no idea, I thought, and neither do I. But I had to hand it to Trey, the first encounter he had with Nathaniel was one of suspicion.

"You just met him, Trey," I said as I finally turned to look at him. Ms. Nethers gave me a warning look from the front of the room so I lowered my voice an octave before I continued. "Just promise me you'll give him a chance? For me?" I said as I smiled encouragingly. "I'll be fine I promise; you don't have to worry about me, k?"

Trey nodded his head reluctantly before whispering back, "Alright, I'll give the guy a chance. Just promise me you'll be careful."

I smiled, thankful that he would drop the subject before replying, "I will." I returned my gaze to the board as Ms. Nethers glared between Trey and me and continued on with her lecture.

"And here is an example of where the comma is used incorrectly. Is there anyone here who can identify the mistake in this sentence?"

Time could not have dragged on any slower as I watched the minute hand tick away the last thirty seconds of science class before lunch. I practically dove out of the doors and nearly took someone else down with me in the process.

"Sorry! I'm sorry!" I frantically said as I pushed my shoulder bag back onto my shoulder and gathered myself together again.

"What the hell, you klutz! If you ruined my new Jimmy Choos, I am so suing."

Then I realized who I had run into. Beth Ryder. Annoyed that she was rambling on about her damn shoes I began to look over her shoulder to see if I could get a glimpse of Nathaniel in the lunch room. I felt a poke/shove on my left shoulder that snapped me out of my trance as I turned to look back at the fuming Beth Ryder.

"I said watch where you're going freak," she snapped.

I took in a deep breath trying to calm myself. I just wanted to find Nathaniel and I didn't feel like getting into it with Beth of all people right now.

"Don't touch me," I replied coldly as I brushed her off and walked past her to get a better view of the lunchroom. The next thing I knew I was shoved from behind and I stumbled forward, but managed to catch myself. She was really pushing her luck and my patience was wearing thin.

I turned back around slowly as she put her hands on her hips and said, "What are you gonna do about it freak. It looks like your brother's not here to help you now is he?" I stared back at her coldly. Now the bitch was getting personal.

"I'm busy," I said flatly. "So back off," I warned one last time. Before I could turn around and walk away for good, a frappachino was flying through the air and landed smack dab on my chest splattering everywhere and creating a gigantic brown wet spot on my brand new shirt. I froze. Everyone in the lunch room had stopped what they were doing and moved their attention to Beth and me. Whispers and 'ooh's' filled the room as they waited to see what would happen next.

That was it; I snapped. I launched myself at Beth and we both went down in a heap of flailing arms and legs. She clawed at my hair as I, having an older brother and knowing how to actually fight; got one good right in before I was grabbed by someone from behind and pried off of Beth. She screamed as she covered her eye that had been punched and got up shouting threats and curses at me. I just looked back at her not even bothering to respond as students around us shouted and cheered; others ran to get faculty members.

I relaxed. Someone still had a hold of both of my arms so I turned to look behind me and I was met with someone whom I was more than grateful to see – Nathaniel.

He grinned as he raised his eyebrows. "I think that's our cue to leave. Let's get out of here." I nodded as he grabbed one of my hands and we rushed out of the school to the parking lot where his car was waiting. We jumped in and peeled out before Nathaniel finally looked over at me and, laughing, started to shake his head.

"What?" I replied as innocently as I could, trying not to laugh myself. I had never been in a fight before and I must say it was a bit of a rush.

"I leave you alone for a few hours and come back to find you brawling with some chic. I can't leave you alone for a minute, can I?" he said as he smirked and waited for my reaction.

I playfully glared at him and motioned to my shirt. "I didn't start it thank you. I actually tried to walk away twice, but then she decided to get personal."

He smiled as he nodded and said "What was the fight over?"

I looked down at the coffee mess that covered my new emerald green dress shirt and said, "She talked about my brother." His smile faded and he nodded in understanding. Just then I felt my bag vibrating and pulled out the phone to answer; knowing full well who it was.

"Hello," I answered trying to sound as calm and causal as possible.

"I can't believe you hit Beth Ryder in the face and I missed it!" Kate screamed on the other end of the line. Then she giddily continued. "Everyone's freaking right now! I would advise you to leave immediately till it cools down, if you haven't done so already." I laughed.

66

"I'm already on it," I replied.

"Good. I'll cover for you in math class but I want details later."

"Deal," I stated before hanging up. I looked at Nathaniel realizing that we were not heading in the direction of my house.

"Where are we going?" I asked Nathaniel curiously.

"I have somewhere I want to take you," He stated, giving me his famous half smile and then focused on driving again. Butterflies started dancing in my stomach as I thought of where Nathaniel wanted to take me; excitedly, I tried to keep Nathaniel from seeing me smile widely.

I was still angry about not knowing what in the world he needed my help for, but at the moment I was just relishing in my fight with Beth, and the fact that I finally did something about it. I was starting to get comfortable around Nathaniel. I couldn't help it; being around Nathaniel seemed so right and even though that scared me a little, there was no one else I would rather have been with at the moment. I felt safe with Nathaniel which considering how we initially met was extremely bizarre.

We drove for some time; passing little towns I had never been to and winding around bends until all that surrounded us seemed to be forest. We parked in a dirt parking lot and got out. The opening in the trees let the warmth of the sunlight through and I noticed a trail to the left of us. I headed towards it instinctively until I felt a hand grab my elbow and stop me. I turned to meet Nathaniel's mischievous eyes.

"We're not taking the path love."

Confused I started to protest a little and asked where we were going, but Nathaniel refused to relinquish any of the details so I followed him apprehensively. We hiked through uncharted forest, over logs and streams and through thick aspens. Nathaniel seemed to know exactly where we were. I, however, was completely lost.

Eventually, a small opening in the forest loomed before us. The small glade revealed the ruins of what looked like an extremely old cathedral church. I stood gaping at it until I realized the church must have been from the 16th or 17th century.

The benefits from taking an art history class in high school and being able to recognize art throughout the ages, I thought as I smiled.

Pillars, columns, and arches surrounded the church, whereas others that had fallen from old age lay scattered about. Most of the outside had been destroyed from weather and old age I gathered. I carefully walked through the ruins examining the moss covered marble as I went.

Nathaniel, whom I could have forgotten was even present at the moment, watched me with gleaming eyes before walking next to me to escort me into the heart of the church itself. We stood before the front of the church – a huge arch where it looked like two gigantic doors had once made for a grand entryway, but was now just a gaping hole.

My eyes widened as I began to fully take in the inside of the church. Chipped and cracked carvings of Cherub angels in white marble were elegantly placed from floor to ceiling everywhere on the walls. Some of the walls suffered from holes and gaps where pieces of the building had collapsed. Most of the ceiling, however, remained intact.

In the center of the cathedral on the ceiling was an enormous hole in the shape of a cross with rounded corners; the stained glass that had once been inside the cross was all but gone now, and a perfect untouched view of the clouds and sky remained. Grass, moss, and some flowers had reclaimed some of the old stone walls, and fallen marble and stones lay in crumpled heaps about the church floor. Yet I could still make out where a podium had once stood so very long ago.

It was enchanting and beautiful at the same time. Even though age and time had deteriorated what was once a grand scale cathedral, it remained elusive and utterly perfect as it was. My mouth hung agape as I tentatively touched a Cherub sculpture on the wall. Admiring every inch of detail it possessed even with its age.

"How do you know about this place?" I asked amazed by the beautiful baby angel and the fact that Nathaniel had wanted to share this with me. Nathaniel had been quiet since we had arrived, allowing me to explore in awe at the colossal formation. When I heard no answer I turned to find him with a content smile formed on his face as he looked up at the cross in the ceiling.

"I've known about this place for a long time." he spoke softly. "This is my sanctuary. Where I became who I was, and where I fell to what I am now; the closest I can get to home."

Once again Nathaniel was speaking in riddles; there were so many things, questions, which I had for him. I wondered if I would ever know any of the answers. Will Nathaniel always be a mystery to me? Or will I eventually find the answers I am looking for?

Chapter 11

I walked over and sat on a fallen pillar and began to fiddle with the birthstone ring my parents had given me for my birthday seven years ago.

"You still haven't kept your promise you know. I want, no, I need to know what this is all about Nathaniel."

Nathaniel looked back at me then, before nodding his head and saying, "Your right, you need to know what this is about. Alright." He breathed out deeply. "I'll tell you what you want to know, but you have to promise you will listen and not just think I'm crazy."

I had no idea why he would think I would think he was crazy, but I was so excited that he would appease me and answer my questions, I nodded my head feverishly in agreement.

He smiled before replying, "You're such a child."

I mini-glared at him before I asked him a question that had been bugging me since I first met him.

"Where are you from?"

"Originally or recently?" he asked unemotionally.

"Both?" I asked.

"Originally, I'm from some place in Europe. A tiny town called Belamire; you probably have never heard of it before because its name has been changed since. I grew up there till I was 18 before I travelled with my mother and father here to escape the conflicts of Spain and France. This was during the Reformation period."

He seemed far off in thought as I cut him off and asked nervously, "You were alive in the 16th and 17th centuries?" Somehow I could not wrap my head around the idea that it was possible let alone probable that Nathaniel was alive back then.

"Yes." he replied without hesitation.

Ok... I thought. You promised to listen, Alex Whether or not you like what you hear is an entirely different thing. At that thought I decided I would have him answer all of my questions first and then I would investigate the information I had been given.

"So, if you have lived since the 16th century what does that make you? An immortal or something?" I questioned him, confused and feeling absolutely ridiculous.

Nathaniel's body tensed a little before he answered. "I guess you could call me that, yes, however, I can still die too."

My eyebrows furrowed as my mind raced through fictional creatures Nathaniel could be. Werewolf? I thought as I laughed inwardly. That's impossible and not likely. I was snapped from my thoughts as Nathaniel continued.

"When I was 19 and 20 I suffered from hallucinations and delusions of angels. I saw them everywhere. When I tried to explain to my parents what I was seeing they thought I had gone 'round the bend'." He chuckled at that before continuing with a serious face.

"What they didn't know was that what I was seeing was real; when I realized this, I knew that I was meant for something more than working on a farm all my life. I was brought to this church one night by one of the angels who I frequently saw watching me. His name was Ezekiel – the archangel of death and transformation. He told me that I had potential. That if I truly wanted it, more than anything else, I could become like him." Nathaniel stopped and looked down at his hands.

The anticipation was practically killing me, so I piped up and asked, "So what did you do?"

"I became like him that night Alex; I was an angel. I was assigned duties which I carried out until I met you." He looked up at me then; his face showed a pained expression.

"What do you mean until you met me? You're not an angel anymore?" I inquired hastily.

"No, I'm what you like to call *in between*," Nathaniel replied as he struggled to find the right words on how to describe what he currently is. He stood and began running a hand through his hair.

"Alex, because I didn't do what I was told to do, I lost my wings; you're now looking at Nathaniel the soon to be fallen angel," he replied aggravated.

Everything seemed to fit into place then. How Nathaniel had enough strength to kill the mountain lion, how he's lived for so long and why he needs my help, or rather why I'm the only person who can help him.

I looked up at him then and asked, "That's why I'm the only person who can help you isn't it? Because it had to do with me? You want me to help you get your wings back?"

Nathaniel turned towards me and sighed. "Now you know," he replied in a sullen voice. "I was an angel and now I'm damned." He stopped pacing and looked at me with glowing eyes. "Does it make you uncomfortable to know that you're basically sleeping with the enemy?"

Now I know, I thought. The thing about secrets is you want to know them badly and when you find out the truth, it's sometimes harder to deal with. I pushed that thought away. I was grateful Nathaniel had taken me here and I was grateful that I finally had a taste of who Nathaniel really was. But on another note, I was just told by practically a complete stranger that he was an angel and now is considered a fallen angel.

Call me crazy but after hearing that and not knowing what to do I wanted him to prove it. That's about the only way I would ever believe him. I looked up at Nathaniel and slowly rose to walk towards him never taking my gaze from his sparkling blue eyes. I had to look up at him to continue to meet his gaze as I got closer. He seemed uneasy as he waited in anticipation for my answer.

"Truthfully, it scares me that I'm not scared or uncomfortable around you. You're a good person Nathaniel, well, minus the whole attempted kidnapping thing; no one has to be an angel to see that. However, if you really want me to believe you and help you; you'll give me a demonstration cause, no offense, but this is crazy," I stated firmly.

Nathaniel seemed taken aback as we stood in silence for a moment; his eyes softened as he stared back at me in wonder. "Fine, but just don't run afterwards. I don't want to have to hunt you down again," he stated only half kidding.

The butterflies in my stomach started to flip flop as I tried to remain calm under his deep stare.

"Oh, and my demonstration will not be done here," he said flatly.

"Why not? Because it's not true? Or because you're afraid of hurting yourself?" I countered.

Nathaniel glared at me before replying sternly, "No, it's because you're shivering so much you're distracting me."

I shivered a little as I noticed twilight had fallen and I knew I needed to be getting home. He made the decision for me and gently but tightly grabbed my elbow and began leading me away from the ruins before I could object.

A thought hit me as we walked back. "Nathaniel?" I asked. "Who were the people you had to meet with earlier?"

His expression hardened then as he slid his leather jacket off and wrapped it around my shoulders while escorting me through the cathedral ruins and back to the unmarked path from whence we came.

"We can talk about that later. Right now you're freezing and your dad might not approve of me anymore if I don't get you home soon." He said as he smirked down at me.

I laughed before saying, "How could he not approve? You're an angel remember? Or so you say," I challenged, grinning.

He huffed back but said nothing.

We made it back to the car as the wind began to pick up more and a chill hung in the air; before I knew it we were back in town and pulling into the farmhouse driveway.

It had been quiet on the way home. Neither Nathaniel nor I had talked. I didn't mind as much however, my mind had been racing through everything Nathaniel had said since we left the cathedral ruins. I couldn't believe that I was somehow involved in what seemed like a story from some mystery or fantasy book. And I continuously scrutinized him the whole way home. His movements; the way he carried himself.

He seemed normal enough, I thought, but besides what he had told me earlier that was supposedly true, what did I really know about Nathaniel? Besides the fact that he had just showed up one day. I wondered what orders Nathaniel could have disobeyed that had to do with me and how it was really possible that he was an angel, or is currently a fallen angel for that matter. I mean sure I believe in angels; I always have ever since I was a child, but angels are always spiritual beings you cannot see. They don't randomly show up in your life at Massage Envy one day and say they need your help so they can get their wings back.

I had to fight the urge to touch Nathaniel's arm to check that he was real and this wasn't some dream I was having. Whatever this was, I decided I was too far in now; the only thing I could do is help Nathaniel - either with getting his wings back, or getting him into an institution and trying not to wind up in one myself. Perhaps then I could find out what the orders were that Nathaniel was given.

We pulled into the drive and I immediately noticed the pearl white mini cooper in the driveway next to my father's black BMW M6 coupe.

"Great," I huffed.

Nathaniel looked at me with raised eyebrows before asking.

"Who owns the..?" But before he could finish asking who owns the Mini Cooper, I answered hastily and prepared myself for the lectures to come.

"My mom."

You know what this means, Alex, I thought, your parents both got a call about you hitting Beth Ryder in the face, and the fact that my dad is home and I never told him about where I was, I figured would also give me a pretty good lecture.

I took a deep breath and closed my eyes when I felt someone come behind me and whisper.

"Don't worry I'll be with you the whole time." This made me smile a little as much as I wanted to be rid of Nathaniel; I was overjoyed having him here at the moment. I knew that my parents would not be as harsh with me if we had company.

We made our way inside the house and I heard my parents arguing in the study.

Here we go again, I thought. When we walked in, my parents automatically stopped talking and turned to look at me.

"Speak of the devil," my mom said exhausted, before her gaze strayed from me to Nathaniel. She turned back towards my dad, eyebrows raised, and he put his hands up defensively.

"Don't look at me."

Nathaniel strode towards her, hand outstretched and charmingly introduced himself.

"I can see where Alex gets her good looks from. I apologize for interrupting. My name is Nathaniel."

My mom glanced in my direction and a smile was placed on her face. I knew Nathaniel had flattered her then and that she approved so far. Smooth Nathaniel, real smooth, I thought, as he looked back at me and winked.

"So young lady... did anything exciting happen at school today?" My dad announced, a little annoyed and already knowing the answer.

"Um, well," I stuttered. "I know what you're both going to say and before you do, let me just get this out. I only hit Beth Ryder because she kept pushing and pushing until I snapped. She talked about Derek and," I motioned to the front of my shirt still covered in Frappuccino, "she did this; so I snapped. It won't happen again I promise."

My parents exchanged a glance. They knew Derek's leaving had affected me a little, they just hadn't known that I would hit someone for bad mouthing him.

My thoughts drifted to Derek then. I had been writing him letters every week now and from the last letter I had gotten it seemed as though his training was practically finished. Just then my dad smiled.

"Well I don't think you'll have to worry about him anymore, hun. He's coming home day after tomorrow; we just got another letter from him today confirming it. He's finished with his training."

My eyes widened as a smile began to form on my lips and I ran to my dad and hugged him. "Are you serious?!" I exclaimed excitedly, as I looked from my mother to my father and back again.

My mom smiled too as she said, "Yep, and I'm sure he'll want to meet your new friend too." I followed her gaze to Nathaniel.

"Right," I said. "About him, mom we're kind of dating right now; Nathaniel is my boyfriend is what I mean to say." I looked back to her for a reaction of any kind.

She smiled and animatedly said, "I thought you two were an item when you walked in. So how did you meet each other?" I opened my mouth only to close it again. Crap, I thought, Nathaniel and I had never talked about the cover story we were going to use. Panicking, I looked to Nathaniel with wide eyes for help. He stepped towards me and wrapped his arm around my waist before continuing.

"We actually met by chance at school, you see I used to live here when I was younger, however, I just recently moved back and because I didn't know my way around the school, Alex was assigned to show me around and be my mentor. We started talking and before we knew it we hit it off." He smiled as he looked from me to my parents.

My parents smiled as my mom declared how cute our story was and I plastered a smile onto my face. We all talked for a little while longer until it was late enough that my mom decided it was time for her to go. I walked her to the door as Nathaniel stayed behind to talk to my dad some more about possible careers and aspirations.

"Would you want to come down to the shop after school tomorrow and help me out?" she asked. "You can bring Nathaniel if you want too. We're over-booked with appointments tomorrow and I could use another hand; what do you say?"

"Of course, I'll be there after school."

I always loved working in my mom's wedding shop. Besides the fact that the dresses were all astonishingly beautiful, I liked the idea that I could make a bride-to-be's day by finding her the perfect gown.

We said our goodbyes and I watched as she pulled out of the drive and her car's headlights disappeared before I went inside and shut the door behind me. I decided I'd better save Nathaniel from any other questions I was sure my father was asking him. I walked in and balanced myself on the doorframe as I watched the two of them animatedly talk about motorcycles. Apparently my dad had already scrutinized his work ethic and so they could now talk about hobbies.

My dad absolutely loves to ride his long raked red Harley Davidson. Most people in my family owned a motorcycle now that I thought about it; Derek has a black Honda CBR600 and my mom has a yellow Can Am Spyder and I have a matte black Yamaha R6.

My dad was the first to notice my presence and he nodded towards me. I walked to Nathaniel and slipped my arm through his before I said goodnight to my dad and they said their goodbyes as well. As I went to walk upstairs with Nathaniel in tow, he stopped me and motioned at my dad's study. I should have known my dad would be waiting to hear the front door open and shut and for a car to leave indicating Nathaniel had left. If he knew Nathaniel was secretly sleeping upstairs in my room and what Nathaniel really was, he would have freaked and called for reinforcements. I'm sure of it.

Nathaniel whispered in my ear.

"I'll meet you in your room."

He seemed to get a little close then and hesitated before he was out the door and in his car in a flash. My head seemed to take a minute to clear the fuzziness away before I was able to walk up the stairs and close my bedroom door behind me.

Why did Nathaniel affect me that way? I couldn't explain what it was about him, but everything he did seemed to have me in a spell.

"He's just a guy Alex," I said out loud as I changed from my now ruined brand new shirt to a turquoise shirt and black sweat pants. "That's all. You're not affected by him at all," I announced proudly as I tried to convince myself the statement was true.

Suddenly, I was interrupted by a voice from my window.

"You're not affected by who I wonder?" Nathaniel inquired deviously as he smirked and made his way across the room to me. Instinctively I moved backwards and cursed myself for saying all of that out loud instead of in my head. Knowing I would collide with the wall soon, I quickly took action and jumped across the bed so I was on the opposite side of Nathaniel.

He stopped and smirked at me before asking, "You wouldn't be affected by me now, would you Alex?"

"Nathaniel," I warned. "I don't want to play any of your games right now, I'm exhausted." I squeaked as he made a move to get to me but I countered it.

"Just tell me the truth then." He grinned. "And I won't have to force you." I rolled my eyes and then squealed as his hand brushed the side of my shirt, but I managed to get away.

"What do you want to know?" I asked nervously, my heart beating rapidly.

"Do I affect you?" he asked flatly.

Reluctant to give him any satisfaction in the fact that he did affect me and embarrassed beyond belief that he had heard what I said in the first place, I refused to answer his question. Call me stubborn or hard headed but I refused.

"I don't think you could affect me if you wanted to," I replied defiantly.

He cocked his head before shaking it and saying, "Is that so? What if I told you I could affect you then?"

"Say whatever you want, Nathaniel, it won't change the fact that you are the last person on this earth who can possibly affect me."

I challenged him with my hands on my hips. But before I could read the reaction on Nathaniel's face I was jolted by a force that pushed my back against the wall. Nathaniel had my wrists pinned beside my face; his expression was one of arrogance and amusement as he waited for my reaction. Infuriated that he had obviously cheated and used some kind of super strength power, I was whisper-screaming at him so my dad wouldn't hear.

"You cheated! You used super human strength to get to me; that doesn't count. And how dare you! Let me go." I was fuming.

"We play with the toys God gives us honey; besides didn't you want a demonstration?" He snickered. "Now answer my question since you obviously can't answer it without being pinned to the wall."

I glared at him. He rolled his eyes and before I knew it he had cupped my chin and held my face in his hands whilst he kissed me. At first I was too shocked to respond and Nathaniel delicately waited for me; his lips lightly parting and touching mine. Something stirred inside of me then, a need, a want, whatever it was; all I knew was that Nathaniel was kissing me and I had to kiss back.

My hands found their way to Nathaniel's neck as one of his hands slid down my side to my hip pushing us closer. The kiss began to pick up in intensity like the start of a fire and before we knew it we were ablaze in an inferno. We kissed vigorously; matching each other's passion. I locked my hands in Nathaniel's hair; responding, Nathaniel's grip tightened on my hip. His minty sweet, earth smell invaded my senses and I could see, hear, feel, touch, and taste, nothing but him.

We stayed melted into one another for a while until breathing became a number one priority. We both panted as we parted from each other's lips. I laid my head back against the wall for support and I was glad that Nathaniel had kept one of his hands on my hip which helped steady me. I was relieved as well when I noticed Nathaniel's other hand was balancing his weight on the wall next to my head.

His head hung in front of me shielding his eyes. Once we both caught our breaths and my mind had come back to earth somewhat, Nathaniel's head slowly rose letting me see his eyes. They were an entirely new force of intensity. It looked as if dark blue icicles were shooting out around his pupils into the rest of the eye. They were practically glowing. We stared at each other until I noticed the familiar outline of Nathaniel's half smile start to creep up. I'm pretty sure by then I was definitely blushing, because the butterflies in my stomach had gone nuts as well.

"So I guess this means I do have an effect on you?" he questioned as he smiled down at me. I couldn't help but smile back.

"So I guess this means I'm not the only one who can be affected." He smirked deviously back at me. Just then a knock sounded at my door, "Alex honey are you ok?" Panicked, I jumped into bed and pulled the covers over me as Nathaniel hid inside my closet just as my dad opened the door.

"Hey, yeah I'm fine dad; I was just reading and dropped my book is all," I said as I motioned to the book I had on my nightstand.

"Oh, ok, I thought I heard something is all, good night hun."

"Night dad," I replied as I looked to my closet and whispered the coast was clear. Nathaniel's head popped out followed by the rest of him.

"That was close," he whispered as he smiled at me. I breathed out deeply and nodded my head before I remembered that I was supposed to ask him if he wanted to go to my mom's shop with me tomorrow.

"Hey, would you want to go with me tomorrow after school to my mom's bridal shop in downtown by any chance? She needs some help tomorrow, but I totally understand if you don't want to go." I quickly finished, hoping that he would say yes. I waited for his reply in anticipation and began biting my lip.

He turned to me and grinned, "I'll go."

"Ok. Cool," I replied. I lay back in bed as Nathaniel finished changing and slid in beside me. Prior to going to sleep, I couldn't help but let my mind race. So what does this mean? What are Nathaniel and I now? Are we really dating or still fake dating? What did that kiss mean? As much as Nathaniel drove me nuts, I was somehow being drawn to him at the same time. How confusing!

Man I hate teenage hormones, I thought as I turned towards Nathaniel who lay on his back, his eyes closed. He seemed completely at ease.

"You know you can come a little closer Alex." He smirked as he kept his eyes closed and moved his arm letting me have access to his firmly built chest. I blushed and I was grateful it was dark in the room and Nathaniel's eyes were closed so he couldn't see. Warmth radiated from his body as it lightly kissed my skin, inviting me in. I couldn't refuse. Whether it was that warmth or the comforting thought of being enfolded in Nathaniel's arms, I discreetly inched a little closer to him, my head lay on his chest, and the front of my body was pressed against his side. He delicately, but firmly curled his arm around my shoulder and I noticed a small smirk on his lips before I fell into the black abyss and began to dream.

Chapter 12

The room was black as I opened my eyes; my body seemed to ache with pain as I sat up from the cold cement floor. I couldn't see anything. I sat on my knees, unmoving. I could feel the unnerving feeling of someone staring at me. Perhaps if I didn't make a sound and just listened, I could detect where the stranger was. I thought, trying to calm my uneasiness; nothing. I slowly got to my feet and kept my hands outstretched to feel my way around the room, but as I walked a voice echoed in the room loud enough that the sound seemed to boom off the walls.

"Alex." The stranger's voice slithered. It was no voice I recognized and it sent an eerie chill crawling up my spine making me shiver. I gathered the courage to answer after a moment of silence.

"Who are you?" I asked, keeping my voice even.

"I am known as a Duke to many, but you may call me Uvall."

"What do you want Uvall?" I asked impatient and uncomfortable with the fact that I still did not know where this 'Uvall' was in the room.

"I believe an acquaintance of mine is staying with you, a Nathaniel Corvx Archais. Is he not?" Uvall questioned.

"Your business with Nathaniel has nothing to do with me; I'm afraid I can be of no service to you Uvall," I answered quickly and harshly. Whoever this guy was, I got the feeling he was someone you don't want to be friends with, let alone in a dark room with.

"Now, now Alex." he breathed, sounding annoyed. "On the contrary, it has everything to do with you." By this point I was sick of playing games with this Uvall and I desperately wanted to get out of this dark room. Just what exactly did he want with Nathaniel, and me?

"Listen pal I'm not helping you with whatever you want me for, ok? So why don't you just show yourself?" I retorted angrily. It was silent for a moment until I felt a cold vice like grip grab my arm firmly and spin me around. Before I knew it I was face to face with a man in black.

Uvall was around Nathaniel's height, with dirty blonde hair and cold eyes that matched those of black onyx. I stood wide-eyed at the man before I tried to wrench my arm from his killer grasp. He was close to my face, smiling devilishly at my attempt to get free.

"I'll be requiring your services soon my dear and you will help me, or the pain in your arm right now will feel like a tap compared to what I'll do to you next; understand?" He spit angrily at me.

Just as I was about to make a sarcastic remark a blinding white light appeared in the room breaking Uvall's grip on my arm; it was followed by a black cawing crow.

The last I heard as white light swirled around me was, "Until we meet again Alex."

I flew up in bed in a panting sweat, clawing, and fighting whomever was near me.

"Alex. Alex! It's me, it's Nathaniel. You're ok; I got you. I got you." It took a moment for me to realize I had just had a dream and that Nathaniel had pulled me in a tight hug so as I could not fight him. I breathed unevenly, but stayed wrapped in Nathaniel's comforting hug as I regained my composure. When I calmed, Nathaniel slowly unfolded me from his arms and looked at me with concern etched in his eyes. Before he could say something his eyes seemed to dart to my left arm, the one Uvall's vice grip had been holding.

Rage replaced Nathaniel's questioning face and I could feel heat rising in his body.

"Who did this to you?" Nathaniel asked. His temper was fuming and his tone was harsh. There was no way I wasn't about to tell him about Uvall. Maybe he would know who he was, what he wanted, and more importantly, how it was possible that from a dream I could have been hurt by someone; that was impossible, right?

"Uvall." It was the only word that came out of my mouth. I stared down at the black and purple bruise that was now steadily forming on my arm. At the mention of the name, Nathaniel's eyes became stormy, like hot blue fire. He got up and walked to the window taking a few moments to breathe deeply and control his rage. I winced as I went to move my arm; hearing me suck in a breath, Nathaniel was at my side again.

"Give me your arm." He gently cradled my arm in between his hands.

"What are you doing?"

"Healing you. If I still can." Nathaniel closed his eyes and a blue-white light radiated from his hands. It was then that I felt a rush of warm energy flow through my entire left arm. It started slowly from the top of my shoulder working its way down to my hand like a wave building momentum and energy before it crashes onto a beach. And just as quickly as it had come, the feeling dissipated, then was gone entirely.

I gazed in wonder at my arm; not a scratch was to be found anywhere on it. The ugly black bruise that would have taken weeks to heal had simply vanished.

"How did you do that?" I asked, mesmerized by what had just happened.

Nathaniel relaxed a little then and a small smirk played at the corner of his mouth as he answered.

"I'm not without my perks still, Alex." I smiled back at him, but the smile faded quickly as I remembered the dream and Uvall. Nathaniel seemed to get what I was thinking about and inquired firmly.

"What happened?"

"We have a serious problem." I answered.

After I had retold what had happened in the dream to Nathaniel, he sighed and ran his hand through his hair. He was aggravated.

"And he didn't say anything else? Or hurt you anywhere else did he?"

"No, at the end he just said 'until we meet again.' But Nathaniel, how is this possible? I mean how could he have hurt me in my dream? That's not possible," I stated, irritated and confused.

Nathaniel looked at the clock; it read 6:23 AM; then he answered.

"Actually it is possible, at least for angels it is."

I furrowed my eyebrows in disbelief.

"Uvall cannot be an angel. The guy has sadistic written all over him," I retorted.

Nathaniel grunted at my comment.

"You're right. Uvall used to be an angel, which means that, like me, he still carries some of an angel's abilities; one of those is being able to appear in a person's dream. Angels can physically touch and influence a person who is dreaming, but angels never hurt humans. Uvall is a fallen angel, so unfortunately those rules - or most angel rules for that matter - don't necessarily apply to him."

I rolled my eyes. "Well isn't that just peachy. So what do we do?" I asked.

Nathaniel turned to look at me then with amusement in his eyes.

"You, Alex, are not going to do anything. You saw what he did to your arm, now I'm not letting you out of my sight nor am I letting you get involved any deeper. This is dangerous." He finished firmly while locking eyes with me.

Defiantly I scrunched my eyes and got up from the bed.

"Excuse me, but I'm pretty sure I'm already too involved; and besides this has to do with both of us so I'm helping, you can count on that."

"No you're not." Nathaniel responded harshly.

"Oh yes I am, you just try and stop me," I replied rebelliously as we eventually stood in front of each other. I scowled up at Nathaniel with my hands on my hips as he looked down at me with irritation, his arms crossed over his chest. He finally conceded and sighed in mock defeat.

"Fine. Fine, you can help, but you have to do exactly what I say, exactly when I say it. There's no fooling around with these guys and I'm still not letting you out of my sight."

I smiled victoriously. "Got it."

He rolled his eyes before storming towards the shower and mumbling under his breath.

"Child."

I sat back on the bed and mumbled, "Stubborn."

I listened to the water running in the other room. A chill washed over me as I thought about the dream once more, but quickly pushing it from my mind, I realized today Nathaniel and I were going to my mom's wedding shop; this ought to be interesting, I thought, as I pondered what I would wear for the day. My long white tank top dress, I think, matched with my long black leggings - pearl necklace – and my black pumps to finish.

As I grabbed my purse and headed down stairs I found Nathaniel was not in his usual place in the kitchen waiting for me. Hmmm, weird, I thought. I walked to the back door and looked out towards the barn. I could see Ajax out in the pasture grazing, his jet black coat gleaming brilliantly in the sunlight. As I turned around, about to call for Nathaniel I nearly lost my breath when I found he had been standing behind me the entire time. I gasped, startled.

"Sorry." Nathaniel said, before I could say anything. The familiar earthy sweet and mint smell hit my nostrils once more and I had to fight to concentrate. He was standing disturbingly close and since our kiss, I couldn't quite figure out exactly what was real or fake between us anymore.

Trying to block out the thoughts of our kiss, my eyes went to what Nathaniel was wearing. He seemed particularly dressed up for going to my mom's shop today. A black button up shirt with dark blue jeans, black shoes, and a small bronze pendant that clung to the base of his neck. As I examined it closer I realized that the pendant depicted a cross with an angel in armor kneeling in front of it, his wings outstretched. The angel's head was bowed and in his hands he held a sword. By the looks of it, it seemed centuries old. I wondered if it was a pendant all angels adorned themselves with.

I was snapped from my thoughts.

"Are you ready?" Nathaniel asked.

I told myself I would ask him about the pendant's meaning later. Having the intoxicating scent of him surround me again, I hurriedly stepped around Nathaniel and made my way out to his car while shaking my head to clear it.

The ride to my mom's shop was strangely quiet. Neither of us were in the mood to talk. Nathaniel seemed to be in deep contemplation, but what exactly he was thinking about, I couldn't be sure of. The White Dove would be full of women and I used that as an excuse to break the silence between us. I decided it would be best to warn him about the fact that he would possibly be the only guy there.

"So I'm kind of surprised you said yes to coming with me today. I mean you do realize you're probably going to be the only male in the entire store."

This seemed to snap him out of his thoughts as he looked at me and smirked.

"I'm ok with that." I rolled my eyes.

"The women who work there are married and the clients are soon-to-be brides, Nathaniel. Hasn't anyone told you, don't break up a happy home?" I stated playfully.

He just smirked at me.

Annoyed, I looked out the window and saw the familiar white sign with the dove. The White Dove was intricately written on it. I smiled.

Upon entering the bridal shop we were greeted with "hello", "it's been too long", "who's the hunk?" and "thank God we have more help" by consultants whom I had helped before.

Consultants with dresses in hand dashed about the store; frantic brides who had not yet found 'that perfect dress' and families 'ooing and ahhing' at their beautiful soon-to-be brides created as much hustle and bustle as a busy beehive.

Nathaniel seemed taken aback at just how much activity was happening. I doubt he had ever been inside a bridal store before. Keeping step with me so as not to get in anyone's way, we eventually made it from the front of the store to the back, past the offices and dressing rooms to the back room where the entire humungous stock of wedding dresses were kept.

There, I found my mother searching for a specific gown and double checking price tags fervently.

"Hey mom! It's crazy today! What can we do?" At the sound of my voice my mom's head shot up and a huge smile formed on her face.

"Alex! Honey, I'm so glad you came! I need you to help assist some of the newer consultants, help them find dresses for their brides." Upon finishing her sentence her gaze turned to Nathaniel and amusement and curiosity swept over her features as she turned to me for an answer.

"Oh, he said he wanted to come, he wanted to help today too, or at least watch," I said smiling. At this she thanked him for being such a gentleman and scampered off with a dress in tow. Nathaniel and I were left standing, looking at each other. I shrugged.

Back out in the front lobby, Nathaniel found an unoccupied chair away from the chaos overlooking the rest of the lobby, and I jumped right into talking with a consultant and bride and began pulling dresses. A half hour passed pulling giant puffy ball gowns, dresses with demure sweet heart necklines, form-fitting mermaid silhouettes, and sleek modern "Grecians". Hour by hour the shop seemed to quiet down as I finished helping a bride named Heather with a dress she deemed 'utterly perfect' to the cashier's desk.

I caught sight of Nathaniel leaning back in his chair smirking at me with his arms folded across his chest. I told the bride how beautiful she was going to look on her big day, then turned and slowly began to walk back towards Nathaniel. I took a seat on the steps in front of the double mirrors next to him; closed my eyes and sighed.

"Hmmm," Nathaniel whispered huskily.

"Hmmm, what?" I asked while keeping my eyes closed.

"You were really good today, I didn't realize how passionate you were about helping people, is all," he said nonchalantly.

"I don't know about that," I replied opening my eyes and looking at him. "I just know if it was my big day, I'd want all the help I could get, too. And the dresses are gorgeous."

Nathaniel's eyes glistened as he looked at me and for a moment he just sat there staring. Uncomfortable, I fidgeted with my hands and my birthstone ring, not meeting his gaze. Finally I couldn't take it any longer.

"Stop looking at me like that." I said unsteadily. This got Nathaniel to smirk deviously at me.

"Like what?" He asked innocently. I glared at him then.

"Like that," I stated firmly.

"What if I can't help myself?" he teased.

I glared, trying to hide the rush of blood forming in my cheeks.

"Try."

Before Nathaniel could reply my mom had walked into the room and exhausted, took a seat next to me on the steps.

"Thank you guys so much for coming, seriously; you helped me out a lot," she stated and then questioned, "So do you two have anything fun planned for tonight?" The way she said it and how she kept looking back and forth from me to Nathaniel made me wonder if they both knew something I didn't. Before I could ask what was going on I was pushed up by my mother and ushered towards an area of dresses in the store that were for special occasions, not weddings. Nathaniel got up and followed us laughing, as my mother persisted to hold up dresses against me.

"Wait a sec." I stopped them abruptly, confused. "Will someone please tell me what is going on?" My mom smiled at me as she put a charcoal grey dress back on the rack.

"Honey, Nathaniel is taking you out tonight and that's all I'm allowed to tell you." She finished winking at me. I looked towards Nathaniel bewildered and raised my eyebrow in question.

"Yes, I'm taking you somewhere; now find a dress and some shoes." He winked and smiled.

"But..." I began, but was cut off by Nathaniel.

"But nothing, now get that butt in a dress; we only have an hour," he stated as he smiled and walked away leaving my mother to fuss over me. I couldn't help myself; I smiled and began sifting through the racks of dresses. An hour later I was in a dressing room staring at a completely different person. My mother was a hobby aesthetician and had taken the liberty of doing my makeup and hair.

"Ok," Nathaniel announced. "I'm going to come back there and get you in five minutes if you're not ready."

I walked out slowly lifting the sides of the silky dress so as not to step on it. I stepped up the double steps and emerged in front of the double mirrors. I looked up, noticing Nathaniel had stopped checking his watch and pacing to look in my direction.

He had changed from a black button up to an all black tux with a silk black shirt underneath. His eyes locked with mine before they travelled to the fitted satin, backless, emerald green dress I had chosen.

My hair had all been pulled back in a twisted bun, with only a few strands framing my face. My makeup, a subtle brown with only a hint of green made my eyes pop.

Nathaniel stood wordless, staring at me. Then he snapped out of his trance and knelt before me. His eyes smoldered a fiery blue as his lips gently kissed the top of my hand. I could only smile as I was led out the door.

"Have a good time!" Mom called after us. In the car, Nathaniel couldn't keep from sneaking glances here and there at me.

"So where are we going?" I asked smiling and curious beyond belief.

"That is a secret. If I told you I'd have to kill you," he teased as he motioned to a blindfold on the dashboard.

"You're kidding right?" I responded bemused.

"Alex." Nathaniel warned. "Either you put it on, or I put it on for you; which I would be glad to do by the way."

Knowing full well he was serious, I grabbed the blindfold and put it over my eyes, but not before announcing, "But I still think it's ridiculously unnecessary." I heard Nathaniel snicker as the darkness from the blindfold became all I could see.

I felt the car make several turns and I wondered where Nathaniel could be taking me. It's definitely somewhere fancy I gathered by our attire, but where? The only occasion I could think of that anyone would possibly get dressed up for was prom, and even that wasn't for another five months or so.

Perplexed, I waited in anticipation until I felt the car come to a halt and heard Nathaniel turn the engine off. I listened to Nathaniel get out of the car and shut the door only to have my door open a second later.

"Give me your hand," Nathaniel told me gently. Still blindfolded, I outstretched my right hand to Nathaniel.

"Where are we?" I inquired curiously.

"You'll see soon enough," Nathaniel replied, and by the sound of his voice I could tell he was smiling. Once out of the car, Nathaniel went behind me and began to undo the blindfold slowly. The soft cotton fabric drifted away from my eyes effortlessly, and I had to squint to adjust to the light around me. From what I could tell we were in a parking garage, but some distance in front of us was an elevator with a red carpet leading towards it and two guards in black tux's standing on either side guarding it. I turned back to Nathaniel and raised my eyebrows in question. A small smirk played at his lips as he popped the trunk of the car and grabbed two objects inside before locking it and walking back towards me.

"You'll need this," Nathaniel said as he slid a mask into my hand.

It was unlike any mask I had seen before. It was gold and black metal that had intricately woven swirls and designs throughout. The edges of the mask swirled together into a hook that would frame the face of any who wore it. The center of the mask was adorned with crystals inlaid into the metal that spread over the brows and below each eye cut-out.

The beauty of the mask seemed to have me in a trance and I found it difficult to express the true uniqueness and sheer exquisiteness it held.

"It's called a Cignetta Venetian Mask," said Nathaniel, as if reading my thoughts. "They are handmade and extremely difficult to acquire. They date as far back as the 12th century."

"It's exquisite," I said in awe. "I can't accept something like this Nathaniel. It's... It's too much," I replied hastily.

"Then I guess it's a good thing I'm not asking you to have it; it's already yours." He smiled. "Besides, for tonight's festivities you're required to wear it." With a smirk he tied a black leather mask around his head and motioned for me to turn so he could put mine on for me. My heart began to race as I felt the mask tighten on my face; I couldn't believe I was going to be wearing something so elegant. Excited for what was to come, I linked arms with Nathaniel and let him escort me towards the two security guards awaiting us at the elevator. To my astonishment they didn't even question either of us as we approached, they merely nodded and watched as we entered the inside of the red velvet elevator and the doors closed behind us.

Not being able to contain myself any longer, I asked Nathaniel where we were going that we would need masks. However, my question was answered when the elevator dinged and the doors opened to an enormous night club.

Everyone was wearing a mask. The cool blue lights were dimmed as mysterious masked figures and couples swirled before us dancing and mingling. As we stepped out of the steel elevator and into this strangely alluring atmosphere I noticed there were dining tables placed along the far walls next to the windows to overlook the city; the dance floor seemed alive with activity as couples floated effortlessly here and there and small circles of people spoke in tones that seemed to match the smooth melodic rhythm of the music. Violins and other instruments echoed throughout the room in a continuous melody.

"Welcome to After Life," Nathaniel whispered in my ear. The coolness of his breath sent shivers racing up my neck. Nathaniel began to escort me onto the dance floor. Nervously I complied, it wasn't that I couldn't dance; it was just that I had been out of practice for quite a while. Without hesitation, Nathaniel grasped my waist with his left hand, and took hold of my hand with his right. Nervously I looked up at him.

"You look nervous Alex." Nathaniel stated smirking.

"I'm not nervous," I replied defiantly.

"Good, cause we're going to have to get a little bit closer," he declared whilst pushing me closer to him; I gasped a little.

Being this close to Nathaniel had its effect on me, I knew that, and after last night's kiss my mind was racing, but before I knew it, we were dancing. He weaved me around the dance floor never faltering. As I danced I recognized the song that was playing, Nothing Else Matters, by Apocalyptica. As I looked back up at Nathaniel, I blushed realizing he had been intently staring at me the entire time.

"So I've been thinking about that kiss from last night," Nathaniel stated callously. My breathing caught and I reflexively stopped dancing. Nathaniel smirked then and kept me moving with his rhythm.

Ok Alex, I thought, don't panic.

"Yes?" I managed to ask. "What of it," I said trying to sound indifferent while meeting his eyes. He smiled and behind his mask his eyes flashed.

All of a sudden Nathaniel came to a halt. His nostrils flared once as his eyes darted towards a set of booths shadowed by darkness off the dance floor. Immediately he grabbed my hand and began leading me in the opposite direction. Whatever it was that he caught sight of, he did not like it. I struggled to make pace with Nathaniel through the throng of masked people noticing, Nathaniel went behind me holding my left hand in his, and guiding me with the other on the small of my back.

"Nathaniel, what is it? What's wrong?" I asked anxiously. He kept looking straight ahead and I couldn't be sure if he had heard me, or if he was deliberately ignoring my question until we'd gotten back to the car. We emerged from the throng of couples and were about to exit through the elevator from whence we had come when two guards stopped us. Nathaniel and I stopped and he protectively stepped in front of me, blocking most of my view.

"Raum, Verin, move." Nathaniel commanded. The seriousness of his tone made me think twice about asking him what was going on.

The stocky man on the left, whom I assumed was Raum, answered. "Apollyon wants to speak with you."

"You can tell Apollyon this is not the time, nor company for me to meet with him." Raum's cold grey eyes looked to me, sending a rush of chills all over me.

"He specifically said he wants to see both of you; he's not asking Nathaniel."

As Raum finished, Verin the taller guard on the right began to speak. "We wouldn't want to make a scene now Nathaniel, would we? In front of your..." he paused and looked me up and down, "...date none the less."

As he finished he looked at me once again and deceitfully smiled. Something in that hungry sadistic smile he held told me that Verin didn't have a problem with the situation escalating. I could feel Nathaniel's body tense and go stone hard under my hands that were pressed against his lower back. He said nothing to Raum or Verin; he only gave a swift nod of his head announcing his compliance.

Raum walked around us and began to lead the way as Verin followed from behind. As uncomfortable as I was with having Verin walking behind us, I decided now was the best time to find out from Nathaniel what was going on.

"What's this about?" I whispered to Nathaniel as discreetly as possible.

Still on edge, Nathaniel replied. "Something I hoped to avoid, however these days it's hard to go unnoticed."

"What do you mean? Who are these guys?" I inquired. Obviously they aren't the kind of people you hope to run in to, I thought.

"Apollyon is a demon and from what I gather now, it seems he's been very busy lately acquiring restaurants, private clubs, and other places for him and his followers; he's a businessman."

"I'm sorry did you just say he's a demon?" Nathaniel rolled his eyes at me before replying.

"You can accept the fact that I was an angel and now I'm a fallen angel, but you can't accept the fact that this guy's a demon?" I glared at him.

"Ok, so he's a demon; what about these two then?" I asked as I motioned towards Raum and back towards Verin.

"Verin is also a demon. He's one of Apollyon's guards and Raum is a fallen angel, another guard of Apollyon's."

As we approached a barely lit back room with a booth I had time to ask Nathaniel one more question.

"What does he want?" Nathaniel tensed again. "I'm not sure, but we're about to find out."

My heartbeat became jagged and irregular as we came within reach of the shadowy booth, where cigarette smoke gathered and hung in the air around it. Just what had I gotten myself into? I could feel the gazes coldly pierce through me as Raum motioned for us to remove our masks while we had a 'chat' with this, Apollyon. Aggravated, Nathaniel complied and helped me remove mine.

Five pairs of eyes gleamed out of the darkness, and as my eyes adjusted to the dim room, I began to make out the people in the booth.

Three women surrounded a man in the middle, with one man at the outer rim of the booth. Of the women, there was one red head, who seemed appalled by my presence, and two brunettes who watched me wearily.

The man in the middle had dark hair with a silver tint to it, signaling he was older, but I got the impression he was no older than my father; or at least that's what I thought. A cigarette dangled from his lips and white smoke slithered fancifully around his face. He smiled cunningly and laughed a deep throaty laugh as one of the brunettes whispered something in his ear. He seemed charming to say the least, but something about him told me he would not appear so reserved if he was upset.

The man on the outer edge of the booth was not reserved at all. His shaggy black hair fell over one of his dark grey eyes and he ignored the fiery red head next to him. He seemed bored and continuously ignited a lighter and slammed it closed again. I gathered him to be younger than the gentleman in the middle and perhaps even related to him.

Nathaniel wrapped his arm around my waist, pulling me protectively to his side as Verin and Raum took their respective places on opposite sides of the booth.

The man in the middle of the booth dismissed the women from the table with a flick of his wrist, cigarette still in hand. The women obeyed, but the fiery red head stood in front of me for a moment boldly, obviously unhappy with the fact that she was being asked to leave.

"You too, Persephone," The man in the middle of the booth announced unfazed. With a turn of her head she looked back at him before storming off. As soon as everyone had dispersed, the man addressed us.

"Awe, if it isn't my friend Nathaniel," the man said as he put out his cigarette.

"Apollyon. We meet again," Nathaniel replied calmly.

"And who, pray tell, is this lovely creature accompanying you?" Nathaniel's grip tightened. The curious man looked from me to Nathaniel and back again before Nathaniel reluctantly answered him.

"This is Alex."

Addressing me, the man smiled. "Alex. Tell me my dear, do you have a last name?" he inquired.

"Do you?" I asked defensively. The man laughed deeply and eyed me for a moment. "How rude of me. I have completely forgotten my manners. My name is Apollyon Demones. Tell me though; you wouldn't happen to be the Alex Fatum Constance everyone is hearing so much about, now would you?"

At the mention of my full name I stood dumbfounded and shocked. How in the world is it that this man, or demon, for that matter, knows me? And what does he mean by everyone? The thought both scared and intrigued me, but my curiosity overtook me.

"How is it that you and everyone else has come to hear about me?" Before Apollyon could answer, Nathaniel interjected.

"Her name is of no consequence at the moment Apollyon. What is it you want to talk with me about?" I looked up at Nathaniel as if to yell at him for interrupting. Apparently there was a lot I was missing that was going on.

Apollyon calmly lit the end of another cigarette and inhaled deeply before looking back up at Nathaniel.

"As a matter of fact, her name is of great consequence. Since you have been back, Nathaniel, you've begun to stir things up for everyone here. People are becoming very interested in your lovely young lady here and even more so, about the past history between you two; rumors have been circulating." Apollyon's eyes flickered between Nathaniel and me.

I began to get the feeling that Apollyon knew something about me and Nathaniel that I had been kept in the dark about.

"People will always talk of rumors Apollyon; you know that." Nathaniel replied calmly.

"Perhaps," Apollyon replied. He took a long drag, dramatically emphasizing the moment. "Either way your presence here has not gone unnoticed, nor has hers. There are some of us, Nathaniel, who don't want you to get your wings back. Some who aren't particularly fond of you." He stated it matter-of-factly.

"So I have gathered. I wouldn't suppose you might know who poses a threat to us that lurks in your neighborhood, would you?" Nathaniel asked.

At his question the man at the end of the table who, up until this point, had been silent, slammed his fist down and sent the table whining back and forth for a moment before it settled in its original position once more. He stood and yelled emphatically.

"Father you cannot think about helping this filth; I will not hear it!" His eyes blazed black with red flames. Unfazed, Apollyon took another drag of his cigarette and blew a cloud full of smoke into the air.

"Corson. We are in the company of guests; control yourself my son."

The younger man's rage spurred at the comment and just as he was about to say something else, Apollyon's wrath ignited. He stood to tower over the full height of Corson.

"You are dismissed!"

Apollyon's rage spread like a wildfire on a desiccated day, and he eyed Raum and Verin as well, cueing them to leave. No more needed to be said. Corson left the table with Raum and Verin hot on his heels.

Returning to his seat once again as if nothing had happened, Apollyon sat. I must have jumped during the family dispute because Nathaniel had grasped me so firmly, I found it hard to breathe.

"Now. I may know of some who have more of an interest in you and Alex, however in our line of work, Nathaniel, the list is overwhelmingly long." He continued as if no disturbance ever occurred.

"What about Uvall?" Nathaniel questioned. The mention of the name sent shivers up my spine and I shuddered. Apollyon was quiet for a moment, before he spoke.

"I do not know of the whereabouts of Uvall, however, his interests surely pertain to you Alex, my dear," he said as he calmly gestured towards me.

"What does he want?" I asked anxiously. "I have nothing to offer him."

Apollyon looked from me to Nathaniel and back again inquisitively.

"Nathaniel has not told you. Has he?" Apollyon smirked. I looked at Nathaniel for answers then, confused at what Apollyon was saying. Surely if Nathaniel knew what he wanted he would have told me wouldn't he?

"What do you mean? What have I not been told?" I asked, anger beginning to rise in the pit of my stomach.

"My dear, it seems Nathaniel has failed to mention the fact that he and Uvall are brothers." My jaw dropped and for a moment I was speechless. I looked at Nathaniel then back to Apollyon with wide eyes before I managed to speak.

"What?" I breathed.

Chapter 13

"Are you kidding me?!" I yelled at Nathaniel as he drove us home. "He's your brother! You could have mentioned that fact to me before; it's kind of important Nathaniel!" I screamed. I was furious. For one, Nathaniel had lied to me, two, not only was his brother wanting to use me for God knows what, but it seemed he was doing all of it to get back at Nathaniel for something that had happened long ago.

"Calm down Alex." Nathaniel ordered.

"No! I'm not going to calm down! A week ago I was a normal 17 year old who only had to worry about school or how her parents' divorce was going, or when she was going to hang out with her friends. Now, I'm dealing with the supernatural! You've got to be kidding me!" I shouted.

"Do you think I wanted you to get involved this deep?! I've been trying to protect you by limiting how much you know!" Nathaniel boomed as he steered the car off the road onto the shoulder. It had become a screaming match now.

"Limiting how much I know! How do you expect me to help you Nathaniel?! Or get out of this mess you put me in!" I questioned angrily.

Nathaniel ignored my question and continued. His hands gripped the wheel so hard I thought he might rip it off.

"I'm sorry that I came into your life and ruined it Alex and I'm sorry that my own flesh and blood wants to hurt you now because of me!" he roared; then his tone began to soften as he continued.

"If I could have gotten my wings back any other way I would have. I hate myself for putting you in harm's way like this, and yet if there had been another way to get them back I would have traded it for just one hour of time spent with you. I'm sorry Alex." Nathaniel had closed his eyes as he spoke the last few words and taken his hands from the steering wheel. His left elbow rested on the door as he ran his hand through his hair.

Astonished at his declaration, I remained silent for a moment. I couldn't quite believe Nathaniel had just admitted he liked me. I was a whirlwind of emotions now. I was furious with him still, but he made it so damn hard to stay mad at him. I swallowed hard as my stomach felt like it would explode with butterflies. I took a deep breath to calm myself down.

"Don't be, I wouldn't have gotten to know you." Nathaniel opened his eyes at my words and looked at me. His blue orbs locked with my emerald ones. I don't remember how long we just stared at one another, but I couldn't manage to tell myself to break away. Nathaniel's small smirk tugged at the corner of his mouth then.

"So I take it this means you like me?"

I rolled my eyes and smiled. "Hardly."

Just as I was about to say something else, Nathaniel grasped me in his arms and pulled me to him. I was met with a passionate and deep kiss. At first I was still so frustrated about everything I tried to push back, but as the kiss deepened, I kissed back and the need for each other seemed to grow with the intensity of the kiss. He kissed my neck and mouth with such fervor it was as if this was the last time I would see him again and his need seemed unbearable.

Minutes passed before we parted, breathless. My forehead rested against his and I realized he must have pulled me on top of him during our kiss because we both were in the driver's seat. Catching my breath, Nathaniel tucked a loose strand of hair behind my ear and gently kissed my forehead. He laughed for a moment.

Curious as to what he found to be amusing I asked, "What?" Nathaniel smiled.

"I was just thinking about how I have to meet your brother tomorrow; I don't believe he's going to like me kissing you." He smirked.

After tonight's events I had completely forgotten about Derek coming home tomorrow from the Marines.

Oh God, I thought. There was quite a lot I had to take in, especially in one evening. I was excited and yet nervous for Derek to meet Nathaniel; somehow I didn't think a Marine infantry man would like the idea of his baby sister going out with a fallen angel, not that he would know Nathaniel was one. In general, I think he would just not like the idea at all.

I pushed the thoughts from my mind as we drove the rest of the way to my dad's house and only made myself think of how everything was going to be just fine – I hoped.

Nathaniel and I managed to sneak into the house without waking my dad. Apparently my mom had told him Nathaniel was taking me out tonight so he would not stay up waiting.

As I changed into my pajamas in the bathroom my thoughts drifted back to the car ride home. I smiled, and yet I couldn't help but wonder how each of us announcing that we liked one another would change everything. What did that mean would happen once I helped Nathaniel get his wings back? Uncertainty lingered in my mind as I turned off the light and stepped out of the bathroom. How did I really feel about him? Someone who just appeared out of nowhere one day and would surely disappear once I helped him.

Nathaniel had already changed and lay on the bed, his bare chest exposed, with his eyes closed. I studied him for a moment, almost trying to memorize every rippling muscle in his biceps, his familiar smirk that always played at his lips, and the ocean blue orbs that formed his eyes. Sighing I climbed in next to him and fell fast asleep.

I was consumed in blackness; not an ounce of light could be seen anywhere around me. Just as I thought I would be lost forever in the black, the darkness began to move as crows flew away opening my eyes to the light. My heart lifted and sank once more when I realized who stood in front of me in the light; Uvall.

With his all black attire and his beady eyes staring down at me condescendingly, I cringed in distaste.

"What do you want?" I spat defiantly.

"You already know that Alex, now why don't we focus on something more important; such as your relationship with Nathaniel." He grinned.

Anger flowed through my body then.

"What is your problem!? How could you even think about destroying your brother's life, he's your brother for God's sake, your family!" I fumed.

Uvall's face seemed to turn dark at my comments, his eyes cold and lifeless as they continued to stare down at me; then he exploded.

"You think you know it all don't you? You have no idea why I'm doing this, but Nathaniel does. He should have been there! They ripped my world from me after casting me out and now I'm going to take this from them! They had this coming for a long time now and I'm going to relish every moment to come. He smiled evilly.

"What are you going to do to him?" I questioned, feeling my heart break into pieces at the thought of him hurting Nathaniel.

"Oh now, you let me worry about that Alex. Don't worry; I'll make sure you have a front row seat at the show when the time comes. Ta ta for now darling." He snarled as a hoard of crows flew at me washing away the light.

"Wait!" I sat up yelling in my bed. I looked around realizing that another dream with Uvall had just come and gone. Nathaniel stood quietly in front of the window with his hands on the ledges of the window sill, his back hunched.

"Uvall?" He stated more than questioned. He must have known Uvall had been kind enough to visit me in my dream again.

"Ugh." I huffed and fell back grabbing a pillow and pulling it to my face while yelling into it. I paused after a moment and laid in silence with the pillow still covering my face. Finally I removed the pillow to find Nathaniel kneeling next to my bed staring intently at me.

He rested his head on his folded arms; it seemed he was having difficulty not laughing at my previous actions. Embarrassed, I bit my lip trying to hide my embarrassment as I felt a wave of blood rush to my cheeks. Nathaniel practically had to bite his tongue off to keep from laughing at me.

"Don't you dare laugh," I threatened, trying to hold back the laughter and humiliation in my voice.

He smirked. "Or what, Alex?" He teased and I glared at him before replying.

"Or I'll, I'll..." I began searching around me for something that I could use to make him fear me. I spotted my pillow next to me and held it like a bat ready to strike at Nathaniel.

"Or I'll hit you with my pillow," I finally stated knowing the threat was weak.

Nathaniel looked at me unconvincingly with raised eyebrows.

"You're going to have to do better than that Alex." He grinned playfully. I glared before hitting him with the pillow and running for my door. I didn't end up making it very far; I probably made it a whole two feet before a force as hard as concrete threw me to the floor in one quick tackle and knocked the breath from me.

I gasped as Nathaniel flipped me over so I was facing him. He straddled my hips and smirked down at me deviously. I huffed, trying to squirm my way out from underneath him, but to no avail. Frustrated I angrily looked up at Nathaniel.

"Really?" I asked sarcastically.

First my dream with Uvall again and now this, perfect, I thought sarcastically.

Nathaniel just watched as I tried to get away. After my second attempt and failure at escaping from Nathaniel's clutches I looked up at him expectantly.

"Can I help you with something? Why won't you let me go?" I asked irritated by his antics.

"Alright fine, I'll make a deal with you Alex." He smirked down at me. "I'll let you go if you kiss me."

I laughed. "Kiss you? You can't be serious right now," I argued.

"Kiss me and I'll let you go, that's the deal. Besides let's stop pretending that you don't like kissing me; you've been quite willing before." He smirked cunningly.

How dare him! I thought, appalled. Why is he so irritating! So what if I liked his kisses before; not that I would ever tell him that to his face, but there was no way he was going to get me to kiss him now. NEVER. I think.

Nathaniel stayed silent as he let me battle with myself inwardly. After ten minutes of being pinned to the floor my butt had gone numb and I began doubting how much longer I could stay there. Not wanting to give him the satisfaction of a kiss, but not wanting to stay on the floor with Nathaniel on top of me for the rest of the day, I caved.

I looked him dead in the eye and laid one on him. I had meant for the kiss to be short and to take him by surprise so I could squeeze my way out from underneath him, but it seemed as though Nathaniel knew me too well. He wrapped his arms around mine and pulled me into a sitting position while still kissing, keeping his grip tight. After a few seconds of doing my best to pull away and resist, I eventually melted into his arms and his grip loosened.

"Why do you even try to fight me?" he teasingly questioned after we had parted.

I just glared at him and moved from the floor to the bed before stubbornly replying, "Because maybe you won't always win. That's why." He chuckled a little and just shook his head at me. I huffed as I lay on my bed and stared at the ceiling.

What was I going to do about Uvall? I wondered helplessly. I felt as if the promise Nathaniel had made to me about my family and friends not getting hurt or involved was completely untrue. I mean we weren't just dealing with some random thugs that we got mixed up with. This was so much worse. All I knew was I could never let something bad happen to the people I loved.

I was shaken out of my thoughts when I felt Nathaniel grasp and hold my hand tightly. I had not even noticed that he had moved from the floor to the bed as well and was now lying next to me, silent.

"I'll get you through this Alex, I promise." He whispered loud enough so I could hear.

I drew in a deep breath. I hope, I thought.

Chapter 14

I awoke the next morning to laughing, things banging, the smell of pancakes and boisterous voices coming from downstairs. I groaned as I looked over towards my alarm clock on the nightstand.

"Ugh." It was 6AM and the sun was just beginning to peak into my room. What is going on! I thought irritably as I dragged myself into a sitting position in bed and looked around. Where is Nathaniel? I wondered as I looked around and found only myself in the quiet empty room.

I began to get anxious after checking the bathroom and still finding no Nathaniel anywhere. I noticed my window to the roof was partially cracked and I quickly went to it to investigate. On the window sill I found a tiny white piece of ripped paper that read:

Had an errand, will be back soon. Nathaniel P.S. Don't worry.

I felt relieved knowing Nathaniel was ok, but telling me not to worry definitely made me worry a little. After all, what I didn't know, in this situation, could hurt me. But I had no choice but to go about my normal morning routine. I rushed to get ready and bounded down the stairs in my black DC's.

"What's all the ruckus? Doesn't anybody sleep around here?" Grinning, I rounded the corner into the kitchen and was stopped dead in my tracks when I was met with Derek, Kate, Trey, and my mom and dad and Derek's girlfriend Jessica.

"Omg!" I shouted excitedly not able to contain myself. "You're home!" Derek just laughed as I ran and hugged him. After we were all done practically interrogating my brother about all that he had been through, who he had met, the things he had seen and how long he would be home for, Derek began to ask how everyone else had been while he was gone.

Only reading letters from us made him eager to know what was new at home and with the people he loved. I panicked a little as I noticed my dad gesture towards me and volunteer me to share what was new first.

"Alex has some new interesting news, don't you honey," he said with a chuckle. I sent a fierce look at him for a moment as if to yell at him. I knew he just wanted Derek to find out about my new boyfriend, or fake boyfriend, so that they both could have their fun and gang up on him. Derek turned expectantly and curiously asked me what was new. Just as I was about to speak up the doorbell rang.

"I'll get it!" I shrilled as I jumped up and skipped to the doorway excited to have the interrogation put on hold. I smiled as I opened the door and was about to ask who it was when I halted and found a smirking Nathaniel in front of me holding a case of beer with 'Welcome Home' written across the side.

Nathaniel seemed to notice I was curious as to where he had been as he kissed my cheek quickly sending a slight chill up my spine.

"Don't worry. I've handled everything for now; enjoy the company of your brother and forget the rest."

I sighed, a little relieved that I might have a normal day with my friends and family since Nathaniel came into my life. I lead Nathaniel into the living room and was met with an inquisitive but scrutinizing stare from Derek.

"Derek this is my boyfriend Nathaniel, Nathaniel this is my brother Derek," I announced, not faltering. Nathaniel and Derek shook hands strongly.

I retold the story we had made up of how Nathaniel and I had met. I was getting pretty good at this whole lying thing, but I wasn't sure if that was a good thing or a bad thing. I really hated lying to everyone; these were the people I loved and trusted and they loved and trusted me. Guilt began to wash over but I pushed it back. I was going to enjoy seeing my brother for however long he was home and I wasn't going to let anything get in the way of that – especially supernatural things.

The day went by as we all talked and laughed and exchanged stories. Derek and everyone had seemed to warm up to Nathaniel a little more. He had told them vaguely about his childhood here and how he had moved back here recently. It was now 8 o'clock in the evening and everyone, especially Derek from his long ride home, were fading fast.

Kate was picked up by Jesse and my mom followed them out and began her drive home. Jessica, Trey, Nathaniel, Derek, my dad and I all stood in the kitchen talking when Nathaniel's pocket began to vibrate erratically. He excused himself as he calmly walked past everyone and answered the phone on the back porch. That's when the 'Talk' came.

"Now Alex," Derek began calmly, "I think it's clear we all accept your new..." He struggled to say the word boyfriend as he still didn't like the idea of his little sister dating..."friend," he mustered. "However, as you probably know I am now considered a lethal weapon by the state and I will have no problem breaking legs, just as dad will have no problem getting rid of the body – with Trey's help of course."

They all snickered and mutually agreed before everyone said their final goodbyes.

"Thanks!" I replied sarcastically as everyone laughed, amused at my annoyed expression. Derek and Jessica went to stay at Jessica's new apartment and Trey went home. Only my dad and I were left in the kitchen when Nathaniel returned from the back porch.

"Well," my dad said walking towards Nathaniel. "You survived us all. I guess this means you're kind of alright," He stated as he smiled and continued walking to his study before turning around one last time. "But you hurt her, you die," he added flatly as I embarrassingly yelled at him.

"Dad!" Nathaniel seemed to chuckle to himself as we heard the study door shut and Nickel Back start to play. Nathaniel winked as he walked past me and out the front door to pretend to leave the house. I turned and walked up the stairs somewhat relieved.

Derek had met Nathaniel and seemed to approve, sort of, and everyone else did too for that matter. It was kind of nice in a way; he was the first guy all of my family genuinely seemed to take to. I smiled at the thought of Nathaniel being a fallen angel and still winning people over. Wasn't he supposed to be a bad guy technically? I wondered as I slipped on my pajamas and slid open my window climbing out onto the roof with a pillow in tow.

The cool night air kissed my skin and felt so refreshing as the night sky sparkled with stars that resembled tiny gems in the sky. A moment later a thud sounded next to me as Nathaniel lay down, his arms folded behind his head. I wanted to ask him where he had been that morning and what errand he had to do that he wouldn't tell me about, but I was too tired and exhausted from everything that I didn't. I told myself I would find out later, but for now, I was honestly just relishing having a day with no supernatural worries.

I felt myself being lifted from the cold shingles of the roof and was laid on a soft familiar comforter. Groggily I grunted to say thank you and fell asleep as Nathaniel whispered, "Don't worry Alex, you have a week with your family where you can just focus on them."

I smiled as I shut my eyes again and sleep overtook me. At least I would be able to be with my family while Derek was home. A week was all he was allotted before he had to go back and complete the second phase of his training as a Marine.

Chapter 15

The week that Derek was home had come and gone in a blur. We had spent the entire week having family dinners, talking, playing video games, and just being around one another. It was nice to feel some type of normal enter my life again, but it all felt like it had ended too soon.

Derek had been back in California for a day now for his second phase of training and our family was trying to ease into the cycle of having him home and having him gone again. We all cried at the airport as we watched him go and wished him well.

I always hated goodbyes. There was something about it that made my insides feel as if they were just ripped out of me. You can't help but feel a little empty when someone you care for goes away for a while.

There was going to be a winter break for the next two weeks, which meant no school and I could hopefully crack down and begin to focus on how I was going to help Nathaniel. Among other things like how to avoid Uvall; how to still keep everything hidden from everyone so that I didn't end up in some psychiatric ward, and how to try and be a normal teenager.

I woke that morning to the sun shining through my window, Nathaniel had come and gone during the week so that my family and I could have time together, but now a week was up and he was sitting on my desk chair intently staring at the brilliant gold pendant he constantly carried with him – the one that depicted a kneeling angel holding a sword.

"Morning," I pronounced eager to get back to business with what had happened with the supernatural in the last week.

Nathaniel seemed to sigh as he put the pendant back in his pocket and turned to face me.

"Good morning." He half smiled. His mind seemed to be weighed down with thoughts.

"So, what's on the agenda for today?" I asked casually. "No goblins or werewolves I should be aware of, right?" I playfully teased, but was only half kidding. I mean I never knew there were demons and angels walking around and buying nightclubs in Denver did I? I was sure there was a lot more I was unaware of.

Nathaniel smiled and laughed as he replied, "No, they don't exist Alex."

Pheww! I thought. Thank god! The last thing I needed was more supernatural or fairy tale creatures wandering around that I had no idea about. Nathaniel finished answering my question then.

"There is someone I need to pay a visit to. Unfortunately, they've been extremely busy this past week making preparations for something."

"Who?" I questioned feeling my brows furrow.

"Uvall," Nathaniel replied in a monotone. The sound of the name sent goose bumps crawling down my arms.

"Why are we going to see your brother who obviously isn't up to any good and clearly has it out for you?" I interjected nervously.

"Because." Nathaniel said. "We need to get an idea of what he is up to. It could help buy us some more time before he does something crazy."

I sat still horrified at what Uvall was possibly capable of and what he was planning.

"That's where you come in." Nathaniel huffed. I looked at him dumbfounded.

"Wait, I'm sorry could you repeat that? You want me to go to Uvall and find out what he's planning? Why would he even tell me? And are you crazy?" I asked flustered, not wanting any of this to happen.

Nathaniel started pacing in front of me and I could feel the heat from his body evaporating from him.

"Alex, if there is one thing I do know about my brother, it's that he is pissed, but for some reason he's been trying to talk to you, to get closer to you. He wants something and you are about the only person besides his minions who he would tell. He won't hurt you. I'll make sure of that."

"But..." I didn't have time to finish my sentence before Nathaniel's ice blue eyes pierced me where I sat.

"Alex." he took a deep breath to calm himself before finishing. "You have no idea how physically painful it is for me to ask you this, but...it's all we've got." His voice seemed to break as the last few words escaped from his mouth. I tried to be reassured by Nathaniel's words, 'he won't hurt you,' but the thoughts of my badly bruised black and blue arm came back into my mind. He did that through a dream, I thought. What could he be capable of face to face? I closed my eyes tightly and opened them again hoping to scratch that thought from my memory.

I shakily finished getting ready in the bathroom as I heard Nathaniel on the phone in the hallway. His tone was serious and monotone with no sense of emotion in it.

"We'll be there," I heard him finish firmly as he hung up the phone. I walked out of the bathroom and saw him standing in the hallway. His head was hung and there were plastic pieces of what used to be a cell phone scattered about the floor around him. It dawned on me he had crushed it when he hung up. Noticing my presence he turned around slowly and ran a hand through his hair.

"I'll get another one," He stated before I could comment on his now torn apart phone.

It was dead silent as we drove in the car. Neither of us could really say anything about what was going to happen at this 'little meeting.' Eventually I couldn't take it anymore.

"You know I agreed to help you Nathaniel. If this helps, I'll keep my promise," I said trying to be casual about the fact that I was basically going into the lion's den alone, outnumbered, to have a chat with a sadistic fallen angel who happens to be the brother of my fake boy-friend. Oh right, it's just a normal Monday, I thought, trying to convince myself.

Nathaniel began to pull the car to the side of the road then. I wasn't sure what he was doing so I just stayed silent and still. The e-brake jerked us to halt. Nathaniel turned towards me, radiating heat.

"You have no idea how badly I want to call this whole thing off. I can't stand the fact that I'm the one who's literally driving you into harm's way for my own benefit!" he shouted. He looked completely torn and helpless.

Just as I was about to respond and try to comfort him in some way, Nathaniel grabbed the steering wheel with his left hand and the other went to his chest. He started to groan in pain. His breathing had increased and the pain seemed to worsen as he let out a thundering shout. The steering wheel was bending from his death grip. Something was horribly wrong.

Panicking, I yelled, "What's wrong?! Nathaniel what's happening?!" Trying to see what invisible creature had hurt Nathaniel.

As moments passed and Nathaniel's body began to relax, the pain had ceased, but his breathing remained jagged. His eyes stayed closed as he hung his head and focused on his breathing.

"Are you ok? Nathaniel? Nathaniel?!" I shouted and grabbed his arm when I got no reply.

Nathaniel opened his eyes and looked at me. They were a slightly darker blue than usual. But he was no longer in pain.

"What just happened?" I breathed. Worry had washed over me as I began to inspect his chest fearing the worst, but only finding hard abs that felt as if they were on fire. I looked expectantly at him for answers before he finally responded.

"I'm starting to change entirely; my body is starting to change." I waited for him to continue. "Basically my body has been changing since I fell and am no longer considered an angel, but a fallen angel. I heard about the transformations, but never actually saw one. They said it happens slowly at first, but eventually I'll have no light left in me; only blackness. What I am now burns the light away."

I sat there helpless and confused as I looked at the twist that was now bent into the steering wheel. I tried asking Nathaniel what he meant by that statement, but he was unresponsive for the rest of the car ride.

We drove quite a ways outside of Denver and the surrounding areas. I stared out the window at the vacant landscape before me, wondering how all of this was happening and fearing what may come. I woke abruptly from the jolt of the car hitting a pot hole. I looked around and realized the once vacant landscape had turned to forest and there seemed to be no civilization anywhere near. I watched as Nathaniel turned right onto a dirt road where an old rusted sign barely hung that read, "Dead End".

I started to wonder if Nathaniel was going the right way. We were surrounded by dense forest and the dirt road seemed to go nowhere until we came to an immense iron gate with spikes along the tops and edges and an intercom box. Nathaniel clicked the intercom box and we waited in silence. The tension was so thick in the air that you could cut it with a butter knife. A moment went by and a voice sounded on the intercom.

"Welcome guests," the voice eerily cooed. "Please come in." The gate groaned as it slowly opened and the dirt road never ended, but the tree line opened just enough for us to arrive at a mansion sized house.

The mansion looked cold; as cold as I pictured Uvall to be. Fitting, I thought. It stood towering over us with a dark grey brick and stone exterior. It resembled more of a fortress than a house. I noticed what looked to be a barn and a few other buildings off in the distance behind the house, but it was hard to make them out as the forest seemed to keep them shaded from view. I took a deep breath and closed my eyes before reopening them. Nathaniel looked at me sternly.

"You're going to be ok Alex, just remember to try and figure out what he is planning." Before I could reply the 8 foot steel doors to the mansion opened and two burly men appeared in black suits and motioned me inside. A panicked look came over my face and I turned one last time to face Nathaniel.

"Right." I tried to muster confidence.

"I won't let anything happen to you Alex." Nathaniel claimed whilst grabbing my arm protectively. I half smiled before getting out of the car and walking up the steps towards the two men. I looked back at Nathaniel one last time, his icy blue orbs never leaving mine before the steel doors closed shut behind me. I turned to look at what lay ahead of me. A grand staircase with red carpet and wrought iron railings seemed to take up most of the foyer. It was dark and dimly lit throughout; all of the windows were covered with heavy black velvety curtains and I noticed large portraits of men and women hung on the walls. They seemed to be glaring at me as the men lead me through a long hallway and stopped at a door. I walked into the room and the men shut the door behind me.

Inside, the room was an octagon shape and there were book shelves lining all the walls with thousands of books. In the center of the room was a black glass desk covered in books and random papers, and two velvet red chairs resembling the carpet surrounded it. Behind the desk was a massive stone fireplace. I could smell the wood burning, and the warmth of the fireplace surrounded by the cold of the stone kissed at my skin giving me goose-bumps. A book lying on the black glass desk caught my attention. I walked to it, and pushing the others aside, examined the title. It was extremely old from what I could gather from the crinkled worn brown leather exterior, and in small black letters on the spine it read, "Et Sanguinem Familiae Constantiae."

It did not have an author nor did it have anything on the front or back of it. I heard the door knob start to turn, so I snatched the book and hid it beneath my shirt in my pants. The door shut hard and I turned to see a figure in the doorway.

"Alex." Uvall half whispered. It was enough to send those same chills up my spine. I stood frozen as Uvall stepped into the dimly lit room. He smiled a sinister smile and began to stride towards me calmly. He stopped a few feet in front of me; his eyes piercing mine the whole time.

"You must be Uvall," I said flatly; trying to remain calm. I took a breath in and couldn't help but hold it for a few seconds; he seemed to notice immediately.

"You aren't nervous are you?" His smile widened at the thought and his eyes examined me closely.

I felt trapped, like I had been cornered by a rabid dog that may attack at any moment. Why did I agree to do this? What the hell is wrong with me?

"I'm not nervous." I lied.

His eyes glistened for a moment with intrigue.

"Good," he stated. "Because I think we can help each other Alex. As a matter of fact, I think we could be great working together," he declared while walking around me slowly.

"Just where exactly do I fit in with all of this?" I asked irritated. I did not want to be near Uvall at all. He turned to face me.

"You mean my dear brother didn't tell you?" he spat sarcastically. Clearly they had family problems. I didn't respond so he continued. "You don't even know what you were destined to do. But I think with my help you will know."

"What do you know about my destiny?" I interjected feeling as if he knew something I didn't, but guarding myself in case he was lying. Uvall just grinned at me and dodged the question.

"Do you know why Nathaniel lost his wings Alex?"

I stared at him, now wanting to know the answer more than ever seeing as Nathaniel hasn't told me anything about what is going on. I walked towards Uvall slowly and stopped a foot from him. Uvall just looked at me knowing he had my full attention now.

"How did he lose them?" I demanded, desperately wanting to know the answer.

"I'll tell you, but you have to do something for me in return," he stated point-blank. I shifted uncomfortably knowing I probably wouldn't like what I had to agree to.

"What do you want?" I questioned cautiously. He motioned me to come closer to him as if it was a secret or something. I cautiously walked towards him. When I was as close as I could muster without practically being sick, he grabbed me quickly and firmly by the left arm. Startled, I tried to hit him with my right, he dodged it spun me around and had both of my arms crossed in front of me. I could feel his body tight against mine and I almost threw up. His mouth grazed my neck and every sensory in my body screamed at me to run. I panicked and slammed my foot down on his causing him to grunt and release his grip on my arms just enough for me to get away. I lunged for a letter opener on his desk and turned to face him. He walked to a red velvet chair throwing himself in it and laughed while his eyes glowed with bits of anger and amusement.

"What the hell!" I shouted furiously.

He stopped laughing, and smiling said, "You'll feel differently about me once you know the truth; that was just a test sweetheart." He snarled.

"You're insane," I said while glaring at him and as I headed for the door he began to speak.

"Nathaniel lost his wings because he disobeyed a direct order to kill you."

I froze, my back still towards Uvall as he continued.

"He hates what he is now but I guess he has you to thank for that, doesn't he? Truthfully, I'm surprised he was able to bide his time for this long before they cast him out completely, but I'm sure they couldn't stand to lose such a good soldier. Tell me Alex, has he already started to change?" He snarled cruelly.

I couldn't hear another word, nor could I stand to be in Uvall's presence any longer. I stormed out of the library with the two burly men hot on my heels. I showed myself out and once outside Nathaniel who had been leaning against the Shelby tensely, straightened himself. I didn't even look at him I just jumped in the car and slammed the door. He hopped in after me, turned on the car and drove quickly out of the driveway and towards home once again.

Chapter 16

I hadn't said a word to Nathaniel for the entire car ride back to my Dad's house, and he hadn't asked either. I'm sure he wanted to know what happened, but I just couldn't understand how he wouldn't tell me that he had been ordered to kill me before! My head hurt from thinking so much.

Why was he ordered to kill me in the first place? I'm not that horrible of a person, I mean sure I don't go to church every Sunday, but I'm not a murderer or anything either! Not to mention my little chat with Uvall was less than enjoyable to say the least. He literally gave me the creeps and seemed to talk in riddles again just enough to where I still have no idea what he is planning or what he wants me for. How does he know my destiny anyway?

Nathaniel got out of the car; I hadn't even realized that we were back at my dad's house already. I got out of the car and Nathaniel went to park the car down the street away from the house so my dad wouldn't know he was staying there. I opened the door and went to head upstairs to my room when my dad's voice called from the office.

"Alex, I need to speak with you." His voice sounded irritated and I knew I was in trouble. I looked at the kitchen clock and it read 9:30PM. I hadn't even realized I had been gone for that long. No wonder he is pissed, I thought.

"Dad I'm so sorry I didn't realize what time it was and I..." I was cut off before I could finish my sentence.

"Do you even realize what time it is? I didn't know where you were and I even had to resort to calling Kate and your mother to see if you were with them! Then it dawned on me, I know you were with him Alex; that Nathaniel kid," he stated harshly.

"I'm sorry I forgot to call you Dad. I was with Nathaniel, I guess I've just had a lot of stress on my plate lately and he was helping me talk through it. I'm sorry I lost track of time," I said feeling ashamed I had let my dad worry so much.

He sighed heavily. "I know you miss your brother, we all miss him, but you can't forget about your responsibilities and just not tell anyone where you're at. I want to treat you like an adult, but you're still my daughter and a kid." I hugged him.

"I know dad, I'm sorry. I'll be better I swear." He just shook his head and half smiled at me; thankful I was home and unharmed but still not peachy about my absence.

I thought I was in the clear until I went to walk out of the doorway and he said, "By the way, you're on hay duty for you scaring me. Make sure Ajax is ok and unload all the bales tonight before you go to class tomorrow."

I rushed back to his office doorway to interject.

"Dad! It's already 9:30!" I groaned.

Before I could say anymore he looked at me and smiling said, "Should have thought of that when you were with Nathaniel."

Defeated, I walked upstairs to change before going out back to unload the new hay bales. I changed in the bathroom since I wasn't sure where Nathaniel was and went out to the barn. The sooner I get this over with, the better, I thought.

I opened the barn doors enough for me to enter and closed them behind me flipping on the lights inside and the radio. I didn't care what station it was on, just that music was playing and I could hopefully clear my head for a while.

There were about 50 bales from what I could make out, stacked on a flatbed trailer in the center of the barn. I walked towards the flatbed and grabbed the first bale; I hesitated for a second knowing Nathaniel was behind me, then continued angrily.

Nathaniel didn't say a word as he grabbed a bale of hay and went to toss it into the hay room.

"What are you doing?" I asked unforgiving.

"Helping you, you need it" he stated, unaffected by my coldness.

"Nope," I replied flatly, "I don't."

Nathaniel threw a couple bales into the hay room. "Really Alex? Why don't you just tell me what happened with Uvall?" he asked getting annoyed.

"Why should I tell you anything? You haven't been so honest with me have you? "In fact, you seem to be in the business of keeping secrets," I accused angrily.

He dropped the bale of hay he was carrying and quickly walked towards me. "What did he tell you?" he ordered. I just looked at him with a cold glare.

"When were you going to tell me Nathaniel? Or did you prefer to just keep me in the dark about it forever?" I was getting even more furious now that I was talking to him about it. Something in Nathaniel's eyes changed just then; the icy blue orbs they once were turned to the darkest blue and black. I froze; something wasn't right.

Nathaniel knocked me to the ground before I could think of what to do. I was pinned to the ground and helpless.

"Nathaniel!" I screeched. "What are you doing!?"

He cocked his head as if even he didn't know the answer to that question and then shook his head quickly; his eyes changed back to the icy blue orbs I once knew. He let my wrists go, but neither of us moved. I was almost shaking and he was breathing heavily.

"Alex..." he whispered. I almost told him to go pound sand until I remembered what Uvall had said to me earlier: 'Tell me Alex, has he started to change yet?'

Nathaniel sat on a bale of hay but did not look at me. He was rubbing the palm of his left hand slowly with his right thumb and his head hung low enough so I could not see his face. I regained my composure, but didn't move; still weary from what had just happened. He started to speak slowly while looking at his hands.

"Uvall told you I was supposed to kill you, didn't he?" When I didn't reply he continued. "You weren't supposed to live past the age of five Alex. It was supposed to happen on a camping trip with your family. You and Derek were playing by the river when you spotted a small island on the other side of the river. You followed Derek across the rocks. Derek made it across safely and you were trying to keep up when one of the boulders beneath you gave way. The river engulfed you and you were swept downstream until your leg got pinned. Your parents said your leg was caught on a stick next to a boulder which is why you could not come up for air, but that's not true. I was there. I was holding you down; watching you under the frigid cold clear water. I watched your brother frantically scream helplessly and your parents come running from the camp. All the while, you just looked up at me. You tried to move and when you found you couldn't it was as if you looked dead at me wondering why I was doing this to you. Something happened in that moment and I couldn't bear the thought of killing you or you not surviving, so I let you go and helped you onto the boulder. You clung to it until your parents saw you and brought you back to camp, and ever since then I've always been watching you. I'm so sorry Alex." he finished, looking at me somberly.

I just stared at him. I remembered that day, my parents scared to death when they thought they lost me; Derek guilt stricken because he thought he was at fault and horrified to see his sister almost die in front of him. I remember gaining strength when climbing onto the boulder, like something or someone was helping me up. Nathaniel got up and took my hand.

"Alex, something is happening to me. I can feel a change in me; I really need your help." I could see he was struggling.

I let out a sigh. I really had no clue what I was doing. Could I really trust Nathaniel? After all he had been the one keeping so many secrets from me. Not to mention that fact that he almost killed me before. I was so confused on what to do, but knew there was no way I could get out of this by just walking away.

Uvall seemed to have some plan for me; Nathaniel already made it clear he wasn't letting me out of his sight and now that half the town of dark angels and demons knew about me – well, let's just say I didn't have much of a choice.

"You need to be completely honest if I'm going to help you any further. I'm dead serious, don't lie to me anymore," I finished coldly.

Nathaniel nodded his head in agreement as worry stamped his face.

"I need to be alone for a while," I said quietly. I needed to gather my thoughts and try to piece all of this together and somehow figure out what we were going to do.

Chapter 17

The cold water rushed over my face; I tried to move so I could reach the surface, but something held me. I opened my eyes and Nathaniel's icy blue orbs were staring at me above the rushing water. I smiled at him under the water at first grateful to see him, but he did not smile back. I couldn't understand; something wasn't right. I struggled more to reach the surface but Nathaniel's face never changed; it held no emotion. I noticed his eyes began to slowly change color, then more rapidly. The once blue orbs changed to a dark glassy navy color. I was desperate for air now; I began fighting with all my might. I had no more air left. I looked up once more and Nathaniel was smiling.

I awoke gasping for air with Nathaniel shaking me frantically and calling my name.

"Alex! Alex! Are you ok?! Breathe, Alex. Just breathe!" He anxiously yelled, trying not to wake my dad up.

Panicked after seeing the sadistic smile on Nathaniel's face similar to Uvall's I pushed away from him. Hysterical and still believing I was dreaming. I pushed back so hard I fell to the floor with a thud.

I could hear my dad wake up down the hallway and rush to my room over the entire racket, but before I could move my dad burst through the door worried.

"Alex, what happened? Are you ok?" He turned his head at me with a curious look on his face. I looked down and realized the curious look was probably due to me being on the floor with all of the sheets around me. Nathaniel was nowhere in the room.

"I'm fine dad, just a bad dream that's all." I faked a smile to reassure him I was alright.

He nodded his head with a worried look on his face, scanned the room for a minute and then closed the door. I waited until I heard his bedroom door shut and the footsteps stop. I sighed deeply and looked at the floor around me covered in crumpled comforter.

I looked up again and saw Nathaniel standing in front of me. He had a worried look on his face and his eye brows furrowed. He stretched out his hand to me offering to help me up and I hesitated for a moment before taking it. He helped me to my feet and I grabbed the comforter off the floor and went back over to the bed before Nathaniel could ask me any questions about why I was acting so crazy.

The alarm clock screamed in my ear; startled and irritated from the lack of sleep, I chucked it off the nightstand. Anything to make that irritating high-pitched droning stop. I definitely got zero sleep last night and I was dreading a day of classes. Then a thought hit me; if I'm in classes I'm not dealing with Uvall wanting to use me for God knows what, nor am I dealing with Nathaniel not wanting to kill me but trying to kill me before, or me having absolutely no idea what is going on and why it is happening to me. Maybe I can actually have a normal teenage day today.

At that thought I dragged my body out of bed and got in the shower hoping the warm water would wake me up. I closed my eyes and let the water run over my face; a flashback of the nightmare from earlier swept over my mind and I threw open my eyes. I wasn't sure where Nathaniel was. He wasn't there when I woke and after my shower when I got dressed.

I had to admit a part of me was relieved for the space he was giving me, but another part of me was terrified of the "episodes" he was having. I wanted to help him, but I still was clueless as to how I could help him. All of this seemed way over my head and I was still trying to get a grip on everything and face reality.

I looked in the mirror and applied some chap-stick. You are just a normal teenager, I tried convincing myself before grabbing my bag and heading down stairs.

My dad had already started the coffee and I could smell the strong aroma hit me as I bounced down the stairs.

"Morning Dad!"

"Morning hun. I made some coffee, figured you could use some after not sleeping so well last night." He motioned to the coffee pot while grabbing his computer bag.

"Thanks, I could definitely use some," I acknowledged trying not to think about that dream again.

"By the way good job unloading all those bales of hay last night; I wasn't sure you'd get all of them done." I looked up at him; then responded quickly.

"Oh, yeah, no problem." With that he said he loved me, kissed me goodbye and headed out to go to work.

I had never finished unloading all the bales of hay last night. I was so exhausted from the day and then the events of the evening I went back inside alone and completely forgot about it. Nathaniel must have finished unloading the rest of them for me. I've got to talk with him again; I just don't know what to say yet.

Before I left, I ran upstairs to find my English book knowing all too well Ms. Nethers would probably be giving a pop quiz from it. As I searched around the room I noticed a book on the floor under some clothes.

Yes, I thought. Found it. I threw the clothes out of the way to uncover a book that read, "Et Sanguinem Familiae Constantiae." I paused before picking it up. I had completely forgotten about snatching it off of Uvall's desk during our little meeting.

My phone began to vibrate and it snapped me out of my thoughts. My alarm stated I had 15 minutes to get to school. Quickly, I threw the book inside my bag, found my English book and ran out the door.

Nathaniel was nowhere to be seen at school either. I waited patiently class after class until I could get to Mrs. Nethers English class. Antsy, I waited outside of English trying to not let Ms. Nethers see me.

I heard Trey's laugh boom from behind me and I watched as he teased a cute brunette. The brunette was just eating it up and couldn't have loved the attention more. Trey noticed me in the hallway then and smiled, waved off the brunette and strutted towards me. I couldn't help but smile and joke with him.

"Look at you; they just eat it up don't they?" I playfully stated.

"Well how could they not?" he replied arrogantly while grinning. I rolled my eyes and then got down to business.

"Can you ditch with me? I need your help with something," I implored. Trey eyed me then with a smile.

"What are you up to? And since when do you ditch?" he questioned, raising his eyebrow.

"I'll take that as a yes," I said while smiling and motioning for him to follow me. Our school library was attached to our main school building, but for some odd reason was rarely used, probably due to the other numerous study wings throughout the school where groups gathered and people studied for tests together. Much to my happiness it would maybe have a few stragglers and give me privacy to have Trey help me read the book I had taken from Uvall without being disturbed.

See, Trey had always loved History and had studied Latin outside of school as well as taken Latin courses. He was the perfect person to help me figure out some kind of clue as to what Uvall was planning.

I walked quickly through the library to a back room normally used for quiet study, shoved Trey inside and shut the door so no one could hear us.

"Ok what's up with you Alex?" Trey asked, starting to get concerned now.

"Nothing, nothing, I'm totally fine," I replied quickly as I opened my bag to find the book. I snatched it up as soon as I felt the leather binding touch my fingers and put it in front of Trey on the table.

"I need you to translate. Can you do that?" I questioned, knowing he could. Trey eyed the book for a moment and tilted his head. He gently ran his fingers over the spine. I grabbed some paper from my notebook and a pen and was ready to write.

"Yeah, but Alex, where did you get this?" he asked intrigued.

"It's just a book I found, but I really need you to translate it for me." I hesitated hoping he would drop the subject and just start reading. He eventually did, although I know he didn't seem to buy into my story of how I found the book.

"Well first of all the title of it is called *The Blood Family of Constance.* He continued to the first page and began reading.

Although the book was not a thick one, the inside held some lengthy lists. Mostly there were names and dates and whether the names and dates corresponded to a female or a male. Trey noticed a timeline on the bottom of each page as well. The timeline was extremely hard to read from so many years of wear and tear but we were able to determine that roughly every century had a gender and a date assigned to it.

Stumped, Trey read on and translated while I feverously wrote down what he was saying, turning pages and pages of dates and genders and names until we reached a few pages before the end of the book.

I sat back and began to stare up out the skylight that lit the room above us. I folded my arms and began wondering if I had just hit another brick wall or a dead end. I heard Trey put the book down and knew there wasn't anything left to analyze or try and figure out. Feeling defeated, I began to thank Trey for helping me translate the book, but was cut short by him.

"Alex, where did you really get this book from?" he questioned sternly.

I looked up at him then and a lump caught in my throat. I had never lied to Trey before, but what was I supposed to tell him? *Oh yeah, sorry but I only had you translate the book because some evil demons and dark angels are trying to use me for something and my fake boyfriend was ordered to kill me but didn't so now he's changing into God knows what and I'm trying to stop that from happening too.* No. I don't think so. I really didn't feel like being taken to have a psychiatric evaluation today. So I tried playing dumb.

"It was just some old book I found and I was curious is all. I just figured since you can read Latin you could help me translate." I did not sound convincing at all. Trey got up quickly from his chair then and put the book in front of me.

"Do you know what this says?!" his voice began to rise now and seemed uneasy.

"Clearly I don't," I stated sarcastically.

Trey pointed to two names hand written on the book on the last page a long time ago. The ink had faded, but was still legible enough to make out the words:

Alexandria Constance - Female + in tiny letters.

It was quiet for a moment. "You don't think that's me do you?" I asked looking at Trey sarcastically.

Trey seemed confused but couldn't ignore it. "Alex, you're asking me if I think this book - which happens to be called *The Blood Family of Constance*, Constance being your last name - and then seeing your actual name in here, that that doesn't mean anything?" I didn't know what to say.

"You know, a lot of other people could be called Alexandria Constance? That doesn't mean it's me, Trey," I stated firmly, mostly trying to convince myself. I really did not want this to have anything else to do with me; I wanted my life to be kept just as simple as it was before. Nothing to worry about but being a teenager who can make mistakes and go to the movies on Saturday's as long as her homework was done.

I closed my eyes and sighed. I started to tell Trey off in order to keep him safe and to keep him out of this mess.

"Trey I just asked for your help, but honestly it's none of your business." I paused when I noticed he wasn't staring at me anymore, but at something behind me. Frustrated I continued. "What, now you're not even going to look at me when I'm talking to you...?"

I turned to see what was so important that he was staring at. My eyes were met with blazing black and red orbs. It was Corson, Apollyon's son. He tapped the window with his nail and a devilish grin appeared on his face. Panic began to flow through my veins as I watched Corson open the door to the study and close it behind him.

"C-Corson?" I managed to squeak out. His smile widened.

"I was wondering if you remembered me." He exhaled slowly.

"Who the hell are you?" Trey questioned from behind me." Corson's attention automatically snapped to Trey.

126

"I need Alexandria to come with me. I have a few questions for her that's all," he lied. The last thing I wanted was for Trey to get involved in all of this. Things were complicated enough and I did not want my family and friends getting hurt. I didn't know what to do. The only thing that would keep Trey safe would be to go with Corson, and that was the last thing I wanted to do. I hesitated, and Trey spoke up.

"I don't think I've ever seen you around here, and Alex has another class beginning soon, so maybe another time," Trey stated firmly, moving to stand in front of me.

Corson kept his eyes locked on Trey intently. "Well, I don't believe we have had the pleasure of meeting have we..." Corson droned.

I cut in between Corson and Trey. "Maybe another time; I completely forgot about my appointment with you today Corson." I walked to the door and opened it motioning for Corson to leave and that I would follow. Corson's smile widened, pleased I was listening. He walked outside of the door and waited for me to follow. I tried shutting the door to the study quickly before Trey could say anything, but Trey lurched forward and grabbed the door to hold it open.

"Are you kidding me Alex?! You're going with this guy?" he questioned in disbelief.

"What about Nathaniel?" he asked. Corson seemed to let out a chuckle and I turned to glare at him before responding.

"Corson is... a friend of Nathaniel's..." I tried to lie again. Then quickly, before Trey could say a word more, I grabbed a piece of blank paper I had brought, tore off the corner and quickly scribbled down the words: *Don't say a word. Find Nathaniel!*

"If you are so worried you can always call me on this number to check in. I'll be fine." I tried to play it off and turned to walk out with Corson. I looked back to make sure Trey had read the note. Trey looked up at me then with anger in his eyes and his fists clenched. He knew I had lied to him and was in trouble; he just didn't know the severity or who I was in trouble with.

Corson grabbed my hand as soon as we were out of sight of Trey and squeezed it firmly.

"So who was that Alexandria? Another lover?" he cooed devilishly.

I scowled at him and reacted to the pain shooting in my hand. I started to panic. Where the hell was Nathaniel? Figures, the one time he isn't around stalking me someone like Corson comes around. Perfect. Just perfect, I thought.

I started scanning the parking lot hastily to see if I could spot Nathaniel's car; nothing. He wasn't at the school. I knew I had to get away from Corson but I wasn't sure how. The death grip he kept on my hand was getting worse as he dragged me across the street to a black lifted 4-door Jeep.

"Get in," he ordered angrily.

Oh no. I thought back to the self-defense classes my dad had taken me to as a child and to the hundreds of movies I had seen where the main hero easily gets out of any situation and single-handedly fights off the bad guy. This was not the movies. Nor was my kidnapper fully human/living either.

"Where are we going?" I questioned sternly not willing to just hop in the car to my death.

Corson grabbed my waist then and proceeded to throw me in the Jeep. I partially screamed and instinctively scrambled to the back seat with my bag. Corson slammed the passenger door and ran to the driver's side and jumped in. Quickly and as sneaky as I could, I grabbed two things from my bag; a pen and the book of the Constance bloodline. I hid the pen under my leg and quickly shoved the book in the small of my back covering it with my shirt.

The Jeep rumbled to a start and Corson practically peeled out of the parking lot hurling me to each of the windows until the car stabilized. I struggled to keep hold of the pen I was hiding. We were on the main road just past the school now and I tried to keep my voice steady.

"Where are you taking me?" I was desperate to know now. My blood pressure was rising by the second and so was my adrenaline. I could see Corson's eyes blazing black and red in the rear view mirror at me.

"Wouldn't you like to know?" he sneered. "Let's just say, for Nathaniel's sake, Uvall better be good at playing Operation." He snickered.

I thought for a moment about the game Operation I had played as a kid. Oh hell no! I thought, I am not about to get opened up or experimented on.

Corson took a hard right that jolted me to the other side of the car again. Suddenly we heard a blaring horn sound directly ahead. I gripped the front passenger seat and looked ahead to see Nathaniel's charcoal Shelby swerve and miss a minivan, then swing the car around to get behind us screeching the back tires with the e-brake.

Corson floored it, but the Jeep couldn't lose the Shelby. Adrenaline ran through my body heavily and I lurched forward and began trying to gouge Corson's eyes out so he couldn't see. There was a struggle for a moment and I could feel something wet running down my fingers; it was Corson's blood.

Corson grabbed my wrist then and dragged me to the center console. I tried to struggle and punch him, but he just overpowered me. Before I knew it a left jab smashed into the right side of my face between my right eye and temple knocking me into the back seat. I struggled to use my right eye.

Nathaniel was right behind us from what I could make out now. I felt my left hand run across something on the backseat then. I gripped it tightly realizing it was the pen I had taken out of my bag before. Without hesitation I turned so I was facing the front of the car again and rammed the point into Corson's neck. He yelled in pain and the Jeep wrenched right, across two lanes right into the path of a semi-truck. We were still moving but it was clear we were not going to make it. I watched in horror from the backseat helpless as the semi came barreling towards us. All of a sudden the back left side of the Jeep was struck. I was thrown sideways and everything went black.

_Chapter 18

All I could feel was this searing pain coming from the right side of my head. I groaned and, putting my hand to my head, tried to sit up. I was coerced to stay lying down by two hands and exhausted, I did not put up a fight but laid back and opened my eyes instead.

I was surprised to see a petite brunette with golden brown eyes staring back at me. I tilted my head in confusion and began to look around the room. I was lying in a queen bed with brown silk sheets that had been freshly cleaned and smelled of lavender. The shades had been drawn to keep out all the sunlight but the room stayed well lit by two bedside lamps and a giant light under the fan above me. I noticed a wall of books, mostly medical books with some literature on an antique looking bookshelf against the wall and an IV bag hanging next to the bed.

"Where am I?" I asked wearily. The brunette took out the IV from my hand and checked my head once more where Corson had struck me before responding.

"My name's Lucy, I am a friend of Nathaniel's. He brought you to my house so we could help heal you up," she stated matter-of-factly.

"Where is he now?" I questioned.

"I'm sure still down in the basement, I wouldn't recommend going down there but suit yourself." She finished gathering the used bandages from the night stand and walked out of the room leaving the door open behind her. I hesitated for a moment and then pushed my body so I was sitting up with my legs over the side of the bed.

I could feel how drained and achy my body was, probably from just being in an accident and getting punched in the face by a full grown man. Ow. I had to talk to Nathaniel though. I was still in the same clothes and I noticed blood stains on the front and side of my shirt. I'd have to change before my dad saw me, that's for sure; he'd freak!

I put my shoes on and walked out of the room quietly. I could hear Lucy in the kitchen, it sounded like she was putting dishes away. Not knowing the layout of the house at all I pretty much had to guess where the basement would be. I walked down the hallway; there were family photos on the walls some old, like black and white old and others newer in color. I continued till the hallway rounded a corner and was met with a door that led to the basement.

The staircase was dimly lit and creaked as I descended to cold concrete flooring, but no one seemed to be down there. I was confused for a moment and wondered if Lucy had really said Nathaniel was in the basement or if I had just imagined that until I heard the sound of a door click.

I peered around a structural beam to get a better glimpse and watched as two figures emerged from a room. They were whispering to one another for a moment and then one of the figures strode back into the room leaving the other behind. It was then that the figure in the hallway noticed me standing there. I paused as I watched the figure motion for me to walk towards him as he lit a cigarette.

Cautiously I made my way forward. As I got closer, I was able to make out his face. He was an older man, I guessed around the same age as my father. When he stepped forward with his hand outstretched I noticed a huge scar running across his face from his left ear to the top middle of his forehead where his hairline began. I tried not to stare at it and shook his hand. There was another scar across the top of his right hand.

"I'm Alex." I said quietly. The butt of the cigarette burned a deep orange as he took another drag before responding.

"I know who you are Alex; it's nice to finally meet you in person. Luther's the name," he replied with a smile on his face. I looked back towards the door where the other figure had disappeared. Luther must have noticed me staring because he followed his introduction with, "You can go in if you like, you know." He motioned towards the door. I half smiled.

I turned the knob and shut the door behind me. Inside, the room was barren, with the same concrete floors and walls, and with one low hanging light bulb struggling to illuminate the room.

In front of me were Corson and Nathaniel. Corson had his arms and legs chained to a metal chair and Nathaniel had been in front of him punching him repeatedly. The click of the door made Nathaniel look back in my direction.

His face was blank at first and then his brows furrowed. Blood trickled from his bruised knuckles as he marched towards me and grabbed my wrist to take me out of the room.

Corson spit a fistful of blood onto the floor and began to laugh. His eyes were black tar glued to us. I could feel the grip Nathaniel had on my arm tighten and he turned as if to listen for a moment to what Corson had to say.

"You can't protect her anymore, Nathaniel. Look at you! The pull of the dark is getting stronger; I can feel it vibrating through you. Pretty soon you'll both be with us and there's nothing you can do to stop it." Corson's laugh echoed inside the concrete walls and was only shut out when Nathaniel escorted me outside of the room.

Luther was putting his cigarette out. "You let her in?!" He seemed furious about it. Luther shrugged and watched as Nathaniel coerced me up the stairs.

"She has a right to know Nathaniel. We need to prepare and there isn't much time anymore." Nathaniel didn't respond. Instead, he moved me up the stairs, grabbed my things, and thanked Lucy.

Thunder clouds began to sound above us; the sky was a dark bluish black. Nathaniel suddenly let go of my arm and pulled me in for a hug. I hugged him back. I felt so lost. I had no idea what was happening or what we needed to prepare for; I had just been kidnapped and had to stab someone in the neck with a pen; I was really starting to lose it.

Neither of us spoke; we just needed one another's embrace. I needed him just as much as he needed me. I could hear his heart beating boldly in his chest. The thump of his heart seemed to calm me and I felt safe. Safe from everything and everyone who was trying to hurt me.

"I'm sorry I was late," he whispered in my ear. The warmth of his breath sent goose bumps crawling up and down my body. I didn't respond to his apology. I just clung to his embrace for a minute before breathing out.

"Can we please talk?" Nathaniel's grip tightened around me after hearing the words and he sighed in reply.

"Yes, we can talk."

We drove to La Bella Lingua, a local Italian restaurant my mom and I used to go to, and Nathaniel pulled into a parking space. The inside reminded me of a place where old time mob bosses would meet. Nathaniel and I didn't say much during the car ride again, but he held my hand the entire time. We both seemed to be fixated on our own thoughts about everything.

My thoughts strayed from the kidnapping and threat of the unknown, to Nathaniel. I wasn't quite sure what to think about how I felt towards him. He was dangerous and getting more dangerous by the day and there was nothing I could do to stop it; of that I was sure.

The worst part is I was the reason he was changing. I was beyond disturbed about the fact that he had been given orders to kill me when I was five. I mean I've told some white lies in my day, but I've never done anything bad enough to justify someone being ordered to kill me. What was so wrong with me that an angel had been ordered to kill me?

We had been seated for several minutes before I was snapped back to reality by the sound of the waitress filling our glasses with water. I looked at Nathaniel and realized he had been staring at me the entire time we'd been sitting. I let a deep breath out feeling the weight of his gaze on me. I had such mixed emotions towards Nathaniel and I tried to ignore the feelings I had for him; at this point I didn't want to complicate an already complicated world.

I'm doing the right thing for both of us, I thought. We'll get each other out of this mess and then move back to a normal life.

Why would Nathaniel want to even be around the person who took everything he had from him? After he gets his wings back, he'll hit the road. I wagered with myself hoping secretly I was wrong.

I looked back at Nathaniel and could see he was studying me greatly. I wasn't expecting it when he reached over and grabbed my hands. My heart skipped a beat for a second but I controlled my nerves so he wouldn't notice.

"Alex, I want to be honest with you." He paused for a second and I could see his eyes radiate a light sharp blue. "Cause, I'm not sure we can make it through this any other way. Luther's right; we need to prepare for what's coming."

I was relieved when Nathaniel didn't try to sugar coat things. Even more gratifying was the fact that I was actually going to start getting some answers. I nodded my head in agreement and let him continue.

"First off, you shouldn't go near your parent's house anymore after what happened today. I've already talked with Luther and arranged a place we can stay and get everything ready." My face sort of dropped.

"How do you expect me to leave? They will know something is wrong," I affirmed, even though I knew I was endangering my parents every second I was around them, and until all of this was over, I had to stay away. I couldn't risk getting them involved and hurt or even worse, killed because of guilt by association.

"The school trip to Washington D. C. is a week away; your parents wouldn't think anything out of the norm if you went on a school guided trip. If they believe Kate is going, do you think they'll buy it?" he questioned, and I got the feeling he already knew the answer.

"Yeah, if Kate goes and we give them all the information on where I am staying, they shouldn't have an issue," I replied.

"Good, then I'll coordinate getting you both tickets. Your parents will think you're out of town and you'll stay with me until we finish this."

I couldn't be sure, but for a minute it sounded as if Nathaniel's voice faltered as he finished speaking, and he sat back against the booth.

"Right. Till we finish this." I bit my lip and averted my gaze from him. I guess I should have been happy that we would be going back to our normal lives after this. But I couldn't help but feel an aching inside hearing Nathaniel speak the words out loud and making them real. I would never see him again after this.

I shifted uncomfortably in the booth as the waitress returned to take our order. I wasn't really hungry but I couldn't remember the last time I had eaten and wasn't sure when I actually would eat next, so I ordered the first thing I could think of; tacos. At this point, what I was eating was the last thing that I cared about. Nathaniel ordered smothered enchiladas and the waitress sauntered off towards the kitchen.

"What are you thinking right now?" Nathaniel asked. I heard concern mixed with curiosity. My emotions were all over the place. The real question should have been what wasn't I thinking or feeling? I struggled to answer and then suddenly came out with it.

"Why were you ordered to kill me?" Nathaniel seemed disturbed that I asked, however he knew it was inevitably going to come out.

"There are speculations that angels, fallen angels and demons alike have heard about you; that somehow you are going to bring an end to the balance and allow the fallen to return to heaven and take over." His voice was monotone and did not hold any emotion. It was difficult to accept the words I was hearing from Nathaniel.

"I don't understand, how could I do that? I'm not an angel or anything else; I'm in high school still for God's sake! How is any of this possible?" My head was spinning. When he didn't respond, I continued.

"Why did you let me live that day if this is what everyone was told I could do?" I asked bewildered. Nathaniel looked me dead in the eye and confidently responded.

"Because I don't believe they're right, and I don't kill innocents," he said firmly.

"You don't know that Nathaniel. I don't even know that." I replied unnerved. "What am I?"

Nathaniel leaned forward. "You're an instrument that fallen angels and demons can use. I don't know how it works or what happens; no one does because it's never been done before. I was supposed to kill you before anything could happen though." His head hung low but he kept his gaze on my face the entire time he spoke. My mouth hung agape and my eyes stuck to a space in the room.

I got up from the booth and ran for the door. I was about to keep running when I felt the grasp of someone's hand and warmth envelope me. Nathaniel had grabbed me and held me close to his chest; I could feel his heart beating rapidly inside his chest and my tears began to flow uncontrollably.

Nathaniel drove me home to my dad's house. The car ride was quiet, but Nathaniel held my hand firmly the entire ride, even when my grip loosened. I gave my dad a hug arriving at the house and muttered something about homework. I didn't respond as I heard him tell me to get some sleep and that I looked tired. If he only knew.

I went into my bathroom, turned on the shower and shut the door. I clung to the bathroom countertop to help hold myself up when the door opened. Nathaniel walked in and shut the door behind him firmly.

"How can you believe that I'm good when I'm clearly bad?" I wondered aloud at him.

"I could ask you the same thing," he replied.

"It's not the same Nathaniel," I responded, irritated. "You're good, you've been good, the only reason you're turning into a fallen angel is because of me. What if I destroy everything?" I asked, shaken.

Nathaniel's lips met mine then. I wasn't expecting it and at first I began to pull away, but Nathaniel held me tightly. I couldn't resist. I felt a heat flare up inside me that seemed to wipe away all of my thoughts. I could just think of one thing. Nathaniel. I kissed him back and my hands found their way to his neck. I could feel the heat of his body against mine; his hands moved from the sides of my face to my lower back then and my body responded eagerly.

Just then a knock came on the door startling us both and causing me to push away from Nathaniel.

"You ok in there, Alex? You received some mail; I'll leave it in your room, k?" my dad called out from the other side of the door.

"Ok thanks dad!" I called back a little breathless and completely embarrassed. Nathaniel and I stared back at each other; his hands on either side of my hips on the counter. I was relieved when he spoke first as I wasn't sure what had just come over me.

"Go ahead and shower, Alex, I'll wait for you in your room." He breathed quietly. I nodded my head in agreement still recovering from the intensity of the kiss just shared between us. He grabbed the handle to the door and added one last thing before leaving the room. "I'm right about you Alex; I know I am. I'm going to do everything to protect you and get you through this. I promise."

The warm water ran down my face and reminded me of our kiss. What did this mean between us now? Feeling confused and not able to take my mind off of Nathaniel, I enjoyed the shower for another 20 minutes before going into my bedroom. My arms and neck were covered in goose-bumps and I wasn't sure if it was because I knew I was getting close to Nathaniel again or if the temperature change caused it.

I couldn't help but notice Nathaniel had already taken his shirt off and had switched to a pair of black baggy Under Armour sweats. He got up from the bed when I entered the room and closed the door behind me.

"You ok?" he asked as I made my way over to my closet.

"I'm ok," I replied not too sure how to respond. I could feel his gaze on me. "I need to change." I saw a grin begin to play at the corners of his mouth and I teasingly glared at him. He reluctantly turned around to let me change.

Afterwards, I climbed into bed and Nathaniel followed. The sheets went up to his hips and he had his hands folded behind his head looking up at the ceiling. I couldn't help but steal a few glances at him again, noticing how defined his body lines were. Nathaniel cocked a smile.

"You know, if you want to see me naked you can just ask." Embarrassed, a flash of red poured into my cheeks.

"I don't want to see you naked!" I squeaked.

"You know it's a sin to lie, Alex. I can tell when you're lying." He smirked as he turned towards me with his hand supporting his head.

I was mortified. I hated how he could just get under my skin like that! He obviously knew me too well. I tried to change the subject.

"I'm sorry, I'm still not used to having an angel in my bed!" I retorted. "We should get some sleep though we've got a busy week."

Nathaniel grunted at my response and nodded in agreement, still grinning.

"Sure. Sure. Get some sleep Alex." I wasn't sure but I thought I heard him say, "I'll be here for you," before a deep sleep enveloped me.

Chapter 19

Red surrounded me, everything was red. I looked around as statues of angels disintegrated in front of my eyes. Huge marble columns and pillars tumbled in my wake. I began to hear whispers. Some of the whispers escalated to shouting and they all began to talk at once, making it impossible to understand what they were trying to tell me.

I ran over the collapsed columns, falling pillars and crumbling statues trying to escape the red destruction that suffocated me; I slid to a stop, my heart pounding through my chest, as I looked past a cliff's edge that I almost barreled over. I could feel the acidic bile forming up through my throat. What was happening?

A flash of light caught my eye; I turned to see it was the sun. I relished the warmth it brought and walked towards it, but with each step I took an eclipse covered more and more of it until everything faded into blackness.

My eyes shot open and I looked around me fearing I was still trapped in the red and darkness, and then looked toward the clock on my nightstand. The intense blue LED light blinded me letting me know it would go off in exactly 3 minutes. Annoyed and shaky from the dream, I turned the alarm off before it could make a sound.

I shuffled my way to the bathroom and let out a mini shriek when I looked up to find Nathaniel naked and just wrapping a towel around his waist.

"Oh my God!" Stunned, my eyes trailed from his broad built shoulders down to his perfectly rippled six pack. Then I turned blushing and bolted for the door. Wow.

I could feel my blood rushing through my body and pooling to my cheeks; my breathing was coming back now and I covered my mouth in embarrassment at what I had just done. I didn't see his, well you know, but let's just say I saw enough to let my imagination wonder. Pull yourself together Alex! Seriously!

As I was mentally scolding myself, Nathaniel walked into the room with a giant smirk plastered on his face. Mortified, I didn't look at him knowing an arrogant comment was coming any second now. That and I couldn't currently look at him without picturing him without a towel now. I tried to push the picture from my mind but knew he wasn't going to be that easy to forget. I grabbed some clothes from the closet and turned to avoid Nathaniel and get dressed in the bathroom. Nathaniel stopped me before I could exit; blocking the door entirely.

"Can I help you?" My cheeks were flaming and I was annoyed that he wasn't going to let this go.

He crossed his arms in front of his chest, amused at my embarrassment.

"We're technically dating you know..." He paused, still smirking. I was so embarrassed still I just wanted to escape.

"No, technically we are pretending... pretending and actually dating are two completely different things," I tried to sound matter-of-fact while I reined in my emotions. His eyes glinted at me and his smirk widened.

"What if I wanted to be actually dating then?" He kept still but his eyes darted across my face trying to discern what I was thinking.

I held my breath in for a moment and felt my heart skip a beat. Was this actually what he wanted? I knew I had feelings for Nathaniel, I just wasn't quite sure what to do with those feelings yet. After all, our relationship wasn't exactly agreed upon from the beginning. What did Nathaniel actually want with me? Was he just using me to get his wings back or did his affections mean something else, something deeper?

"Nathaniel, I'm not sure...what if..." I started to question him and Nathaniel unfolded his arms and began to counter me.

"Is it so hard to believe I want to date you? His eyes glistened a light sea blue as he waited for my reaction.

"No." I paused unsure of how to respond. But truthfully, yes, I thought it was pretty hard to believe. Any girl would kill to date him; he was smart, good looking - make that amazingly good looking - and had the personality of a bad guy with good guy morals. He literally was an angel. What did he want with me?

"I guess I thought you just wanted to get your wings back so you didn't really have any other option." I stated, uncertainty hanging on every word. What did Nathaniel really want? The thought made my stomach flutter.

He watched me carefully and I couldn't tell what he was thinking.

"I want to get to know you again Alex, and I want you to get to know me." Heat rushed to my cheeks and my thoughts raced at the notion of getting to know Nathaniel on a deeper level.

Ever since he'd come falling into my life, my world had been turned upside down to say the least, but I had also uncovered secrets about myself and a world that I still couldn't quite comprehend. I had been kidnapped, lied to Kate, Trey and my parents and was now involved in something way over my head and out of my control, but I couldn't deny the pull I felt towards Nathaniel. Anytime he was near I was acutely aware of his presence drawing me towards him; the tone of his voice - deep and velvety. Was it because he was an angel that he had this type of power over me? Or did it foretell of something more? I knew there was only one way to find out, I just wasn't sure I could take the emptiness if it turned out to be nothing.

My heart and mind reeled in two different directions.

"If it isn't meant to be we'll go back to being just friends?" Nathaniel nodded continuing to watch me.

"If you change your mind, we'll just be friends," he confirmed.

"Or if you change your mind."

"It's very doubtful I will change my mind about you Alex." He answered unequivocally.

I took a deep breath in and answered on the exhale. "Ok. I'll date you."

A smile swept across his face and I could feel it making one tug at the corner of mine. Before I could finish he grabbed my waist and pulled me towards him. A fire deep inside of me awakened then. Whatever this was between us, it seemed to spark to life when we were close. It felt true and faultless, and it was irresistible.

I met his lips eagerly and wrapped my arms around his neck deepening the kiss. I felt myself plunge head first into the unknown, deeper into him and his world.

Nathaniel responded instantly grabbing my hips tightly and then running his hands over the small of my back. Everywhere he touched ignited a spark and grew into a wildfire. Reeling myself back, we parted, breathless. He continued to hold me and looked down at me then.

"I knew you couldn't resist me." He smirked triumphantly. I rolled my eyes at him and smiling headed to the bathroom to change, not wanting to reveal that I wasn't sure if I could resist him even if I wanted.

"Wait, so now that we're actually dating..." He called after me, expecting me to change in front of him. My eyes widened and the heat rose in my cheeks again.

"Nice try!" I shouted back before closing the door.

Nathaniel and I had arrived at school late, and I could not have cared less. He walked me to my class and pulled my face in for another kiss before sending me in. I turned to give him a look for a minute and he smiled.

"I'm allowed now." He smirked playfully. And with that he turned and disappeared down the hallway.

I could feel a tingling spark his lips had left on mine and it dazed me for a moment before I snapped back to the dreary thought of school. I wasn't sure how I was supposed to focus on my teachers or class work when I was practically preparing for war against fallen angels who were hell bent on using me for their cause. Complicated was a delicate way to describe my life these days.

I turned towards the classroom door, stopping the thoughts of last night's dream. Now to be ninja, I thought, hoping no one in class would recognize my tardiness; specifically Mrs. Nethers. I tried to be inconspicuous but as soon as the click of the door was heard all heads turned to acknowledge my tardiness. So much for ninja I thought. Defeated, I took my seat next to Trey who had been glaring at me ever since I came in.

Oh crap. I thought, how was I going to explain what happened with Corson? There was no way I could lie to Trey again, he would know if I wasn't telling the truth in a heartbeat and pry it from me anyway. Besides, Trey was one of my best friends; I had never lied to him prior to yesterday about Corson. His glare seemed to confirm my suspicions that he was pissed, not disappointed or sad, but fuming.

"What the hell happened yesterday Alex!" He tried to speak quietly but it came out loud enough for a few other students to turn and stare for a moment. I looked at Mrs. Nethers scrutinizing me under the bridge of her glasses in disapproval.

"I'm sorry, but I'm ok, everything is fine." I threw a smile his way when I finished to sound convincing.

"You can't call once? I was practically ready to go file a missing person's report!"

I thought about what to say to Trey. I had to tell him something! I wracked my brain for an excuse of some kind that he would buy, but I didn't get a chance to respond before Mrs. Nethers called on me from the front of the room. Her tone suggested she was less than thrilled about my tardiness and lack of attention.

"Alex! So generous of you to grace us with your presence today!" she exclaimed. "Why don't you answer the question for everyone seeing as you interrupted those who are here to learn to begin with." I squinted at the projector on the board.

"Um, what does the relationship between Heathcliff and Clara symbolize?" I read it aloud stalling and unsure of the answer.

"Maybe you don't know the answer because your textbook isn't even out; start paying attention Ms. Constance," she accused before moving forward with her lecture.

Wow someone is in a sour mood today, I thought before nodding my head in acknowledgment. I could feel the class's eyes boring into the back of my skull and I kept my eyes forward until the room settled and everyone turned their attention back to Mrs. Nethers.

The remainder of the class went slower than molasses and I kept stealing glances at Trey who hadn't looked at me since Mrs. Nethers had interjected earlier. I counted down the seconds as I watched the clock tick down before the bell sounded. Everyone jumped in response as if the start of a sprint was announced and they all headed for the door.

Trey motioned for me to follow him out the door so we could "talk". He stopped in the hallway and began again.

"So what happened to you? Who was that guy yesterday?" His tone had quieted but the intensity was still present.

"He was looking for Nathaniel. They aren't the best of friends but he knew I would know where to find him," I exclaimed partially telling the truth.

"Are you lying to me Alex? Are you in some sort of trouble?" Concern was etched in his face now.

I shook my head. "I'm fine Trey. Talk to Nathaniel about it if you want. He'll tell you what happened."

"Were you involved in that car crash outside of school at all?" He continued to pry. "After you left there was a huge accident with a semi just 3 miles from here, I thought you could have been involved." Trey continued to search for answers from me. Great, lie after lie is what I was feeding Trey.

Just then I heard a scream down the hallway. "Oh My God! Where have you BEEN!" Kate yelled running towards me. She gave Trey a brief hug before grabbing me and interrogating me as she walked us towards our next class leaving Trey behind.

I looked back and gave Trey an "I'll talk to you later" look and mouthed "I'm sorry" as I was escorted away. He nodded curtly in acknowledgment, but I could tell he was worried and wasn't about to drop it until he got all of the answers he wanted and was satisfied with them. He knew I had lied to him and because I had lied, he knew whatever I was mixed up in was dire.

Everyone associated with me was in danger. I had to begin to put distance between us so that Nathaniel and I could prepare for the week and whatever chaos was to come.

I cut Kate off for a moment. "Do you think you can cover for me for about a week?" I turned her so she was looking at me.

"Cover you for what? What are you...?" Then she stopped. "Are you going somewhere with Nathaniel?!" She tried to compose herself. I thought about it for a moment and decided it probably wasn't a bad idea if at least Kate knew where I was.

"Yes, he asked me to go to his cabin with him for the week. I'll get to meet his family there too," I said smiling. Technically I was telling the truth, I was just leaving out the whole angel, fallen angel, and demon details.

"You little hussy!" She slapped my shoulder trying to contain her excitement. "What do you need me to do?"

"Can you confirm with my parents Ajax will be staying at your Aunt's house all of next week so he gets exercise while you and I are in Washington D.C.?" She seemed confused. "That's the story I'm telling my parents," I stated. "You and I are supposedly going on the school trip next week to D.C., but I'll really be with Nathaniel at his cabin for the week."

"I'll get them to buy it, but why aren't you telling your parents about it? Do they not like Nathaniel or something?" she questioned curiously. I had never really asked Kate to do anything like this before. It was definitely unlike me to lie to my parents and run off to a guy's cabin with him and even she knew it.

"You know what my dad will think; he would rather put me in a nunnery than let me go away for a week with Nathaniel, but I feel different with him. I have to see where this goes."

Kate's smile widened. "You've got it bad girly, but I want all the insider details when you get back." I smiled at her; I knew I could rely on Kate to help me when I needed her.

"Absolutely," I replied.

"Ok, I'll call them before our math class and let you know if they bought it." With a wink and a grin, she turned on her heels and darted off to her next class.

I spent the next few classes scribbling incoherent notes in my notebook and thinking of what would happen next week. I wasn't sure I was ready for what was coming. What would happen to me? What would happen to Nathaniel? What exactly would come of our new relationship? The bell shrieked and I practically pounced for the door scanning the halls for Kate. I reached the entrance of Mr. Kritch's math class and practically shoved two girls out of my way into the doorway. I found her in her seat with Jesse leaning over her proclaiming his innocence to something.

"I'm just saying you could take me on secret trips too, you know?" Kate accused arms folded. Jesse held his hands up not wanting to argue.

"You told him!?" I approached the two of them, accusatory. Kate gave me her 'my bad' face.

"I can't lie to him Alex; he always gets it out of me somehow," she said giving him a sideways wink. I rolled my eyes.

"Do you think the both of you could manage to NOT tell anyone else?" I questioned, annoyed. They shook their heads in agreement when Kate interjected.

"Not even Trey?" She asked. "I'm sure he won't care." I looked at her dumbfounded.

"Especially Trey." You have to promise me you won't tell him or anyone else," I pleaded.

"Ok fine, we won't say anything," Kate assured me as Jesse gave her a kiss and headed to his class. "Oh, and your parents totally fell for it!" She gleamed in triumph.

"I owe you one," I said as relief filled me. I could be as irritated at Kate as I wanted for telling Jesse but I didn't really blame her. They had an open relationship that anyone would be jealous of.

"No, you owe me a girl's night when you get back to tell me everything." She countered, smiling as the bell rang and I took my seat.

Math class about killed me; who even cared about finding X and Y when there were angels and fallen angels running around? I thought, wondering how people would react if they knew the truth. Freak out, mass panic and hysteria, that's how they would react.

So much had happened lately it was hard to feel normal sitting in a class listening to Algebra when the night before I had just been told that I was somehow the key to destroying heaven. Who knew, I thought, trying to joke with myself to mask my own fears. It was too late to turn back now and I couldn't even if I wanted to. Somehow I was a part of this whole other world I never knew of and I needed to find out who I truly am.

The bell rang one last time and I could practically taste the freedom. I told Kate I would call her over the weekend to finish setting everything up and with that I bounced out of my seat and briskly walked towards the school entrance where I knew I would find Nathaniel. A firm hand encased my hip moments later.

"Looking for me?" Nathaniel inquired in his low velvety voice. I tried to hide my smile.

"No actually I was looking for someone else." I pretended to scan behind him for another person.

"Oh is that so?" he questioned, a hint of jealousy in his voice. I stopped scanning the crowd of students and looked at him.

"Hmm, I suppose I'll have to settle for you then," I stated playfully. He eyed me for a moment with a grin on his face.

"I guess I better take you with me before that other guy comes to claim you then, after all, I can't let someone else capture what's mine."

My heart fluttered at the way he seemed to claim me protectively and he escorted me outside and into the Shelby. I let a deep breath out and relaxed and looked out the window; my arm resting on the door's arm rest.

"What's Heaven like?" I asked suddenly, continuing to gaze at the sky and passing trees. We stopped at a light and I looked back at him when he didn't respond. His eyes were closed and he seemed to be picturing it.

"It's beautiful; more peaceful than you can ever imagine. There is no such thing as pain, fear, anger, or regret." A pinch of sadness hit me when he finished and I gulped. I couldn't bear the thought that I was the reason all of that could be destroyed. He opened his eyes as the light turned green and continued to drive.

"I think I saw it in my dream last night, only differently," I said, sighing. Nathaniel looked at me then and his brows furrowed.

"What did you see?" he questioned. "I'm not sure; there was a lot of red," I replied vaguely not wanting to reminisce on it. Telling him I saw crumbling statues of angels probably wouldn't help either of us right now.

"Did you see an eclipse?" My eyes shot towards his.

"How did you know that?" I questioned, feeling as if he knew more than he was letting on again. He shifted uncomfortably in his seat as we pulled into a driveway and parked before he responded.

"Because I've been seeing it too." My mouth was somewhat agape.

"What does that mean?" I asked, afraid to know the answer.

"It means..." he paused, "we have less time than I thought." We sat quietly for a moment, neither of us stating the obvious. He was changing fast, that's what it meant. How long would I have with Nathaniel? And what would happen when he finally turned all the way? I wondered.

My gut wrenched in my stomach and I looked around to stop any nausea from taking hold. To my surprise we were not at my dad's house.

"Where are we?" I asked.

"Luther's house. We need to grab some equipment before we head up to the cabin. We should leave tomorrow instead of Monday. Can you make that happen?" He stated more than asked, making me feel as if an hour glass was counting down the time we had left. I knew I could probably convince my parents that I was spending the night at Kate's house so that we could pack up and leave the next morning, but there was a part of me that felt guilty for still having to lie to them.

I had never needed to lie to my parents before, but lately it seemed that's all I had been doing. My reasoning was sound, but that didn't keep me from feeling terrible about it.

"Yeah, I can convince them," I responded quietly. Nathaniel placed his hand gently under my chin and turned my face so I was looking at him.

"I promise this will be over soon, and when it is, things can go back to whatever and however you want them to be," he said, a small smile on his face, but his eyes showed something I had not seen before; fear.

Nathaniel's face turned towards the house in front of us then.

"You ever shot a gun before beautiful?" a grin appearing on his face. I cocked my head in confusion, not knowing where he was going with this.

"Yeah, I used to go shooting with my dad and Derek, but I haven't been in a little while; why?" I questioned. His smile widened and he motioned for me to follow him inside the house. We stood outside on the concrete porch and rang the doorbell. It was a two story home and besides its light blue color and blood red front door, it didn't differ much from the other cookie-cutter homes nestled on the same block. A few seconds later we heard a lock click and Luther pulled open the door.

"I was wondering when you were going to come by," Luther stated with a grin on his face. He nodded and welcomed us inside. "It's good to see you again my dear," Luther said walking us through a brightly lit hallway towards a basement door and grabbing a cigar and lighter from a chair on the way down.

The scuffed grey stairs down to the basement creaked as we descended and one light dimly lit the pasty white wall around us, allowing just enough light so as not to miss a step. At the bottom, cold concrete floors led two ways, to the left and to the right. Luther made a left and stopped when he reached a concrete wall in front of him.

The deep cracks in the concrete floor and walls indicated that the house had shifted over the years. I watched quietly as Luther ran his hand over a large vertical crack that ran eye level with him and stopped at his chest. He ran his thumb from the top of the crack to where it ended and pressed it for a moment. A break sounded, causing the wall to groan followed by a rush of air and dust exiting the cracks. Luther pressed his hands against the wall and pushed forward. It was a hidden door.

I followed Nathaniel and Luther inside. My mind brimming with curiosity as to what was so secret it needed to be kept in a room like that. Why would anyone need a giant concrete secret door? What were they hiding? My questions were soon answered.

The room could not have been bigger than the living room at my dad's house. Probably 15' x 15', but the walls were decorated with every type of gun and knife you could want. I scanned the room as I picked out bolt actions, handguns, rifles and knives. In the center of the room were stacks upon stacks of ammo cans ranging from 7.62x39 to 9mm.

"Holy shit," I exclaimed, not meaning to cuss out loud.. I was in shock at how many weapons I was in the midst of. Luther and Nathaniel chuckled at the irony of my comment. "I'm sorry, did I miss something? Are we going to war or...Afghanistan?" I asked bewilderment on my face as I touched the stock of an AR-15 that hung low on a rack.

Luther and Nathaniel looked at me. "Trust me; you're going to need a little help dear," Luther stated puffing the end of his cigar to keep it lit.

Great, I thought, what the hell did I get myself into? Luther tossed two black duffle bags to Nathaniel and Nathaniel began to fill one with ammo. The other, I assumed, would be for weapons. Nathaniel looked up at me then.

"Pick your poison love," he said devilishly. I was nervous about why we needed such artillery, but when I thought of Uvall and Corson, a shiver ran down my spine.

I began casing the room for my weapons of choice. I'd definitely feel much safer with a weapon around, just in case. I grabbed the M4 rifle from the rack in front of me; it was completely decked out in Magpull furniture with an EO-Tech sight. It was lighter than the rest and felt good in my hands.

Then I proceeded to grab a full size nickel plated 45mm Sig Sauer 1911, a stainless Sig Sauer P938 which I figured would be a great conceal carry due to its smaller size, a few boot knifes, and an ankle knife and laid them on the table in front of Nathaniel. His sly grin reappeared as he eyed my selection approvingly.

"Good choices," he said. I smiled back. I was actually pretty excited that I hand-selected some of my favorite guns, but had never had the privilege of shooting before.

After selecting our artillery, we lugged our bags back to the Shelby and Nathaniel loaded the car with the ungodly amount of ammo and weapons that filled the duffle bags. I hugged Luther and thanked him, the smell of cigar smoke suffocating my lungs.

"Be careful my dear; Nathaniel will take care of you. I'll be seeing you two in a few days," he said as he released me from the hug. "Try not to worry; you're with the best of the best." He finished, motioning towards Nathaniel. I smiled back at him, thankful that he was on our side.

Luther had been very calm and polite since I met him, but something told me I didn't want to be on his bad side. Nathaniel swapped places with me and I hopped in the car as the two talked for a moment. Sitting there, I remembered I hadn't had my phone with me since the car accident. I opened the center console hoping Nathaniel had grabbed it and that it wasn't broken from the crash.

Sure enough, the silver and black iPhone 4 lay there. I grabbed it and checked the battery life. 20%. Ok, I thought, that'll be enough. I checked the screen and realized I had missed 10 calls. Four, split equally between my mom and dad wondering where I was and if I had everything ready for my school trip, and the rest consisted of Kate and Trey; Trey who portrayed his anger at lying to him over the phone and leaving school with a weirdo, and Kate who wondered if I was completely ignoring her or just on my rag. Lovely.

As I finished listening to the messages I looked up and noticed Luther pass something bright and polished to Nathaniel discretely. The exchange happened so quickly and unnoticeably I questioned whether or not I had just witnessed it happen. I was going to ask Nathaniel about it when my attention was drawn to my vibrating phone in my hands. It was my mom. I took a breath and quickly answered fearing she was upset with my recent lack of communication.

"Hey mom!" I tried to sound cheery and nonchalant.

"There you are!" she exclaimed. "Your father and I have been trying to get a hold of you! I want to see you before you leave. Are you all ready for your trip? Do you need anything before you go?" She asked seeming ready to jump at a moment's notice. I hadn't really thought about bringing anything to the cabin, but I was sure I was down to the last squirt of shampoo and conditioner.

"I think I may need some shampoo and conditioner but that's it."

"Well call your father and tell him I am stealing you for the night, we can get you some toiletries and go to dinner, just us girls." She finished emphasizing her need to see me.

"That sounds perfect! And mom, Kate was wondering if I could just stay at her house tomorrow night since we'll be leaving the next morning. Is that ok?" I asked hoping I knew her answer.

"That's fine. Just be sure to include your dad in the planning, he'll want to know where you are too. I'll pick you up in a couple hours ok?"

My mom and I finished our goodbyes over the phone and I dialed my dad's phone. The voicemail picked up and I gathered he was in a meeting. I finished my voicemail just as Nathaniel slipped into the driver's seat next to me. His eyebrows rose and he nodded towards the phone in question.

"My mom wants to see me before I go," I stated, a half smile on my face. To be honest I was pretty unnerved at the thoughts of what could happen this week. There was an eclipse scheduled to occur Friday night and after my recent dream with one in it, I had an eerie feeling. I shook away the thoughts quickly. If I wanted to make it through whatever this was, I was going to have to be strong; really strong.

Nathaniel noticed my uneasiness and reached over and cupped my face in his hand. For a moment his gaze just seemed to stare straight through me.

"You're strong enough to make it through this Alex, I know you are." Before I could respond he moved his hand to the shifter and putting it into gear began to back out of the driveway. My heart rate had increased a little and I could feel my skin tingle where he had touched me.

"I can get through this," I replied with a breath, but I wasn't so sure yet. The undisclosed and secret things Nathaniel had been reluctant to tell me were beginning to outweigh my confidence. After all, I really didn't know just how bad things were quite yet, or how bad they could get.

Nathaniel pulled into the driveway of the farmhouse and leaving the engine running, we both got out of the Shelby. I began to walk towards the house when he caught my wrist gently and pulled me against him.

"Spend some time with your mom for a bit; take your mind off things for a while, I'll come get you afterward," he said as his hands held my hips in place firmly; his eyes never leaving mine, but trying to read my expression. A small smile played at my lips.

"For what it's worth, I wouldn't have made it this far without you Nathaniel; so thank you," I said genuinely. He smiled slowly, and I could tell that even if he thought all of this was his fault, he appreciated my remark greatly.

"You're stronger than you think Alex," he said giving me a wink as a devilish grin showed on his mouth and in his eyes. He pulled me in closer and my heart beat faster as his lips brushed mine, but he didn't kiss me. I leaned towards him my body wanting desperately to mold against his and my mind beginning to fog. Nathaniel's mouth moved towards my left ear and velvety whispered to me.

"I'll see you later beautiful." With that he turned and got into the Shelby and was gone. I sighed and headed towards the house. Inside, the smell of roasted garlic chicken wafted through the house and had my mouth watering. My dad rarely cooked and I wracked my brain trying to remember if it was a holiday or birthday, but nothing came to mind.

"Is it a special occasion or something or..?" I yelled from the doorway but stopped dead in my tracks when I entered the kitchen and saw my dad, Renee and Trey all gathered. My mouth hung open but I couldn't speak. I hadn't even noticed Trey's black Dodge Ram 2500 parked in the street in front of the house.

"Alex you're home!" My dad and Renee spoke in unison and a little too overly eager for my liking. I looked towards Trey a questioning and demanding stare appearing on my face for an explanation as to what was going on. Trey caught my death stare and immediately put his hands up in defense to plead his innocence. My dad and Renee seemed to notice.

"Oh, Trey just stopped by for a moment, he said he had a school paper to talk with you about before you left for your trip, and we thought it would be nice to sit down and all have dinner together. Maybe get to know each other a little bit better?" my dad finished; the end of his reasoning sounding more like a requirement than an option. When I didn't respond right away Renee jumped in.

"I didn't want to impose or anything, but I really want to get to know you more Alex and I think it's only best if you get to know me more too." I just stared back at her a look of displeasure creeping over my face. Were they really serious right now? I had no intention of sitting down and 'getting to know' each other. Not now, and definitely not in the near future. I know people get divorced, it just happens. Some people grow apart or simply are never on the same page and end up splitting, but that doesn't mean I can't be pissed about it either. My parents may have separated, but I was not promoting strange men or women to fill their places just yet. I mustered the fakest smile possible.

"Mom's picking me up tonight remember? So as much as I'd love to stay she's going to be here in about half an hour. So...rain-check?" I asked sarcastically. My dad's eyes narrowed at my response.

"Oh! I had no idea she was coming by tonight, maybe another time then," Renee said smiling, but I could tell this was news to her.

My dad checked his voicemail for a moment and scratched his head as he responded. "Looks like I did miss your call earlier; when you get back from your trip I'd like to give this another shot." We all nodded in agreement and I towed Trey towards the stairs to my bedroom.

"So what do you want to know about that paper?" I asked my stare cold. Trey was quiet until we entered my room and shut the door.

"Alex..." he began to say while massaging the back of his neck uncomfortably.

"I had no idea about the dinner; I didn't even know she was over here until your dad let me in." He sounded sincere and innocent. I put my hand up before he could continue and threw my body onto my bed.

"I know Trey. This was all my dad trying to get me and Renee closer." Her name came out like a bad taste in my mouth. Renee had never done anything to me or my dad, but my parents' divorce was still a fresh wound and I wasn't ready to kiss all my hopes away that my parents would get back together. Call me a hormonal teenager or a snob, but I just wasn't ready for Renee even if my dad was.

Trey plopped himself down on my bed next to me and we both

stared at the ceiling for a minute silently.

"Have you talked to Derek lately?" he asked me hopeful. "No." The answer made my eyes instantly water for a second. I missed my brother so much it hurt and the no communication thing while he was in training was beginning to weigh on me and everyone else.

"You?" I asked back nonchalantly.

"No," he responded. Another moment of silence settled between us. "Are you going to tell me why you lied to me?" Trey spoke, but his voice was even; almost quiet.

I turned my head to look at him, his arms were folded behind his head and he didn't turn to meet my gaze. I chewed my lip nervously. Could it really hurt to tell Trey? Not that he would believe me, but I could really use another human to talk to about it.

I decided I would tell Trey a grey story about what was happening, not the whole truth, but not a complete lie either. I couldn't risk him blowing my cover for the D.C. Trip or thinking I was mentally unstable.

"That guy who came to school the other day was a previous acquaintance of Nathaniel's. They were never what you would call friends though. He came to collect the book I was having you translate, he said it was his, and thought that Nathaniel had taken it from him. I was that bargaining chip for him to get the book back since Nathaniel and I are dating; he just didn't know I was the one who had it all along. Anyway Nathaniel worked it out with him so I don't think he'll be coming back."

I watched for Trey's reaction, he seemed to somewhat buy my story, but I could tell he still had questions.

"Why was your name in the book?" he questioned searching for his answers.

"I'm not sure, from what I've been told, it's just an old book with my family bloodlines in it." He nodded his head in understanding, stood up and helped me up off the bed. He didn't release my hands though.

"I was just worried about you Alex. I've been worried about you. I guess I sort of took over that job while your brother's been away." I smiled. Trey was a good guy and it was comforting knowing I had another person who was looking out for me.

"Thanks Trey," I said appreciatively. "But you don't have to worry about me; I'm a self-sufficient sort 'a girl. I said giving him a wink. He rolled his eyes.

"Yea I know," he said sarcastically but with a grin on his face.

"I'll call you when I get back from my trip and we'll catch up again, k?" He nodded while walking towards the door.

"Sounds good. Oh and you may want to clean your room, it smells like a guy in here and it looks like a tornado touched down." He shut the door and I looked around for a minute. My room was definitely beginning to resemble a war zone. I sighed and threw a load of laundry in the wash and picked up so it was somewhat clean before I left. I threw some toiletries in my duffle bag so I would only have to pack clothes later and I heard the doorbell. It was my mom.

Silently dreading her reaction to Renee in our home I pushed it from my mind, grabbed my leather jacket and bounded down the stairs to meet her. My dad beat me to the door and they were talking quietly in the doorway when I came up behind him.

"Ready to go mom?!" I asked hastily. My mom looked less than pleased and nodded her head. It wasn't what I pictured happening, but I knew from the look on her face that she was distressed Renee was there. We hopped in the pearl white mini cooper and were off. It was silent until we got onto the main road.

"You ok mom?" I asked genuinely concerned. She smiled at me, but I could tell it was forced.

"I'm fine. Now, what do us girls want to go do?" she asked, trying to change the subject.

Three hours later my mom hugged me in the driveway and said good-bye, we had gone to a steak restaurant downtown and then she had taken me shopping for some last minute trip necessities and a few outfits. It was refreshing to not have to think about angels and fallen angels or any of the other incredulous beings or things I had learned about recently. We had laughed, talked about Nathaniel and school and overall just had a good time. I had needed the space and breathing room from it all and I waved goodbye to my mom from the front door and went inside.

Renee must have gone home for the night as the kitchen was clear and the house was fairly quiet minus the dim light and sound of the radio coming from my dad's study. I knocked on the door before entering and plopped myself in a sofa chair across from my dad's desk. He smiled up at me.

"You're back. Did you guys have fun?" he asked. I smiled and told him what we had done and he nodded finishing typing something on his computer. "So about earlier tonight..." he began and looked up at me.

"Dad..." I started to say but he put his hand up to let him finish.

"I know you're not particularly fond of Renee just yet, but I want you to make a conscious effort to get to know her." I let out a sigh.

"Yeah but dad you can't just push her on me, I'm not comfortable with this whole thing yet, you know?" I pleaded hoping he would not push this issue. He leaned back in his chair.

"I know it's weird and I don't want to push you into liking her, but I'm just asking that you give her a fair chance. She's not your mom, I get it, but she also means something to me. Understand?" I nodded feebly.

"Ok. I'll try to play nice, but I'm not promising I'll be any good at it," I stated folding my arms across my chest. He smiled.

"Thank you. You all packed?"

"Just about, I just need to pack some clothes and that should be it."

"Ok well be safe, call me when you get to D.C. and have fun. Do I need to take you to Kate's or anything?" I hugged him.

"I will. No, Nathaniel is going to take me to her house." My dad's face crinkled at his name. "He wants to say good-bye too dad," I added.

"There is such a thing as a phone these days," he stated disapprovingly, but didn't push it.

"Love you dad."

"Love you."

After saying good-bye to my dad I ran upstairs to finish throwing my clean clothes in my duffle bag. I heard a creak from the window and almost jumped out of my skin when I saw Nathaniel there. My hand immediately went over my heart.

"God, you scared me." He grinned mischievously at me.

"I have that effect. You ready?" He turned his head questioning. I scanned the room one last time wondering if I was forgetting anything.

"Ready," I concluded. Nathaniel took my bag and loaded it into the Shelby. As we pulled out of the driveway I couldn't help but feel an aching in the pit of my stomach. I wondered if I would ever see my family again and if our plan would work to keep them all safe. I said a small prayer in my head hoping the man upstairs would hear me, but unsure if He was listening to me; or even if He would help me. Wasn't I ordered to be dead a long time ago so this whole mess wouldn't happen? I tried to push the thoughts from my head as the Shelby's headlights rounded the next corner. My head rested against the window pane and I closed my eyes. Before I knew it, I had drifted asleep to the rhythmic changing of gears.

Chapter 20

Red was all around me again. I could hear the cries of angels and fallen angels as they were battling each other. I looked down realizing I had a dagger clutched in my right hand. The metal glistened a bright light and the handle had twisted gold designs and engravings splayed across it. A blinding light cast down on me, suddenly making my grip on the dagger loosen and I shielded my eyes. Slowly I moved my hand away from my eyes but was still unable to look directly at the illumination before me.

"Use it. Use it!" The voice bellowed deeply at me.

"Use what?! How do I stop this?!" I screamed at the light desperately.

"Use it Alexandria! Make us believe in you!"

I was jolted from my sleep. Nathaniel's hand was cupping the side of my face and his eyes showed concern.

"We're almost there; you were dreaming weren't you?" My breaths came out jagged and I looked around at the black forest surrounding us. We were definitely far from the city. The time suggested we had been driving for the past 3 hours. I nodded my head to Nathaniel's question and massaged the kink out of my neck.

"I think they're getting worse," I stated flatly.

Nathaniel turned the Shelby onto another dirt road or what was once a dirt road. Weeds and small bushes had grown in the roads

159

place and it looked like nothing could lie beyond. Nathaniel eased the Shelby forward and after 15 minutes the trees parted and a dirt road appeared circling around a tiny log cabin with a front porch. A barn sat about 500 yards away and I could see a dark glistening reflection of the moon on a lake in front of the cabin.

"What is this place? Where are we?" I asked disbelieving that this cabin lay before me. There was no way anyone would find this cabin if they did not know about it, and even then they would have difficulty finding it. Nathaniel sat and looked at the cabin for a moment before responding.

"It's a safe house; one that hasn't been used in quite a while."

"Why would angels need a safe house?" I questioned.

"For times like these," he answered looking back at me. "And to re-group. We're about 3 hours northwest of the city."

We both exited the Shelby and grabbed the bags. The cabin door creaked and Nathaniel and I stood in the dark entryway.

"Stay here; I'll find a light." He disappeared into the dark ahead of me and moments later the lights in the cabin flickered to life.

I looked around gathering my bearings. The whole cabin had been built with logs and had minor updates done to it over the years I gathered, eyeing the electricity that had been added. Wood floors and simple undecorated wooden furniture lay about. A quaint kitchen appeared to the left of the entryway with a small wooden dining table and 4 chairs in front of it. To my right I walked towards a lit bedroom located down a stretched hallway. I passed a bathroom with a free standing tub, sink and toilet and continued to the bedroom with my duffle bag; stopping at the entryway.

Nathaniel's voice sounded from behind me.

"I know it's not much, but it'll do for now."

I smiled at him. "Hey it's got running water and electricity, I'm not complaining." I tossed my duffle bag on the floor beside the bed.

He smiled at me and followed me into the room tossing off his black jacket and stretching out on the bed. It must have been a full size, because seeing Nathaniel stretched out on it made me laugh a little and wonder how we both would fit; his feet hung over the end of the bed and he folded his arms behind his head a grin plastered on his face.

"What are you so happy about?" I questioned. "You barely fit in that bed," I said smirking and unsure of his sudden happiness. He grinned at me.

"Because, we're going to have to be really close in order to sleep in this bed together. No couch doll." My heart kicked up a notch at his words. He was right; I didn't remember seeing a couch when we had come in. I was nervously excited thinking of being that close to him this entire week.

"I'm not going to have to worry about you am I Nathaniel?" I asked a small smile at my mouth with genuine nervousness protruding through my words. He locked eyes with me.

"Don't worry love, I won't do anything you don't ask me to." The small smirk was still playing at his lips, but his eyes were icy and intensely focused on me. I looked away trying to calm my heart beat. His eyes sliced through me like a smoldering blue fire.

I changed into my black yoga pants, tank top, and a zip up hoodie in the bathroom. The cabin may have had electricity, but it was far from being warm. I checked my phone; little to no service and the time alerted me it was almost 1 AM. I put the phone back in my duffle bag knowing it was close to useless to me now. I really am off the grid here, I thought.

When I entered the bedroom again Nathaniel had kicked off his shoes and was now wearing black sweats and a plain white t-shirt that hugged his muscles nicely. I sat crossing my legs facing Nathaniel on the bed.

"So what's the plan while we're up here?" I asked tying my hair back into a pony tail. He turned to look at me, leaning against the large wooden dresser behind him, his palms pressed against the dresser as if to steady him. His muscles flexed and I could see every outline of his abs, arm and chest muscles; momentarily, my train of thought was distracted.

"I want to teach you a few things I think may come in handy, focus on some hand to hand combat, shooting skills and possibly some knife throwing." My eyebrows raised and I couldn't hide the small smile on my face. I was actually kind of excited to learn some self-defense techniques; especially since there were people after me. I needed any confidence boost I could get.

Nathaniel closed the gap between us, his hands were fists on either side of me bracing him as he lowered his head to mine. His eyes held mine.

"I need to make sure you can defend yourself in case there is ever a time where I'm not there to protect you. I can't let anything happen to you. I won't." His voice was low and velvety and his eyes blazed a fiery blue. I didn't respond, I just pulled his face to mine and kissed him deeply.

The need to be close to Nathaniel was more than I could bear. My fingers laced behind Nathaniel's neck and I felt his body lay forward onto mine. His hands pulled my waist in towards him and his thumb brushed against my skin by my navel spreading heat all over like a wildfire. The intensity of the kiss increased causing our breathing to come out jagged and uneven and eventually we parted our eyes never leaving each other. His arms possessively continued to hold me close and the palm of his hand gently held my jaw line. A small smile appeared on his face and I couldn't help but blush and smile in return.

"You'll be the death of me Alexandria, I swear," he said shaking his head slowly.

The sound of him saying my name sent a wave of heat over me again as my stomach flip flopped at his words, and I knew Nathaniel could feel what I was feeling. Whole. Like no matter what happened if we trusted this, if we trusted us, everything would be ok. My head may have been telling me all of this wouldn't last, but my heart wasn't listening anymore, it was leading me straight into Nathaniel's arms where I belonged.

Nathaniel and I lay entangled together throughout the night. His protective hold on me never loosening until the methodical rise and fall of his chest and intoxicating scent drifted me to sleep. I woke to the sounds of birds chirping outside the window and a flash of relief filled me when I realized I could not remember my dream from last night; no dreams were better than nightmares any day.

I noticed Nathaniel had already gotten up so I quickly got dressed, freshened up in the bathroom and headed towards the intoxicating smell of bacon and eggs coming from the kitchen. I rounded the corner to find Nathaniel with two hot plates of eggs, bacon, biscuits, and orange juice ready and on the table. I took a seat and smiled at the food in front of me.

"You must really like to cook?" I said, raising an eyebrow at him. A playful smile confirmed I was still scratching the surface and getting to know him. He joined me at the table.

"Normally I never have time; I take advantage of it when I'm able." I nodded.

"I have an idea about how to make our training more interesting," he began.

"Mhmm? How's that?"

"Anytime you shoot a target, hit a bull's-eye, or successfully attack and defend yourself I'll answer a question you have. If you don't, you answer one of my questions."

"I can ask you anything and you'll answer it?" I inquired, liking the idea of getting to know Nathaniel more.

"Anything," he confirmed taking a bite of his eggs.

"Ok, deal."

Chapter 21

An hour and a half had passed since breakfast and my body lay sprawled out on the mat, sweaty and exhausted. We had been training inside what looked to be a barn from the outside, but the inside was covered in gym mats, punching bags and target boards. Nathaniel had decided to begin training with hand to hand combat which had turned into me so far answering about 50 questions of Nathaniel's and him answering none of mine. I huffed in frustration and Nathaniel circled me on the mat smiling.

"Any previous ex's I should know about?" I pulled my body up off the mat and faced him for an attack. He faked right and plowed my torso to the mat where he straddled me. Even though he had equipped me with padded head gear and sparring gloves, my body hurt like hell. I glared at him and he looked down at me playfully.

"Maybe, maybe not," I spat defiantly, refusing to answer his question. I had not gotten to ask him one question yet and my frustration had boiled to its maximum level now. He grinned down at me.

"Now Alex, that wasn't part of the game. Answer my question," he prodded, clearly enjoying himself, but letting me up to my feet again. I tucked my head low and dodging his frontal attack jumped onto his back attempting to put some kind of a sleeper hold on him. He struggled to un-wrap my clenched legs from his waist and for a moment I felt pleased at the progress I had made. The next moment happened so quickly I could feel my head spin. I was on the mat facing up at Nathaniel who was smirking down at me again. He had thrown me over his head and back onto the mat which I was getting to know all too well. Defeated and exhausted, I caved and answered his question.

"I dated a few people growing up, but nothing special." He smiled at my answer and handed me a water bottle and towel.

"We'll take a break before we switch to shooting. I'm hoping you'll have an easier time with that," he teased, knowing he was getting a rise out of me. A fierce look shot across my face.

"In my defense I'm fighting an angel and I'm a human. I think the odds are just a smidge out of my favor," I retorted sarcastically. He nodded in agreement.

"You're cute when you're angry," he stated, the same grin on his face. I rolled my eyes at him and chugged more water.

Nathaniel hauled the two black duffle bags we had gotten from Luther's house out to the mini shooting range conveniently located behind the cabin. There were cans, bottles, and even some water vapor Tannerite explosives stacked on logs and tree limbs. Some were close up, whereas others where anywhere from 25 yards to 150 yards out. I smiled remembering all of the concealed carry classes my dad had urged me to take and all of the times camping Derek had given me pointers.

There was a small wooden slab about seven feet long and waist high where I laid my guns down on. I decided to start with the 1911 first. Nathaniel stood just behind me and on my left to observe. I grabbed a can of 45mm ammo and loaded the magazine; once finished I slid the magazine into the gun and racked the slide back, switching off the safety with my thumb at the same time.

I aimed for a beer can resting on a log first; one of the closer targets to start. Taking a breath in and letting it out slowly, I squeezed the trigger. An eruption sounded from the barrel of the gun and the bullet shred through the middle of the can. I smiled and turned to see Nathaniel who was grinning.

"What do you want to know?" he asked.

"Any ex's I should be worried about?" I mocked, but eager to finally get some answers. He laughed, but his eyes turned serious.

"None." I took another shot and was rewarded with another hit.

"You mean you've never dated anyone before?" He nodded meeting my bewildered look.

"Angels aren't supposed to date, especially guardian angels. Our job is to protect and watch over the people we are assigned. It's our life. There isn't time for personal relationships and even if there were, I never met anyone I was interested in dating until you,' he said casually. I could feel my skin heating up with his words. I squeezed the trigger again and the sound of a glass bottle breaking echoed with the blast of the gun.

"How is it possible that Uvall or fallen angels could use me to enter and destroy heaven? Everyone in my family is normal from what I can tell." I looked back at him intently searching his face for answers I desperately needed. He sighed.

"You're family's bloodline dates back way before I ever became an angel. From what I've been told and what I've heard, your family's bloodline has always been connected to angels in one way or another. Your great, great, great grandfather is said to have prayed and called upon angels to help protect him and his family during a time of war and famine, specifically, to protect them from fallen angels who sought to gain power and control over everyone and everything. At the time, fallen angels were disciplined, but not banished from heaven yet. His prayers were eventually answered; he and his family lived and thrived in peace, angels decided it was best if fallen angels were cast from heaven for good and stripped of some of their powers, but the help came at a price. In return for the help given, the angels gave your grandfather and grandmother a baby girl; hoping to forever link humans and angels and to help monitor and stop the spread of fallen angels holding power on earth. The girl was meant to be used as a peacemaker between humans, fallen angels and angels. However, the gift backfired on the angels when fallen angels learned that every so often a girl with the right blood, just before her 18th birthday and during an eclipse, could be used to enter back into heaven and take over.

As a result, guardian angels were ordered to "deal with" the female children who possessed the power in their blood. Some of your ancestors had that blood and other times decades would pass before the right heir would be born again."

I swallowed hard taking in this new information on my history. I cringed at the thought of all of my female ancestors who had perished not knowing what type of blood coursed through their veins or how it had endangered them. I tried to focus for a minute and hit a tree branch holding a Tannerite explosive. A boom sounded and a puff of grey water vapor evaporated into the air where the target once hung.

"Does that mean part of my blood is mixed with angel blood? How could we be used if we are fully human and not angel?" I countered, wanting to understand what was so special about some of the females in our family.

"Every so often, a female is born with the same blood the first baby girl had. It's a mixture of human blood and angel blood, but there is not enough angel blood flowing through your veins to cause any effect on you, you are just as you said, fully human still."

I nodded letting him know I understood. Another shot, another hit. "What happens when you change completely and you're a fallen angel?" He hesitated. I could see a mixture of hidden doubt and fear behind his eyes, but his voice was velvety and calm.

"I don't really know to be honest. What I do know is that certain loyalties can change. There is a strong bond that holds all angels together and all fallen angels together; allegiances change and I know most newly fallen angels go through a sort of 'break in period' to find their rank and occupation among fallen angles based on their previous set of skills as angels. I've heard of respectful acquaintances between angels and fallen angels, but typically the two never mix."

I turned to shoot again, but my fingers had stopped listening to commands. All of the new information I had gotten had helped piece together some of the big questions that had lingered with me for so long, but I couldn't help but hate some of the answers I got. The thought of Nathaniel changing was terrifying. What if he wasn't the same person afterward? I was pulled from my thoughts when I heard the sound of a car pulling up in front of the cabin. I turned and raised an eyebrow at Nathaniel questioning who else knew where we were. He smiled and grabbed my hand escorting me towards the front of the cabin.

"Come on, I have a few friends I'd like you to meet. They're here to help with anything we may need; Luther should be with them." I smiled at Nathaniel.

"Friends huh?" A black escalade with a New York license plate was parked in front of the cabin and four doors opened. Luther got out of the driver's side door followed by a slender woman with shoulder length jet black hair and hazel eyes. Two heavily built men in dark blue jeans and t-shirts followed suit.

"You all made it," Nathaniel exclaimed a part of him sounding relieved.

The woman with the jet black hair sighed, seeming not too thrilled with the trip.

"Had it taken any longer to get here you may have been short a few people," she stated motioning towards the two heavily built men beside her. She pushed past them and opened the back of the Escalade to grab a few bags.

The two men grinned at her annoyance. "So is this her?" One of the men asked quickly motioning towards me. Nathaniel looked back at me and smiled.

"This is her." He gave me a wink.

The man in the blue t-shirt who asked grinned widely at me then turned towards the man next to him in the white t-shirt.

"I told you! Now pay up!" The man in the white t-shirt shoveled some money out of his pockets and slapped it into the other man's hand reluctantly.

"Alex, I'd like you to meet Lahash," He pointed towards the man in the white t-shirt, "and Caim," he finished motioning towards the man in the blue t-shirt.

"They're fallen angels, but very good acquaintances who have never held the same wants or needs that most other fallen angels have." Lahash smiled.

"We prefer to call it having fun our own way." His green eyes flicked to mine and a mischievous smile played at his lips.

"Please." The woman with the black hair huffed, dropping the bags at their feet.

Caim gave a husky laugh. "Uh-oh I think we've upset her again." But instead of looking sympathetic, he seemed pleased.

"I'm just glad the damn bets are over and I'm not stuck in a small space with either of you anymore," she stated irritated by their presence.

"What bets?" I asked. She strode towards me, carrying one bag over her shoulder her other hand outstretched towards me.

"This is Seraphina," Nathaniel introduced. "Seraphina, I'd like you to meet Alex." I shook her hand and she eyed me a few times over.

"They were making bets on if you were hot or not. For once, rumors are true." She finished smiling at me, but I could tell she hadn't given me a once over for my looks, she had sized me up to conclude how strong I was to make it through this.

"Seraphina is an angel. She wants to stop fallen angels from taking over Heaven and believes that we can stop all of this differently than other angels believe we can," he explained.

She smiled again. "Here to help."

"And you already know me." Luther exclaimed, smiling widely and embracing me in a hug for a moment. I smiled back.

"So what's on the agenda now?" I questioned not sure how many more surprises or answers I could take, but feeling a bit relieved to know there were others on our side who wanted to help.

"Now we train some more, but this time you'll be going against them." He nodded towards, Caim, Lahash and Seraphina who had already disappeared inside the barn. I looked at Nathaniel then, my eyes wide and a bewildered expression on my face questioning his sanity.

"You're kidding right? I could barely stay off the mat just fighting you!" I cried out. He grinned.

"They're going to show you some more techniques that will help you in case you have to go against a fallen angel or an angel. Keep in mind; both kinds of angels aren't particularly fond of your wellbeing currently." His voice came out smooth but serious. I breathed out a sigh.

"Right." We finished with the gun training Nathaniel and I had started earlier. Seraphina had brought moving targets for me and after a brief period setting them up; had me run through drills over and over again; running and ducking objects she had thrown my way, until my groupings were within five inches of one another.

"You did well," she said, pleased with my effort as she began cleaning my AR for me.

"Thanks." I replied. I took another chug of my water feeling the heat of the mid-day sun baking my body. "So how do you and Nathaniel know each other?" I inquired curiously. She didn't hesitate giving the answer, almost like she expected me to ask it.

"We were both initiated as angels around the same time. We were in the same classes with one another; he's been like a brother to me and ever since then we've always just had each other's backs. I thought he was crazy when he didn't follow through with the orders given, regarding you. But, I know Nathaniel and if he believes in you enough to risk everything he's always loved then that must mean you're pretty extraordinary." She finished. Her sparking hazel eyes examining my reaction to her words carefully.

I looked away for a moment; I wasn't sure extraordinary was a word to describe myself lately.

"And what do you believe?" I questioned. She shrugged her shoulders.

"I stand behind Nathaniel's judgment. It's everyone else you need to prove wrong." Seraphina and I cleaned the remaining guns in silence. Nathaniel had brought out some lunch to help re-charge me for the next round of training.

Afterwards, Caim and Lahash sauntered over. "Time to train with us now Alex," they both said in unison. I swore if Caim and Lahash hadn't looked so different from one another they could have been brothers.

Caim had the olive skin tone of an Italian with dark brown hair and brown eyes, whereas, Lahash had dark green eyes, a pale complexion and blonde hair cut similarly to Caim's. However, both always seemed to know what the other was going to say, they were both built similarly, and they each shared the same taste in clothes, among other things from what I could gather. I nodded in concurrence and followed them towards the barn.

"So how do you guys know Nathaniel?" I asked, curious as to how an angel would have become friends with two fallen angels. They both smirked at my inquiry.

"We've been in bar fights against him a few times." The two exchanged a look with wide eyes for a moment. "All I can say is the man can definitely fight. And then he saved our asses once with the angels. Gave us a chance to get out of town and lay low for a while; just told us to stay out of Colorado," Caim stated.

"I've never seen him fight. I sparred with him this morning, but he's never mentioned anything about fighting," I stated out loud as we pushed the barn doors open. Lahash and Caim looked at me.

"He's one of the best I've ever seen," Caim retorted. "Angel's used to use him to track down and intercept some fallen angels before he transferred to be a guardian angel." I took in this new information.

"Why did he transfer?"

Caim shrugged his shoulders. "No one knows, but, rumors surfaced after word got around about your identity that he transferred because of you." Caim and Lahash and I exchanged looks for a moment. I looked away quickly and decided to change the subject.

"What did you guys do to have angels after you? Or Nathaniel for that matter?" I asked curiously. Lahash shook his head and grinned devilishly.

"I don't think you want to know sweetheart." I didn't reply; something about the look in Lahash's eyes told me I really didn't want to know.

_Chapter 22

An hour had flown by training with Caim and Lahash and my skills had increased considerably. I was still a human fighting against fallen angels and angels alike, so I was definitely at a disadvantage, but I had learned new tactics to at least help me injure my attacker long enough for me to get away and if I'm lucky, eliminate them all together if need be.

Nathaniel, Luther and Seraphina had watched as Lahash and Caim gave pointers and drills to defend and attack at the appropriate moments and the best places to injure my opponent that would do the most damage. Only significant amounts of blood loss and weapons created and designed by angels could kill them. Guns and knives cannot kill fallen angels or angels, but they will definitely slow them down.

I was told that if you injure them enough, they will be forced to flee and heal themselves before they die of blood loss. I thanked everyone for their help and headed towards the cabin. I was utterly exhausted and I was beginning to see and feel bruises forming on my body from the day's arduous activities. Caim, Lahash, Seraphina and Luther stayed to talk with Nathaniel. In the bathroom, I turned on the faucet and let the water fill the tub; struggling to shrug off my clothes. Sure enough, a muddle of green, black, blue and purple bruises covered the backs of my arms, the outsides of my legs and my hips from being tossed around like a rag doll.

I grimaced at the throbbing pain smothering my body and then climbed in the tub letting the steam and water envelope me in a soothing hot embrace. The heat and water felt good on my sore achy body and I rested my head on the back of the tub. Closing my eyes, I began to re-play the entire day over again in my head.

The things Nathaniel had told me about my family, our mysterious bloodline, and the things I had learned about Nathaniel from Caim and Lahash. It was a lot to take in along with the physical beating of the day. Fatigue consumed my body and after a half hour of soaking in the tub, I decided it was probably time to get out, get dressed and get some sleep. I slowly stood up and stepped out of the tub, wrapping a towel around my midsection.

I peeked my head out of the doorway searching for any sign of Nathaniel; when I found none, I tiptoed my way into the bedroom and shut the door behind me. I heard Nathaniel clear his throat and I immediately sighed in frustration and moved slowly towards my side of the bed.

"Can you turn around?" I pleaded quietly, too exhausted to protest his presence in the room while I changed. He smiled, but his smile quickly turned into a thinly pressed line of concern.

"Are you ok?" he questioned, knowing I wasn't. My arm moved to stop his chest from coming any closer when he caught sight of my bruises.

"Lay back on the bed, now," he commanded, his hands delicately guiding me back onto the bed.

"You should have told me you needed to be healed," he announced, a tone of anger seeping through his words.

"Sorry," I breathed. He shook his head, but his tone softened.

"You did great today; I think you're a natural." He worked his way healing the bruises down my arm. I grinned a little.

"Coming from a professional, that's quite a complement," I replied. My body was beginning to feel better by the minute; the pain was slowly fading away as light filled me. Nathaniel stopped for a moment and his gaze caught mine before he continued.

"Are you bruised anywhere else?" he asked. I gulped for a minute feeling vulnerable in only a towel.

"My hips and the outsides of my legs," I responded not taking my eyes away from his, but feeling my heart rate raise.

"I need to see the bruises so I can heal you," he said, his icy blue orbs piercing through me. I nodded and swallowed hard. I positioned the towel so it wasn't revealing anything except the outside of my right hip and leg. With only a towel on, it was the best way for me to have him heal each side of my body without exposing myself.

To take my mind off of my racing heart beat and Nathaniel examining my body while practically being naked, I decided to get some more questions off my chest.

"Did everyone else leave already?" I asked. He smiled faintly. "It's just you and I love. I have everyone else keeping watch on Uvall and his men to give us a heads up on their movements." I nodded and continued to try and distract my wondering thoughts.

"So, did you enjoy what you did before you became a guardian?" It was the first question that popped into my head and I immediately regretted asking it. "I'm sorry, I didn't mean to..." I stated instantly.

Nathaniel's hands moved from my thigh to my hips and I stiffened holding my breath for a moment. I could've sworn I saw him smirk, but I wasn't sure. His expression was soft when he looked back at me.

"I was good at it; I've never really enjoyed it though," he replied nonchalantly.

"From what I hear you were exceptional at it." He smiled slowly.

"Let me guess? Caim and Lahash told you about what I used to do?" I moved the towel so Nathaniel could heal the left side of my body.

"Yes, they vaguely described how you used to track down fallen angels and intercept them for angels," I said. His eyebrows furrowed for a moment and he looked back at me.

"That's the kid's version of it, yes," he said coolly, his voice taking a more serious tone.

"So what did you used to do then?" I questioned. He raked his hand through his hair for a moment and leaned back against the bed frame.

"I used to intercept fallen angels, interrogate and eliminate them if necessary, then I became a guardian and my job changed to protecting whomever I was assigned," he said. I already knew the end to the story now; Nathaniel had been reassigned as a guardian and was then sent orders to kill me but didn't go through with it. We were silent as Nathaniel finished healing my left hip.

"You're fully healed now, you should get some sleep," he said getting up from the bed. He pulled his shirt off and threw on a tank top before exiting the room. I lay on my back and examined my arms where horrible bruises once existed. Then I grabbed some pajamas and climbed into bed. It was clear Nathaniel didn't enjoy speaking about his past and I didn't push the issue.

Chapter 23

I woke the next morning to Nathaniel's warm breath on my shoulder. My guess is he hadn't come to bed early and was getting his few hours of much needed sleep in. His broad chest heaved up and down in rhythmic fashion. I slowly slid out of bed making sure not to wake him. It was early morning; around 5 AM I gathered, from the faint blue light outside, and a slight chill filled the air. I collected some clothes, my phone and silently headed for the bathroom.

After getting dressed I left the cabin and taking in a breath full of the crisp air decided I would try to locate a place with cell reception to call my parents. I walked around the lake and followed a trail that lead uphill to a set of rocks that looked like they were being used in a Jenga game. Holding my phone up and checking for service bars I climbed higher on the rocks hoping to get a signal. Two flashing bars lit up my screen and I smiled, quickly dialing my dad. A few rings later he picked up.

"Hey dad! Just checking in, we got to the hotel pretty late yesterday so I'm sorry I didn't call sooner. I'm still getting used to the time difference." I lied.

"I figured." he said. "So how is D.C?" He asked. I wracked my brain remembering the itinerary for the trip and told him about what was on the list for today and how I'd check back in with him soon. Then a thought hit me,

Could my parents know about our background? Our bloodline? Was there any way they were hiding the truth from me to possibly protect me?'

"By the way, I was wondering, all this history and stuff really has me thinking about where our family came from and our history. Was there anything very significant that happened to our family?" I questioned wearily.

"Our ancestors originated in Europe, but other than that I can't say there is anything astounding about our history besides coming to America or things of that nature." I nodded, feeling bad for thinking that my parents had lied to me about anything. I was the one who was lying; me. My parents were just innocently unaware of our bloodline's history and how much danger it currently put me in.

After finishing both calls to my parents I slid the phone into my pants pocket and gazed out at the astounding sunrise in front of me. I rested my elbows on my knees and watched the brilliant orange, yellow and pink hues splash over the mountains ahead of me; then reach the tree line and eventually the rocks where I sat. I saw movement out of the corner of my eye and was met by the outline of Nathaniel's body.

"You know you shouldn't wander off without me." He began, taking a seat next to me.

"I'm not used to needing a body guard." I said with a smile. But, it was true; I really wasn't used to someone knowing everywhere I was, who I was with or what I was doing. Although I knew Nathaniel was protecting me, I felt a sort of invasion of privacy at times.

We sat and watched the sunrise together in silence. It was the most peaceful moment I had found since all of the craziness had entered my life. I relished in the moment, appreciating the silence and Nathaniel's presence. The sun finished rising over the mountains.

"So I take it knife throwing is on the agenda today?" I finally asked. Nathaniel nodded and helped me down off the rocks and we began to make our way back to the barn.

There were taped lines on the mats facing targets of life sized people. Nathaniel handed me a black case of five inch throwing knives and instructed me on how to hold and throw them properly. Then, placing me behind the 1st white line indicating seven ft. he instructed me to throw one of the knives at the target. My first thousand throws were pitiful to say the least, but after a while of working on my form, I was sticking the knives left and right into the target wherever I aimed.

Dusk came swiftly and we called it quits for the night, closing the steel barn doors. A blue hue had settled over us as night quickly approached.

I met Nathaniel in the kitchen after each of had showered and heard the sound of a cell phone close shut when I rounded the corner to the kitchen. Nathaniel stay leaned against the counter with the phone in his hand. He gave a faint smile when he saw me but I could tell something was wrong.

"What is it?" I asked concerned. His face furrowed in confusion and thought.

"Nothing. Luther, just checking in." He said still suspicious.

"Is something wrong?" I pressed wondering what he was thinking.

"No; absolutely nothing has happened so far for anyone to report on." He replied apprehensively.

"Wouldn't they be scrambling to make a move as soon as possible, especially since the eclipse is just three days from now?" I asked in disbelief that absolutely nothing was happening. Something didn't seem right. Nathaniel's eye brows furrowed and he looked at me.

"That's what bothers me. It's too...calm." He declared uneasily. "You should get dressed, in case we need to move quickly." He stated worry and distrust etching his features. I swallowed hard and nodded. I paused to ask Nathaniel a swarm of questions entering my mind, but stopped and headed towards the bedroom to change.

I changed into a pair of black pants, boots and a warm black long sleeve with a zip up neckline. Then, after sifting through the black duffel bag from Luther's I secured a boot knife to the inside of my boot and found Nathaniel back in the kitchen. He was in dark blue jeans and a black long sleeve shirt that was rolled up to his elbows and molded his body perfectly.

I perched myself on the corner of the countertop and peered back at Nathaniel who let out a breath and watched me as the counter continued to support his weight. Feeling his gaze I looked away for a moment as another question flashed across my mind that I had been wondering about since we first met. I hesitated and looked back at him.

"So after all of this is over, what then? I take it you'll return to being a guardian angel?" I asked. The words were like sand paper in my mouth, but I tried not to show it. Nathaniel never took his gaze from me, but something flashed behind his eyes that I couldn't quite make out. He straightened so his body was no longer leaning on the counter and he was facing me directly.

"Is that what you want?" He searched my face intently. I couldn't unlock my eyes from his and truth be told, I didn't want him to go after all of this was over. I may have been thrown into this conflict because of my ancestors, but a part of me was thankful to have met Nathaniel through it all. I chewed my lower lip nervously, unsure if he felt the same way I did.

A soft, "No," was all I could say in response to him. I surveyed his reaction. His eyes locked with mine and he walked towards me and stopped when his legs brushed mine.

"Good. Cause I don't think I could have stayed away even if you wanted me to." He breathed low and velvety. My pulse increased with his touch and presence. He continued, "I'm drawn to you in a way even I don't understand. I don't know what this is, but I'm not letting go of you Alex. No matter what." He stated absolutely. I smiled at Nathaniel and pulled him in for a kiss.

Whatever this was between us, I couldn't explain it either, but our connection was too powerful to ignore. The nerves throughout my body tingled sending shooting bursts of bliss through me as our kiss deepened. I laced my fingers through his hair and the back of his neck. He responded; his hands gripping my legs, securing me closer to him. A wave of heat washed over me and we separated breathing deeply.

Nathaniel's pocket began to buzz and he helped me off the counter and kissed my neck; pulling the phone out of his pocket to check the caller id. I pointed towards the bathroom as he picked it up and he nodded.

Inside the bathroom I eyed myself in the mirror, a smile and blushed cheeks forming on my face. This is crazy, I thought and my heart jumped as I thought of Nathaniel's words again. After a few moments in the bathroom I figured I would try and check my phone for service again to call Kate and Trey. I felt a rush of excitement pour through me and I was giddy to tell someone about Nathaniel and me.

I punched in the numbers swiftly when a force thrust me towards the mirror violently, causing the phone to drop from my hands into the sink. A hand clamped down over my mouth muffling my screams and I felt the edge of a blade press into my hip.

"You scream I'll slice your hip open." My attacker whispered hostily in my ear. I heard Nathaniel call my name from the kitchen and my attacker edged us out into the hallway.

"Alex, we need to go now, Luther..." Nathaniel's words faded abruptly as he rounded the corner from the kitchen and was met with me and my attacker. The rough hand that covered my mouth moved away and replaced itself under my neck, but the knife remained.

Nathaniel's body stiffened ahead of us and his head was hung lower.

"Cassius, that you?" Nathaniel questioned sarcastically taking a few slow steps towards us. My attacker grunted in response and shifted his weight uneasily.

"Word is you're gonna be one of us soon. Why fight it Nathaniel? Isn't this what you angels like to call fate?" He spat unsympathetically and amused.

Nathaniel took another step forward causing Cassius's grip to tighten and the knife to pierce my skin. I groaned and winced.

"You remember what I told you last time we met don't you?" Nathaniel's voice was dark and warning him. Cassius laughed patronizingly.

"I hardly think you're in a position to threaten me." He argued, but before he could hear Nathaniel's response, a knife from the back of Nathaniel's hand had been thrown and pierced Cassius's neck.

Nathaniel crossed the gap between us knocking Cassius out from a blow to the head with his knee. I was stunned for a moment until I felt Nathaniel bring me to my feet and shove me into the bedroom. He grabbed a rifle and shoved a handgun into the back of his pants, while equipping me with the same.

"Whatever happens, you run. Don't try and come back here. Keep running; I'll cover you." He ordered. I nodded in response trying to prepare myself for what was next.

"What about you?" I asked anxiously. We exchanged looks briefly and he paused before answering.

"I'll catch up to you. Remember, these weapons won't kill them, but it should buy us enough time to get you out of here." He finished shoving a magazine into the AR and pulling the charging handle back. We crouched low to the floor in the cabin and headed for the back door. It was eerily quiet. Blood stains caked the floor from where Cassius had lain, but his body no longer rested there; he was gone. My heart raced and I held the rifle tight against my shoulder.

We eased out the back door of the cabin and that's when we heard the alarming shouts. I could barely make out the black figures moving towards us from the tree line; we were being surrounded.

"Run Alex!" The sounds of gun fire echoed behind me and I bolted for the cover of the barn. If I could make it to the tree line, I may have a chance. I threw my back against the side of the barn catching my breath for a moment as I thought of which way to head. I remembered the rocks where I had dialed my parents and bolted that way. A shadow blocked the path ahead of me and I instinctively aimed at their center mass and squeezed the trigger. The figure slumped to the ground in agony.

"You bitch!" I was terrified I had just shot someone, but remembering who I was fighting against I sidestepped the fallen angel and clambered my way up the hill. Shouts rang out behind me and I knew I was being followed; a pang of sadness hit me as I wondered where Nathaniel was. I careened down the other side of a hill and saw a giant meadow filled with waist high grass surrounded by a tree line. I had to keep going. The shouts were getting closer now and I bolted for the cover of the tall grass. As soon as I reached it I fell flat to my belly and listened for a moment; hoping no one had seen me.

The sound of the ground crunching beneath feet absorbed my attention and I brought the rifle slowly to the crook of my shoulder again. A few shots rang out and it was silent until I heard a familiar voice reverberate across the meadow.

"Come on out Alex, you know you're not going to make it to that tree line." Uvall snickered. I didn't move. I could hear multiple footsteps coming from both sides of the meadow. They were trying to flank me and flush me out.

"We don't have all night Alex. Either you come out or I sink this knife through Nathaniel. Oh and did I mention it'll kill him?" A lump closed my throat hearing the words. Uvall had a knife crafted by angels, one of the only things that could kill them. I wracked my brain on what to do; I was cornered with no backup. Uvall was right, there was no way I was going to make it to the tree line and there was no way I was going to let Nathaniel die either.

"You have 10 seconds to come out my dear; I've never been one to go back on my word." His voice turned low and impatient as he began to count down from ten. I slowly turned over so my back lay against the grass, the two men scowering the grass hadn't discovered me yet, but they were close now.

When I was barely able to see the outline of their chests I squeezed the trigger and they both fell to the earth groaning and cursing. I stood up and aimed the rifle at Uvall who was standing next to Nathaniel. Nathaniel was on his knees and was bleeding; he looked like he had taken several shots to his shoulder and chest and without healing he appeared weaker. Uvall smiled; the gleam of the blade shinning as he laced it back inside its sheath on his hip.

"Good girl." He stated pleased to see me. The feeling was not mutual.

"Let him go Uvall." My voice warned. A man on his right took a step forward and I reacted shooting him in the leg.

"Nobody move!" I yelled. Uvall's face held a smile.

"You can't kill us Alex and eventually you're going to run out of bullets." His eyes glistened like a predator's watching its prey. I swallowed. Nathaniel took me by surprise then when he pulled a knife from under his shirt and stabbed Uvall, then turned to attack another fallen angel behind him. Another shot rang out and Nathaniel's body slumped to the ground as Uvall cursed in pain and moved towards him.

"Please don't hurt him!" I pleaded, knowing I was all out of ideas and desperately wanting to keep Nathaniel alive. Uvall looked back to Nathaniel.

"You giving up then Alex?" He cooed.

"Yes!" I replied hastily as Nathaniel objected from the ground. I was grabbed from behind roughly and my hands were bound behind my back. Two trucks and a van pulled up behind Uvall and he instructed his men to put Nathaniel and I in the van. The man who had grabbed me threw me into the van violently and I hit the floor with a thud. I turned to see who it was and was met with Corson's devilish eyes.

"You're going to pay for those bullets." He sneered and I eyed his shirt. There were three bullet holes and stains of dried blood from where I had shot him. Uvall looked at Corson.

"Nothing happens to her until we get access to heaven, do you understand?" He warned motioning towards the knife on his hip. Corson's face furrowed in anger.

"Understood." He replied coldly throwing Nathaniel in the van beside me and slamming the doors shut. Nathaniel was bloody and they had secured his legs and arms with chains. We heard the doors shut up front and felt the van begin to creep forward. Nathaniel winced in pain and then gave me a small smile to try and reassure me.

"You need to heal I said." Worry dripping on every word. He nodded.

"They'll heal me when we get to Uvall's, they won't want to risk transferring me with my full strength." I nodded, but his words couldn't give me much comfort seeing how much pain he was in.

"What are they going to do to me?" I asked, suddenly terrified. Nathaniel hesitated and closed his eyes before looking back at me.

"I don't know how they plan to do it, but I know they can't open the portal to heaven unless your blood is mixed with fallen angel blood. They have to change you to make that happen." He paused coughing up a mouthful of blood.

"Uvall will keep you safe until after the portal is open to heaven; after that he won't need you anymore. You'll be outnumbered and everyone will be trying to kill you. I'll find you by then, but if I'm late find Seraphina or Luther, they will keep you safe. Do you understand?" Concern and sorrow filled his eyes. I nodded.

"What do you mean they will try and 'change' me?" I questioned warily. He rolled onto his back and I saw a 9mm casing push itself out of his body. He winced in pain as it fell to the floor of the van. His body was slowly trying to heal itself and was rejecting the bullets he had been shot with. He smiled at my horrified expression.

"I've had practice at this love." I wondered what he meant by that for a moment. 'Was he used to being restrained by chains in the back of a van with bullet holes in him?' It wasn't too difficult to picture this being his typical Tuesday night, but I was petrified. Nathaniel turned back to me and touched his forehead to mine.

"I'm not sure what will change; this has never happened before, but I do know a lot of people are going to pay for doing this to you." His eyes had darkened and his threat made me stiffen. I knew he wasn't bluffing. An hour and a half later the van jolted to a stop and we heard the sound of footsteps on gravel and men shutting car doors. The van's back doors opened and bright lights blinded us. Nathaniel kicked one of the men in the head who tried to grab me and the man retaliated with a blow to Nathaniel's face. The burly man pulled me to the edge of the van and swung me over his shoulders in a fireman carry.

"Remember what I said Alex." Nathaniel managed to say before I was hauled away from him. Tears stung my eyes as I looked back and saw them drag Nathaniel out of the van next. He took a few more blows to the body and looked up to find me. When our eyes met a tear had escaped my eye and rolled down my cheek. He mouthed something to me silently, but I wasn't sure what he had said. His face disappeared as I was carried inside Uvall's mansion where the giant double doors closed behind us. I tried to control myself from sobbing.

The burly man carried me up the stairs, down a long corridor to the end of a hallway and unlocked a door. Once inside, he tossed me on the bed and ignoring my shouts of protest exited the room locking me inside. I chased after him and kicked at the door shouting at his cowardice and then turned to face my accommodations. Still bound, I remembered I had a hidden boot knife on me. I pulled it out and sliced through the ropes binding my hands. I hid the knife back inside my boot and glanced around. There was a giant king sized bed with large wooden posts extending to the ceiling.

The walls matched the golden and brown bed spread and a wooden vanity and mirror sat against the wall with a small stool. I ran towards the window on the far side of the room and throwing the curtains aside opened the window only to find iron bars preventing any type of escape. I saw a doorway and tried that; it lead to a bathroom with tiled floors and one mirror covered the entire wall above the double sinks with a toilet and a tiled shower. I couldn't focus; the adrenaline that had coursed through my veins back at the cabin had perished and I could feel the stress and exhaustion override my body.

I couldn't stop thinking about Nathaniel or about the eclipse. We only had two days until Uvall would try and change me seeing the clock on the nightstand that read 12:30AM. I prayed Luther, Seraphina or Lahash and Caim had known we had been taken and that they would come to our rescue. But how could only four of them take on an entire army? Doubtful, I decided I would try and do anything I could to escape and save Nathaniel. It was the only thing I could do. For all I knew we were already dead and I wasn't about to go out quietly.

I bent down beside the bed and entwined my hands together; looking up I said a small prayer. With that I got up and pounded on the door demanding to speak with Uvall. After over an hour of pounding and no answer, I laid back on the bed; my fists aching, and fell asleep from exhaustion.

Chapter 24

Our capture was replayed in my dream and I looked back at Nathaniel to see him mouth something to me. He smiled and I felt his gentle touch caress my face and the heat of his kiss. 'I love you.' He breathed as we parted and his eyes locked with mine. I smiled and before I could respond he was all of a sudden being taken away. And I was being taken from him. I shouted in protest and kicked and clawed trying to get back into his arms again, but he disappeared into the black. Nathaniel!

I screamed and was jolted awake to a sitting position. I was startled to see Cassius leaning against the bedpost eyeing me with his arms folded and I jumped to the other side of the bed to put more distance between us.

"What are doing in here!?" I questioned alarmed by his presence. He raised an eyebrow at me and grinned.

"I was told some irritating little half-blood kept making a racket demanding to see Uvall." He stated chidingly. When I didn't respond he snickered. "So what do you want to see him about?" He pressed.

"That's for me to ask him." I replied frigidly. Cassius stood upright and walked around the other side of the room towards me. "Wh..What are you doing?" I questioned not trusting him and uncomfortable. It wasn't long ago he had a knife pressed against my hip and the last thing I wanted was to be trapped in a room with him. I could feel the scab already forming over the cut. He stopped when he was a few feet in front of me.

"So you and Nathaniel huh? I never pictured he'd give up his wings for anyone, but..." He droned looking me up and down. "You're not just anyone are you? Half-blood." His dark charcoal eyes flicked over me again and his question sounded more like a statement.

I took another step back and he took a step forward. I could feel the wall against my back; I had nowhere to go and Cassius was disturbingly close now. A grin appeared on his face as he noticed my vulnerability and leaned towards me.

"There is something about you though..." He continued, and a fleck of curiosity flashed across his eyes. Intrigued, he bent towards me and lifted my jaw to him. I locked eyes with him and then sent my knee into his privates. He coughed and lurched backwards and I smiled.

"You'll never know what that something is Cassius." Distain drenched my words and I bolted for the door. I didn't have a key to lock the door so I bolted down the hallway hearing the door slam behind me; I looked back to see Cassius enraged and hot on my heels. I scrambled down the corridor but was brought down by what felt like a freight train before I could make it to the stairs. Cassius pulled me to my feet and threw me against the wall laughing threateningly.

"I think I like you even more Alex, you've got some fiery spirit in you." He cooed as one of his hands held my wrists above my head and the other closed around my windpipe. I was defenseless and the more I tried to squirm away from him the more his grip on my neck tightened. I choked and he smiled. Just then, we each heard a voice breaking us out of our state.

"Cassius, let her go, you remember what Uvall said." The voice warned. Cassius's grip loosened on my throat and I gasped in air. We turned to see the same burly man who had locked me inside the room. He wore military style pants and boots with a black plain shirt. The outlines in his face indicated he was older, but he looked ready for battle. His entire aura screamed killer. Cassius smiled ruthlessly.

"We were just playing Azza, I'm taking her to see Uvall." He stated callously.

"Then take her already, or I will." Azza declared. Cassius nodded and we watched as Azza disappeared down the stairs. Cassius turned to me then.

"You're lucky half blood, and just a little piece of information, I always get what I want." He sneered releasing me and grabbing my arm to lead me down the hallway. Cassius towed me into a dining room and let go of me when we saw Uvall at the table. It was a stretched wooden table that looked like it could seat 12 people. He pushed his plate away from him and stood up.

"Alex! I heard you wanted to see me?" He exclaimed walking towards me. His eyes darted to my throat when he got closer and his eyes narrowed at Cassius.

"I thought I made myself very clear... she is not to be touched until after the eclipse." He exclaimed.

Suddenly a shot rang out and I covered my ears at the unexpected sound. Uvall re-holstered a 1911 and guided me to my seat; then turned back to Cassius who had staggered towards the wall to support himself, cursing.

"Do I make myself clear now?" He asked calmly. Cassius straightened himself holding his shoulder and nodded.

"Perfectly clear." He hissed through his teeth eyeing me one last time. "Good, you can go now." Uvall replied taking a seat across from me.

"Sorry about that Alex. We've got a lot of new recruits and, well, sometimes they have a hard time taking orders." He stated irritated by the lack of discipline.

"So what did you want to talk to me about?" He asked finally; leaning back in his chair.

"What did you do with Nathaniel?" I questioned. Trying to remain calm and focus with the sound of ringing in my ears. Uvall eyed me.

"He's here at our lab." He replied.

"Lab?" I inquired not liking the sound of it. He smiled, but didn't respond to my inquiry.

"So tell me, what is the story between you and my brother?" He

188

asked. Silence filled the air between us and I shifted in my seat uncomfortably, 'I hesitated not knowing what to say.'

"We were both helping each other." I stated simply, trying not to divulge too much information Uvall could use against either of us.

"So you like him then?" I opened my mouth and then closed it not knowing how to react.

"It's complicated." I managed to reply.

"Isn't it always?" He added grinning. 'Was I seriously divulging my personal relationship with Nathaniel to Uvall? What was wrong with me?!'

"I want to see him." I said definitively. He let out a sigh.

"I'm not too sure that's a good idea."

"You promised you wouldn't hurt him." I stated my voice raising. He nodded.

"And I haven't; but like you witnessed before, my recruits don't exactly listen at times and Nathaniel has his own history with a lot of the people here." He said nonchalantly.

"Take me to him now." I demanded. He thought about it for a moment and then nodded for me to follow him. I was lead outside past a field and to a steel structure that passed as a barn, but with much more security.

The exterior of Uvall's property was filled with fallen angels; packing and unpacking supplies and weapons from trucks. Uvall had an army and I was his greatest weapon. I frowned at the sight of all of the men and women. There was no way I would be able to escape undetected if I found a way out of the room.

Two men stood guard outside of the structure and Uvall slipped a key card into the door; clicking, it allowed us to enter. The walls and floor were all white and the word lab came to my mind that Uvall had said previously. He definitely had a lab all right. A long hallway lead us to an elevator. Inside there was only B1 & B2 levels to choose from. I watched as Uvall clicked B2 and the elevator doors closed.

We stepped out onto level B2 and I followed Uvall down a set of identical white hallways fishing left and right and eventually coming to a halt at a room that was labeled observatory. We entered and a glass pane allowed us to view Nathaniel in the other room. He was chained to a steel chair and his head hung low. From what I could tell, his bullet wounds from before had healed as well, however there were fresh cuts and bruises to his face now.

"Nathaniel!" I yelled and pounded my fist on the glass to get his attention. His head jerked backwards at the sound of my voice and he gritted his teeth, but he didn't respond.

"Nathaniel?!!" I yelled out again; this time with more desperation in my voice. Nathaniel's breathing was erratic and he looked like he was in severe pain, fighting some unknown assailant.

"What's wrong with him? What did you do?!" I turned to Uvall accusingly; fury flowing through me. He didn't turn to engage me; instead he was quiet and then replied monotonously.

"He's changing. It takes several months for the entire process to transpire. By my count, he will be a fallen angel by the end of the week." He affirmed, knowing from personal experience. I looked back at Nathaniel.

"What will happen when the change is complete?" I questioned anxiously. Uvall shrugged.

"Everyone's different. Some have suffered from amnesia, loss of control at times; others change easily or seek out refuge with other fallen angels. Everyone goes through a break in period with our kind; see where you fit in and where you can be used to help our causes."

I huffed when he said the word 'causes'. "Am I your cause?" I asked sarcastically. We exchanged a look for a moment before he responded.

"Something like that. I should take you back to your room." He said motioning towards the door.

"Can I speak with him for a minute?" I begged, desperately wanting to stay with Nathaniel. Uvall shook his head and his tone darkened a little.

"Absolutely not. He's unstable and unpredictable right now. Seeing you could set him off or endanger you." I sent Uvall a confused look, but he had me outside the room walking towards the elevator before I could protest. We were silent as he escorted me back to my room. Before he turned to leave I blurted out a question that had been hovering in the back of my mind.

"Would you have killed your own brother?" He turned back to face me and I continued. "Back at the cabin, would you have really killed him?" I tried to make sense of Uvall's emotionless face.

"I wouldn't have wanted to." Was all he replied before closing the door and locking it.

I sat back on the bed and looked at the clock again. 3:30PM. its sinister red numbers seemed to be counting down to my ultimate fate and all of my fears. The rest of the day and Thursday came and went in a blur. I spent my time practicing some of the hand to hand combat techniques I had learned, eating meals that Azza brought into the room and wishing I had more time. More time with my family, my friends, and Nathaniel. I wondered if I would ever see any of them again. They would never know the truth, where I had been, the truth about our heritage, or what had happened to me. I would just simply disappear.

Eventually, sleep overtook me again. I woke to a knock on the door startling me out of the same dream about Nathaniel that had haunted me for the past several nights now. I slipped out of bed wearily and responded to the sound.

"Yes?" Azza opened the door holding a set of clothes for me.

"Uvall thought you may want a fresh pair of clothes." I nodded and he set the clothes on the bed then exited locking the door behind him. Azza wasn't a talker, I had tried to get under his skin numerous times, even tried to ask him questions over the past several days and the most I got in return was a few grunts or guttural sounds. If I hadn't known better, I would have thought he was mute.

I sniffed my clothes, they were the same ones I had had on the night Nathaniel and I were taken; slipping them off and locking the bathroom door I let the steamy water roll off my skin in the shower.

Today was it; my judgment day for lack of a better word, I thought. After the shower I quickly dressed and hid the boot knife again. The pants Azza had brought me were similar to the black ones I had previously on, and a black tank top replaced my long sleeve with a zip up neck line. I sifted through the drawers first in the bathroom, then in the vanity for a hairbrush; trying to busy my mind and think of something else besides my impending demise. Finding one, I went to slide the vanity drawer shut when a small black and white picture caught my attention.

It was wallet sized and depicted a beautiful brunette woman looking back at the camera and smiling. Strands of her hair seemed to be blowing in the wind as she turned back and in the background I could see the same golden walls that decorated the current room I was trapped in. I turned the picture over and in tiny black letters at the bottom it read: Blyth -1992. I wasn't sure why it was important, but I slipped the photo inside the back pocket of my pants.

There had been no sign of Luther, Seraphina, Caim or Lahash and with time dwindling down to the wire, I doubted any sort of rescue was imminent. It was only me and Nathaniel against everyone else; if Nathaniel was even the same person still.

Chapter 25

At 4PM I heard a knock and the turn of a key unlocking the door to my prison. Azza, Cassius, as well as several other men I didn't recognize stood outside the door.

"It's time, Alex." Cassius stated, grinning slightly. I gulped, but held my head high not wanting to show my apprehension or distress and let them escort me out. There was no use in putting up a fight right now. I was outnumbered 4 to 1 and against fallen angels for that matter. They were stronger, faster, and most were practiced killers.

I needed access to the lab to get Nathaniel out; I decided that would be the place I made my move. If I had even the slightest chance of getting Nathaniel and myself out, I was going to take it. I counted the number of men we passed from the room to the steel structure outside.

There were at least 20 men and women keeping watch at all times as the others prepared for the battle to come. Inside the lab, I tried to memorize the way we had entered, where Nathaniel was being kept and this new location Uvall's men were taking me to now. Cassius followed closely behind me; the two strangers bringing up the rear as Azza lead the way.

"You nervous yet half-blood?" He antagonized. "I heard it's going to hurt like hell." He stated provokingly, but his tone told me he wasn't bluffing. I glared at him, but didn't respond. I had to keep it together. We stopped, as Azza slid his key card across a panel causing the two giant frosted glass double doors to open electronically. I hesitated moving forward and Cassius gave me a push from behind. Inside the room, bright fluorescent lights illuminated the spotless white walls and floors.

In the center of the room lay an operating table and directly across from it were assorted tools, syringes, drugs and vials of liquids I couldn't identify. I felt as if I had walked into a huge science experiment, only I was the test subject. So far, it was just me and the four other men in the room. I couldn't wait any longer, now was the only chance I would get.

I backed myself up towards a counter and grabbed a scalpel and slid it up my sleeve discretely as Cassius dialed Uvall to let him know I was ready. Suddenly, the doors opened and Uvall, along with several other men entered the room.

The two strangers, who had helped escort me to the lab left, and a man and a woman dressed in scrubs replaced them. Uvall smiled at me, but apprehension was in his eyes.

"Prep her." He stated shrugging his coat off and rolling up his sleeves. The two men Uvall entered with moved towards me and I stuck one of the men closest to me in the neck with the scalpel. Taking them by surprise, I was able to follow up with a slice to the chest on the other man until two strong arms physically overpowered me. The scalpel dropped to the floor as I winced in pain from the grip Azza held on my wrist and I lost it. I fought and kicked and did anything I could to get away, but it was no use.

The two men I had injured were healing themselves as the man and woman in scrubs cleaned and sanitized the floor of the blood. Cassius and Azza forced me onto the operating table where my wrists and legs were bound by metal shackles. I cried out and cursed, knowing it was hopeless now.

Chuckles sounded from across the room and my face fell when I turned to witness who it was. "Apollyon." I said, my tone was cold and menacing, but surprised. He looked pleased enough to take a bow.

"Alexandria, my dear." He replied as if we were old friends.

"Just a neutral party huh?" I spat accusingly. He smiled and went on to explain himself.

"I saw an opportunity for our kind and fallen angels to join forces for the same cause. Ever since I met you that night at the masquerade I knew you had angel blood in you and were the key we all had been looking for, for so long. I'm not one to waste an 'opportunity' such as this." He said plainly.

"Screw your opportunity! I won't open that portal no matter what you do to me." I argued defiantly. He grinned at my response as if knowing something that I didn't and motioned to the man and woman in scrubs to begin. I watched helplessly as a syringe was filled with a thick reddish brown substance and I struggled trying to break free of the shackles.

My heart was pumping wildly as I watched one of the men pin my right arm to the operating table to steady it. The syringe was prepped and I shrieked in horror as I felt the prick of the syringe and fluid entering my blood stream. By the time the entire syringe had been emptied into my body I was already suffering from bursts of uncontrollable shaking. That's when I felt my pulse begin to slow; I could feel myself fading in and out from lack of breath. I heard some shouts around me as the doctors rushed to my aide.

"Her body is rejecting the blood; is she strong enough to survive this?" Someone questioned uncertainly.

"She'll make it; she's a survivor this one." Another stated convinced. I felt the light fading around the corners of my vision and then it was as if someone had stuck me with an adrenaline needle. My breathing began to increase rapidly; violently my body began to try and either fight or accept the new fluid that had been introduced in my body and a searing pain began to grow inside of me. It felt as if I was being burnt alive and ripped apart at the same time. The pain grew and moved from my feet, to my legs, my arms, and eventually stayed concentrated at my chest and back.

I screamed out in pain and quivered violently. I couldn't focus on anything but the pain; it was tearing at my back now, clawing deeper and deeper through to my organs. Tears streamed down the sides of my face as the worst part began to creep to my shoulder blades. I felt sharp piercing stabs and I shrilled in agony as the bones in my back shifted and pierced my shoulder blades. I began to see pictures flash across my mind as I cried out in anguish. A red eclipse followed by visions of bright light, Nathaniel, angels and fallen angels, a blade with an engraved hilt, and my brother and parents, all blazed across my eyes.

My breathing was jagged and irregular as I felt the pain slowly become more bearable and I tried to comprehend what was happening to me. A hot liquid had seeped from my back and I grimaced. Something about me was not the same. I didn't know what that was, but instinctually, I knew I would never be the same again.

From this point forward I was never going to just be Alex Constance. Whatever Apollyon and Uvall had injected me with I could still feel it coursing through my veins like hot dye. I lay motionless, my eyes closed for a while and then I felt the metal shackles restraining me fall away. I didn't move, but my eyes opened. The first thing I noticed was my sight. It was sharper, colors appeared vividly bright and objects more prominent. What had they done to me? I looked around taking in this new mode of sight and my eyes landed on Apollyon and Uvall.

Everyone in the room remained silent, still piecing together what they had just witnessed. I analyzed the looks of astonishment, surprise, shock, and satisfaction and rose from the operating table slowly to face them. One of the men from before went to grab me but Uvall placed a hand in the air to protest. I wavered for a moment and then straightened myself clenching and unclenching my fists and wiggling my toes trying to feel out this 'new' body. Inside, I could feel something settle deep inside the pit of my body; it smoldered with something I could not identify; something mysterious and dark. I hardly felt like I was in the same body as my mind grasped the sensations of this 'new' me.

My attention shifted towards an unknown weight on my upper back and I reached back to feel what was causing the disturbance. My fingers brushed against something soft and feather like. Reacting on their own from my touch the mystifying objects rustled causing my back nerves to twitch and I finally caught a glimpse of what the objects were out of the corner of my eye. Wings.

There was a set of massive white, flecked with black feathered wings protruding from my upper back. I felt my nerves and muscles connected to the wings move and the wings moved in response. I eyed them in trepidation and wonder as they billowed out past the width of my body and curved in towards my spine again before brushing across the floor slightly. Even with the extra added weight of the wings I felt more balanced than ever before and stronger somehow.

I fixed my attention back to Apollyon who began to clap loudly. His smirk showed he was more than satisfied with the results of his experiment as he looked me over appraisingly.

"Shouldn't we restrain her?" Cassius questioned; uneasy with my new form. Apollyon shook his head disapprovingly.

"No, she's partly one of us now; we will escort her outside where the portal can be opened." He looked down at his watch then, eyeing the time before continuing. "She won't put up a fight." He stated confidently and I smiled back at him. Inside, I was practically screaming at the top of my lungs with rage. Uvall turned to Apollyon then.

"We need to inform the army; the men will want to know the injection was a success. Then we'll have exactly 20 minutes before the eclipse will be over." He stated hastily. Apollyon nodded and evaluated me one last time with cold delight.

"I need a few minutes so I can be ready to open the portal." I declared nonchalantly to them hoping they would buy my con. They shook their heads and all but Cassius and another man headed for above ground. I hesitated before moving until they were all gone, then I moved towards the counter to steady myself. I rolled my shoulders cringing at the tender pain still lingering in my shoulder blades. That's when I remembered the boot knife I had kept hidden. Cassius approached me nervously.

"Are you really on our side now." He asked. I turned back towards him and smirked.

"Wasn't that the idea?" I replied unperturbed.

"Prove it." He pressed. I noticed the knife in his waistband and casually stepped closer to him, twinning my fingers through his belt loops. Cassius froze for a moment and then responded seizing my face in his hands and kissing me roughly. I went along with it, slowly moving my left hand from his belt loops to his knife.

Abruptly, I gripped the knife and plunged it into his chest twisting is slightly. Then, holding Cassius up to cover me, I reached for my boot knife and swiftly flung it across the room directly into the other man's throat. Cassius was wide eyed as I let him fall to the floor.

"I'm on no one's side." I stated grimly. My senses heightened as I listened for others outside the door. Hearing none, I knocked Cassius out and grabbed his key card. A part of me had enjoyed what I had just done and I could feel it burn and stir wildly inside me with life. I didn't stop to wonder about it, I had to find Nathaniel and we had to get out. I was going to have to rely on my new strength to get us out of here.

I grabbed a long white doctor's jacket before exiting the room hoping to conceal my wings as much as possible and re-traced my steps back to Nathaniel's room. Keeping my head low and walking briskly I focused on remembering where he was being held; down the hall to the right, then left, another left and right again and I would be there. None of Uvall or Apollyon's men were in the halls and I suspected they were all above ground awaiting for the portal to be opened. Finally, I saw the observatory sign and went down one more room.

Sliding the key card over the door I entered and shut the door quickly and quietly behind me. Nathaniel starred at me as I entered the room and I hurriedly went to unchain his arms and legs. I had no key, I looked around the room for a minute hopelessly, then that same feeling that had me enjoying what I had done to Cassius and the other man rose inside me again; like a steady hum. With both hands I grasped the chains and after a few heaves, the chains fell to the floor.

"Nathaniel! We need to get out of here; Apollyon and Uvall will be back to get me soon to open the portal. There is only 20 minutes left of the eclipse and we have to get as far away from here as possible." I said out of breath anxiously. He rose from the chair and tilted his head in question.

"A-Alex?" He breathed uneasily. My eye brows furrowed and I remembered what Uvall had said earlier this week.

"Yes, it's me Alex; don't you remember me?" I asked impatiently but suddenly feeling a cold shiver run up my spine. His eyes were unreadable and still an icy blue. My eyes widened as he lunged forwards with sheer force knocking me back into the wall. I grimaced in pain and my wings fluttered in response.

"Nathaniel! I swear it's me!" I shrieked. His attention turned to my wings and confusion filled his face; his forearm moved to my throat and instantly applied pressure as he gazed into my eyes untrustingly. It was then I couldn't take it, after everything I had been through, I just wanted to be near him again. I desperately pulled him into a kiss. Instead of pushing away I was surprised when Nathaniel returned the kiss. Slowly at first, like a flame, then our kiss spread into a wildfire out of control. The mysterious feeling inside of me grew with the intensity of the kiss and it was euphoric. Between breaths I could hear him repeating my name over and over again.

"Alex. I remember now, I remember everything." He said cupping my face between his hands and then embracing me protectively as if he would lose me again at any second. I smiled and ran my hands through the back of his hair not wanting to let him go. My feelings and need for Nathaniel had been intensified in my new body. Tearing me away from my thoughts and the rush of heat that flooded my body, Nathaniel grabbed my hand and led me to the door.

"We need to get out of here, but first, I have to retrieve something they stole from the cabin." He said as he re-secured the doctor's coat over my wings and grabbed a set of the chains that had restrained him.

He escorted me through the halls, seeming to have memorized them himself and peered around a corner.

"There's a guard, we need to get close enough to take him out." He said placing the chains on his wrists and winking at me. I nodded my head knowing what he was getting at and guided him down the hallway. He pretended to stumble and groaned as we approached the guard.

"Step aside please; I need to dispose of this one." I said motioning to Nathaniel." The guard huffed and eyed me suspiciously. Nathaniel suddenly had the man's holstered handgun and twisted the man's head into a headlock discharging the weapon twice. The guard fell limply in Nathaniel's arms and I opened the door as Nathaniel drug his body inside the room.

The walls were stacked with weapons of all kinds and we loaded up with anything we could carry, but Nathaniel grabbed for one weapon in particular hanging by itself on the far side of the room. A knife with an engraved handle that I had remembered Uvall carrying not too long ago and the same shiny blade Luther had passed to Nathaniel back at his house. He hid the knife in his waist and turned to me as I shrugged off the doctor's coat.

"This is a knife crafted by angels; it can kill any of us now, including you." He said his tone stern. I nodded suddenly acutely aware of the dangerous shiny blade he held and fearful of it.

We pushed back into the hallway again, making our way to the elevators as alarms began to shrill relentlessly and red lights flashed. Everyone would know by now that I had lied, that somehow I was still Alex inside. We braced the rifles to our shoulders tightly and entered the elevators, preparing for what awaited us on ground level.

Chapter 26

The elevator doors opened and we were already surrounded by Apollyon and Uvall's men. They had been waiting for us, knowing the only way out was the elevator.

"Hold your fire!" Apollyon announced. "I seemed to have misread you Alex. Let's not make this any more time consuming than it's already been. Willingly or not, you will open that portal." He announced snidely.

Nathaniel and I glanced at one another still keeping our rifles up. It was a look of desperation and despair as we both knew we wouldn't make it out of here.

It was then the pictures that had flashed across my vision previously, reappeared again and took over my vision like a hallucination. I shut and reopened my eyes trying to flush out the images, but a searing sharp pain filled my head and I dropped to my knees with a cry while holding my head in my hands. Nathaniel rushed next to me holding the rifle in one hand and touching my back with the other.

"Alex? What's wrong?" He pressed, trying to understand. "What have you done to her?!" He shouted at Apollyon and Uvall furiously.

"It's not us, Nathaniel. The transformation and eclipse are taking hold of her. It won't be long now. It's like I said, willingly or unwillingly, she's going to open that portal." He said unperturbed at my frantic outbursts.

A shout came from me again. "I can hear them calling for me; they want me to open it. Nathaniel!" Nathaniel turned back to me and took my head in his hands firmly.

"Can you fight it?" He asked fear lighting his eyes. I shook my head helplessly as I was forced to listen to the voices filling my head; 'come home', they urged over and over. I could feel a strange pull in my gut and my body and wings trembled uncontrollably.

It was then, the images in my head shifted to just that of the eclipse. I could see its brilliant orange flames turn to a deep burgundy and I could feel its pull; too strong for me to bare and I was unwillingly heaved towards it. I whispered to Nathaniel faintly.

"Kill me." Nathaniel's body went rigid and his eyes widened.

"Alex, no. I – I can't." His voice low and protective. I writhed again in pain. And his eyes glistened with moisture as they turned to a darker shade of navy.

"There's no other choice, do it now! I can't hold it off for much longer." I breathed helplessly. He embraced me in a protective hug and whispered in my ear and kissed my cheek.

"Please forgive me. I love you Alex." A sharp and swift pain pierced my stomach and I fell towards Nathaniel, my head resting against his shoulder as I felt my body quiver and the blade creep deeper into my abdomen. I choked and coughed; unable to fill my lungs with air, feeling the pull of the eclipse releasing me with each passing second as a hot liquid oozed out of the wound. My blood slowed and my veins began to pack with ice making my body gradually get colder; like someone had stuck me in a freezer. Inaudibly, I faded into the blackness.

Chapter 27

It was dark and as I blinked to try and see anything a blinding light surrounded me, but nothing and no one was there. I couldn't make out a single thing. I felt a door knob and pushed it open stepping into a room that was brightly lit, but not blinding. The room was all white, except for a row of pictures that hung on the far side of the wall. I made my way over to them cautiously.

The first one depicted my parents holding me when I was first born; their faces overwhelmed with love and joy. The next depicted my brother and I fishing together when we were young; I had been bitten by the fish I was trying to unhook from my fishing pole and Derek had come to my aide. I smiled at the picture recalling the memory and continued to the next photographs hanging down the line.

After viewing ones of my parents, my brother, Trey and Kate, I came to the last one on the wall; Nathaniel. It showed him looking back over his right shoulder, his dark black hair matching his black jacket. The picture looked to be black and white except for his icy blue orbs that looked startlingly more than just a likeness to him. I touched the painting delicately with my fingertips, but jerked away when a soft but low male voice spoke. His voice carried throughout the room equally and I turned around to find an angel standing in the center of the room.

"Why did you sacrifice yourself?" The stranger asked me.

Gold armor adorned his chest plate that wrapped around his shoulders and back, but left his arms bare and several blades were in view on his black pants. His bright sea green eyes assessed me under shaggy brownish blonde hair.

"Who are you? Where am I?" I asked still remaining watchful.

There was no answer from the tall heavily built angel as his wings rested un-opened, close to his body. The feeling in my gut told me that I was not in any danger, that the stranger whomever they were, was no threat.

The angel spoke again. "My name is Ezekiel, the angel of death and transformation. Now tell me, why did you sacrifice yourself?" He questioned gently. I looked back at the photograph of Nathaniel hanging on the wall.

The sight of him sent a tingling sensation through my nerves. And I trusted my instincts that I was not in any danger here.

"I did it to save him. To save everyone." I said, looking back at the photograph of Nathaniel hanging on the wall. The room was silent before the angel spoke again.

"Indeed you've saved a great deal, but some are too lost to be saved right now." My eye brows furrowed hearing the words.

"What do you mean? Who could not be saved?" I asked, feeling a lump in my throat and the tone of my voice raise a little as I thought of Nathaniel.

"Answers will come in time. You're different from the rest of us Alexandria, but you have the same potential I've seen in others. The rules have been re-written now and it is not your time to perish." He stated.

"So if I'm not dead what happens next? What am I?" I questioned, feeling relief that I wasn't going to die, but not knowing how I would return to my previous life this way.

"That's up to you to decide. You need to understand though that you're no longer just a human; you need to tread carefully from here on out when you are around others. We'll be watching over you Alexandria; we'll be here if you need us." Ezekiel stated fading away.

I was jolted awake, coughing as I lay on my back on the cold damp soil. It was almost dawn and a misty fog hung low to the ground creating eerie scenery.

I sat up gathering myself and immediately pulled up the tank top to view where the knife had once laid. There was no blade now, only a hole in my tank top and a thick white scar almost 3 inches wide. The grass around me and some of my clothes were layered with dried blood, but I was somehow healed.

I looked around for Nathaniel then, my arms and wings helping me to my feet quickly as alarm began to come over me. In the distance I could hear gun shots and screams. I didn't think; I just bolted towards the reverberating sounds. I ran as fast as I could and my wings twitched to carry me. It was painful for a moment but I slowly felt my feet leave the ground, my wings picking up more speed and gaining more confidence. I landed surprisingly gracefully in front of the steps to Uvall's mansion; hitting the ground with a pounding sound. I stood in place for a minute listening to hear the shouts or gun shots again.

Instead, the front doors had been flung open and a man tumbled violently down the steps to my feet. He had been beaten quite a bit from what I could tell of the gashes, cuts, and bruises on his arms and neck and as he turned over I discovered who he was. It was Uvall; he watched me intently as he got up from the ground holding his midsection which had been cut.

"It's not possible." He breathed in disbelief; eyes wide with shock. Footsteps sounded on the steps and I turned to meet their owners when my eyes locked with Nathaniel's. He held a knife and stopped, frozen in his tracks by my presence.

"Alex?" His face was full of anguish and disbelief as he said my name. My eyes darted over the blood stains across the side of his face and covering his hands.

"Nathaniel it's me." I said a small smile on my face grateful to be back with him again. "I don't know what happened, but I'm here." I could see Nathaniel's eyes water and two tears slid down them before he dropped the knife and crossed the distance between us and embraced me.

I molded into him and he held me protectively and tightly. We parted and he cupped my face in his hands to look at me again. His eyes were filled with a mixture of remorse, grief, suffering and relief. He kissed my forehead delicately and held me close; like he would lose me again if he released me even a little bit. He eventually released me, moving me behind him and turning to face Uvall, who stood dumbfounded.

Nathaniel drove his fist into Uvall's face, a popping sound rang out and I cringed in response, but he didn't stop at just one punch. Over and over he beat Uvall with his fist; appalled and frightened I screamed for him to stop and grabbed his arm. He stopped at my touch and looked at me confused before he turned back to Uvall.

"Why? Why did you do this? You weren't in it to take over." He said flatly curling his fists. Uvall spit up a mouth full of blood and faced us.

"You know why. They took her from me Nathaniel! When I changed, I didn't know what I was capable of, but they did! They let me go to her!" Uvall yelled dropping to his knees and covering his face.

Nathaniel's vengeful and frightened eyes looked back at Uvall sympathetically for a moment and I stepped in.

"Blyth? How did she die?" I asked holding out the small black and white picture I had placed in my back pocket to Uvall. Uvall gripped the picture and looked up at me, tears streaming down his face as he silently sobbed.

"I only did it to get back at the angels who cast me out. I loved her Nathaniel and because of what I became she died. I was only trying to save you from the same pain." He said solemnly looking at his brother and then to me.

Nathaniel was silent for a moment. Taking one last look back at Uvall he scooped me up in his arms and began to carry me away from the mansion, muttering a warning as we left.

"Come near her again and next time, I'll kill you." The words sounded more like a promise than a threat. Uvall did not reply to Nathaniel, he just held the picture in his hands and stared at it.

Nathaniel carried me to the front of the mansion where a black escalade sat parked. It was dissonantly silent as we passed blood-spattered bodies on the ground. Most of which were Uvall and Apollyon's men from what I could tell.

What had happened here after I had been stabbed? I wondered; too disturbed to ask Nathaniel. At the SUV he set me on the ground gently and Luther, Seraphina, Lahash and Caim approached us from the car; their eyes wide with shock and questions filling their minds. Lahash spoke up first.

"Holy shit! She's alive!" He said with a smile ecstatic and bewildered.

"And a..Hybrid?" Seraphina questioned aloud, gazing over my wings. I remained quiet, unsure of how to answer them. I didn't even know who or what I was anymore, but I was beginning to feel like a freak show on display.

My wings reflexively moved behind me more. Nathaniel motioned to speak with Luther and the two walked a little ways from the car to speak in hushed tones. I was left standing there, eyes on me.

"What happened here? After...after I...passed?" I questioned, trying to find the right words. I still couldn't quite believe that I was still alive after a knife that was meant to kill me had been rammed into my stomach. I pushed the thoughts from my mind quickly as Caim answered me.

"You're man over there went haywire." He stated pointing towards Nathaniel.

"That's an understatement." Lahash retorted with a grunt. I cocked my head confused and turned to look back at all of the bodies we had passed again. A cold chill made its way up my spine and sent goose-bumps across my skin.

"Nathanial did this?" I asked in disbelief and horror. Nods followed my question.

"What about Apollyon?" I asked.

"He and his men fled, along with a few of Uvall's. We tried to track them, but lost their tracks five miles from here." Seraphina said, a look of sorrow filling her eyes as she gazed at me.

My body felt weak as I stood there, suddenly exhausted from the events that had passed earlier. I felt my wings lay against my back and stretching my shoulders back, they folded in tightly and disappeared. I stooped forward catching myself as the weight of the wings left me;

and I groaned in pain for a moment. I reached back, but could not feel them anymore; before panic could overcome me, Luther helped steady me.

"Don't worry, it always hurts the first few times your wings retract, but it will get easier." He said hoping to comfort me. "We should get you home." He finished. My eye brows furrowed as he helped me to the car. I looked back to see Nathaniel standing where he and Luther had been talking; he stood motionless, watching me.

"Wait, what about Nathaniel?" I questioned, looking back confused. "Aren't you coming?" I asked shrugging out of Luther's hands and walking towards Nathaniel. Nathaniel was silent for a moment.

"You have to go Alex, Luther and everyone will take care of you and watch over you." He said his voice sullen and morose.

"What do you mean? Why can't you come with me?" I asked feeling a grip on my heart tighten and a lump surface in my throat. He cupped the side of my face tenderly with his hand; his eyes seemed torn with emotions I could not read.

"I'm not...well...right now Alex. I can't be with you for your own safety." He stated, sifting for the right words to say.

"News flash, I'm not 'well' right now either. You can't just leave!" I stated, anger beginning to seep through my words when he didn't respond. "Is this about what Uvall said? About what happened to Blyth?" I asked.

'How could he be doing this to me? We were in this together and now, I needed him with me more than ever and he was going to leave!?' I thought angrily.

Nathaniel looked at the ground, struggling to respond.

"Uvall killed Blyth by accident when he changed. He lost control and couldn't remember her; that's something he has to live with now. I couldn't live with myself if I ever did anything to hurt you. Look at what happened when I thought I had lost you Alex." He stated grimly motioning towards all of the bodies that surrounded us. I gulped for a moment.

"You won't hurt me; I know you won't." I replied confidently; not wanting to lose him. Nathaniel pulled me in for a kiss which I succumbed to immediately. I didn't want him to go.

"Please, why are you doing this?" I begged pulling away. "I need you; I – I Love you." I said a tear streaming down my face.

Nathaniel looked back at me, remorse written on his face, but a small smile touched his lips at my words.

"I have to do this to keep you safe," he said pulling me into an embrace and whispering into my ear. "I love you Alex, but you have to go. It's the only way I can keep you safe right now; from me." His grip tightened around me before he pulled away and escorted me into the car with the others. He uttered one last thing to me before kissing me on my forehead.

"I promise I'll come back for you." His tone was serious and I wanted to believe his promise, but it hurt too much that he was leaving me. I watched him as the car pulled away, until the mansion was out of sight. Nathaniel was gone.

I felt a jacket slip over my shoulders as the pitter patter of rain began to hit the windshield. We made our way back to the city and I sat motionless with my head leaning against the window.

The raindrops had turned to frozen pellets that slammed against the windshield, eventually turning to thick snowflakes that blanketed everything, emphasizing the deathly silence in the Escalade.

I used to be an ordinary teenaged girl. Now, everyone seemed to be uncomfortable in my presence. I could feel the edgy tension. As I drifted unwillingly off to sleep, my head was filled with questions. When would I see Nathaniel again? Would my life ever be normal again? Where do I go from here?

But my dreams were not unpleasant. Nathaniel and I soared above the world with wings outstretched, gliding effortlessly on the warm spring breeze. I was happy. Nathaniel smiled at me and we kissed in mid-air.

Perhaps this portent would be where my life was headed. At least it was something – an image I could hold on to.

Epilogue

There has never been a hybrid before – part angel, part fallen angel. Many before me had been killed because they were gifted with angel blood. It was feared that they could be used by fallen angels to open a portal to Heaven, giving them the means to take over.

But because my guardian angel – Nathaniel – had disobeyed his orders to kill me when I was young, I was now an unpredictable supernatural being, transformed into something that was supposed to be impossible. And that terrified me as much as it did everyone else. No one – angels and fallen angels alike – knew what I was capable of.

I worried about Nathaniel. Uvall had killed his only love, Blyth, when the change took him, and now Nathaniel was a fallen angel, too.

I felt like it was my fault. He had defied his orders to kill me and now it had changed him to the point where he had to get as far away from me as possible to keep me safe. Safe from what he thought he might do to me.

Pictures of Nathaniel and my family and friends danced across my vision relentlessly, then the words Ezekiel had spoken thundered around me:

"Some are too lost to be saved right now... You're no longer a human; you need to tread carefully from here on out when you are around others. We'll be watching over you Alexandria; we'll be here if you need us."

I shuddered reflexively. Somewhere deep down I had to still be Alex Constance.

ASHLEY
LUCERO

Redemption

THE NEXT BOOK IN
THE AWAKENING SERIES

readersfavorite.com/book-review/absolution-the-awakening-series
facebook.com/AshleyLucero.TheAwakeningSeries